Interior Designed By

1st Edition

ISBN: 978-1-964324-00-5

The Winter Solstice Series

Winter Solstice

The Crone

The Lady of Brighton

Summer Solstice

Summer Solstice

Candace Meredith

Chapter One

Hanna holds the crystal orb in both hands. Cracked, the essence of forever seeps from within; the omnipresent white light reveals her grandmother's face.

"Go to Reese," Grandmother says, and Hanna blinks.

"Grandmother…"

Hanna begins but senses that she needs to rush.

"Take the children to Reese…," and Hanna's mind whirls. Her thoughts become like the wind against oblivion – a deep vastness between time and space. When her mind wanes from spinning, she is in a small room in a well-kept house. Her children are already there, but she did not take them. Aly is almost three. At a year-and-a-half old Lucas walks, wobbling, between furniture; his feet touch the hard, slate floor. Reese emerges from behind a curtain that conceals her magic.

"There is a lot to tell you…" Reese says, and Hanna takes her son into her arms.

"My Grandmother…" Hanna speaks softly.

"LaQuinta," Reese speaks smoothly.

"Who?"

"LaQuinta. She changed her name when she wed to Pratt."

"I'm so confused…."

"Grandall, along with the Elders, have moved on."

"To where?"

Lucas coos and drools simultaneously; he is eating a piece of candy.

"They have incarnated, to become human again, to relearn the ways of magic and sorcery."

"Incarnated? But…"

"The only one allowed to return was Sterling."

"But why?"

"She had an ethereal body."

"In the flame…."

"Yes. That you saw with sorcery."

"Yes."

"Her ethereal body has materialized, and her memories are before the loss of…."

"But your memories…."

"Survived the time warp; a lapse in time affects us all differently based on the needs of the soul."

"Can you explain?"

"Depending on the needs of the soul, in their path to attain enlightenment, all souls have decided where they desire to be on this journey."

"Go on…"

"Of course, some of us know some of the pieces of the previous journey, like yourself, but others, according to the needs of their development, while in spirit, asked to begin anew."

"Oh my gosh," Hanna whispers, still feeling lost, afraid, and uncertain. She sits on the floor among her children when Lucius enters the room, and he kneels aside Hanna; he takes her hand into his and peers into her eyes…

"I'm here, Hanna," he says, placing her hand on his chest, "for whatever you decide to do."

"About what?"

"Jace … is still the disembodied soul of the underworld. A phantom of the night."

"The darkest night," Reese says in the background.

Lucius continues…

"We think he wanted the Lady … he wanted a Queen to be his…."

"But he chose Aly," Hanna demands.

"Yes. And he gave us the map."

"Where?"

"To the Lady of Brighton…"

Lucius turns to Reese, and she moves toward them.

"There is a great deal your grandmother could not tell you."

The orb glows faintly from within, and Lucius rolls it toward him and picks it up. Her grandmother's face is like amber, and she speaks slowly, calmly, and with reassurance; beside her are two men, one older and the other younger; they are Pratt and Tristian, reunited and forgiven. Pratt always loved her, and in their death, they could live eternally in spirit where neither magic nor religion could separate them. They are eternal in nature. LaQuinta tells Hanna all she knows of The Craft and of Hanna's mother's concerns regarding magic, how she blamed Tristian's death as a curse in black magic; in a way, Alayna was right.

"I was cursed," LaQuinta admits, "hexed by the Mother of the Dark."

"But if Jace is…"

"We will get to that soon…." LaQuinta tries to assure her.

"She broke the Witch's Creed." Reese says, "The Doctrine of the Witch that binds her to her Coven." She explains. "So in death, she now lives...." Reese takes the orb into her hands and places a pendant into Hanna's palm; she sees a cat with jade-colored eyes.

"Is this Rajah-Jade?" Hanna peers at its familiarity.

"Rajah, the Great Cat, named by Grandall is known by many; the pendant is his image. The insignia, the eyes like an ancient Pharaoh, bring about his great prowlness to accompany a witch on his or her journey – now Hanna too can summon him," and Reese smooths her palms over the orb and whispers a quiet *good night*.

A tear trickles from Hanna's eye and Lucius kisses her cheek.

"She needs us now..." he whispers in her ear.

"Who?" Hanna is still confused.

"The Lady..."

"My grandmother's sister?"

"Yes," Lucius says, and Reese nods, then enters her bedroom.

On the map is an insignia of a single rose – that is the destination, but something different about it stirs in Hanna's soul. She frets the subtle sense of déjà vu but shakes it off. The Lady of Brighton, Rose Grace Worthington, a daughter of blood relation to an intolerable banker, as the legend goes, must be saved by midnight on the eve of the Summer Solstice when the most evil of witches wishes for blood to be used to cleanse and purify their own soul – the blood of the most innocent to sanctify their allegiance to the dark and make them a family of darkness.

"Does Goldie wish for immortal power?"

"She wishes for power – in any form, she can get it." Lucius sighs.

"Then I feel like we are back to the beginning."

"You are…" he nods, placing the dim orb into a satchel.

Hanna hears scratching at the door; outside, she sees Thor covered in snow from the blizzard. Once inside, he shakes his coat, and they can feel the frost. Hanna hovers to examine him when she hears a disembodied voice.

"Tully?" Reese returns from the bedroom. In the corner of the kitchen, beneath a light shaped like a ball of yarn and oscillating – it gives off a spectrum of radiant light, and they hear the voice again.

"We can't hear you clearly, Tully," Hanna says when the voice becomes softer.

"Your vision," Hanna says, reaching to touch her. She can feel radiant energy, like heat given off by a light bulb. The light embraces her at the fingertips. Hanna recounts the vision she had when her daughter was born; how the Goddess and the Prince of Peace were visible and the demon was among them. Reese explains

11

that her vision was a foresight that would eventually unfold. Lucius adds that in the birth of their son they split them so the energy would be shared among the siblings and Lucas would be born to protect his very own sister; how they would not have the spirit of the Goddess and the birth of her son in one human body – with the diversion of their energy Goldie would have to end both their lives. The derision was effective. Through the vision of the demon, Hanna learned that there is a balance between the good and evil.

As Hanna continued to share a mental image of her vision, she also learns that Aly was blessed and cursed at birth; that Goldie could hate so much that she hexed the only family that showed her kindness – the only family The Lady had known – her illegitimate sister and cursed the beautiful young woman so that she aged and through her she would find her family and commit an evil curse against them. Hanna understands that her grandmother hid in her home where the curse would not affect her; but to leave meant that she was in danger so she tried to live as normal as she could to bless her children with the gifts of life – but those gifts had consequences too and Goldie chose her family to sacrifice in the name of the darkest hatred; she with the demon would choose the child and claim the rights to her immortality. Hanna's vision and her keen sense of intuition saved her daughter and her son with the help from her husband, but to banish the evil entirely is a matter they have not settled.

"She wants a baby," Hanna says, still focusing on the twilight of radiance in front of her.

"Goldie hadn't known the Crone carried a child…" Tully's voice is soft.

"Yes, The Lady of Brighton," Reese says when a portal opens in the far corner and a coolness from the underworld engulfs them. Jace emerges in his ethereal body that is opaque in the face of transparency where there would be skin. He then manifests into a material body and Hanna goes to him – he is cold to the touch.

"The story my mother told me as a kid…"

"What story?"

Hanna is eager.

"The beautiful Lady is taken by a demon from the dark underworld and in her womb is the infant she carries."

"She can't possibly…"

"In the light of the New Moon," Jace continues, "a sacrifice is happening all over again."

"Oh no." Hanna is awakened. Alert.

She darts her eyes to Reese …

"Mind over matter," Lucius says firmly.

The orb of light flickers and Tully's voice is gone. Hanna feels as if she is looking for the needle in the haystack, again, but alongside Lucius and Jace she is valiant – there is no one else. She ponders over the map when she turns to ask Jace; in the material body he can interact with Alysiah. She is beautiful like her father. He is regal despite his youth, and Hanna loves him as the father of her first born. She loves Lucius deeply and feels they are both her best friends. Together they prevail. They must. But she questions … *where do they begin?*

Jace holds his daughter with fatherly affection and Lucius takes notice. Thor licks at his paws at Jace's feet. The house is warm. Hanna thinks of Sterling's face and how fire scrying kept them bonded – and now she must return to her, to the little store, and she will be absent of those memories. She feels complete within the home and she cringes because she'll be called to duty – does her grandmother blame herself? She must. But Hanna cannot allow it. She takes a deep breath and when she exhales she smells a fragrance like a day lily and she muses over the scent, knowing it is winter, but somewhere else, in some other time perhaps, it is summer there and Hanna longs for spring. She thinks about if Jace

15

longs to be human again. Reese secures her place as Guardian of the North Coordinate but explains she'll relinquish the duty to care for the children. Hanna feels she will be needed – her intuition enables her to understand what is before her. Tully sent the reminder of her vision to move her – to recall that the Celestials have a divine plan.

The veil between the two worlds will be at its thinnest when the Samhain festival will celebrate the dead and Jace must commence a word of peace - but how will they get the dark others to listen?

Followers of the darkness feel the presence of the impending power and Jace has his work before him but for the night they must rest. Hanna appreciates the quiet. The peace.

Sterling opens the store at six o' clock AM in conjunction with the opening of *The Witches' Brew* located next door; the new location will complement the new sign hanging out front: *High Tide* has become *Mystic Mountains*, and Sterling is feeling exuberant over the change. She prepares to close the doors after dusting once again before the opening in the morning.

The next morning the bells clang as the door opens; Hanna notices that Sterling is radiant and her positive energy is infectious (in a good way).

"Welcome back," Sterling smiles and she rearranges the collection of scarves she has on the rack.

"Have I been gone for a long time?" Hanna is trying to grasp the lapse in time.

"You okay?" Sterling doesn't look up from the shelf.

"Yeah." Hanna musters a smile... looking for what to say... "You changed the sign," she is hoping the sign wasn't changed a year ago and she takes a seat behind the counter. She can remember how to open the register.

"You helped me pick it out yesterday."

"It's befitting," Hanna sighs, needing relief.

"I love it." Sterling stops arranging the shelf. "Did you take the kiddos to Reese this morning?"

"Yes," Hanna replies with a nod and she feels perplexed.

"Would you like to go next door to get us a cup of coffee?" Sterling asks and Hanna is eager.

She takes her satchel; the orb is contained within.

The bells clang, and she finds the glass doors are welcoming; the interior is decorated for Samhain. Candles are lit, the walls are adorned with sconces, they reflect from mirrors and the lighting adds an aura of ambience throughout the space.

Patrons are seated among the bar and the tables. Hanna takes a seat to be noticed when the worker asks "What are you having?"

The male bartender wears a black vest with printing that is reflective – *The*

Witches' Brew imprinted on it. His fingers are adorned with clunky metal rings and his ears are pierced. He wears a necklace with a black onyx that caresses the stubble of hair behind the gray v-neck.

"Two cups of coffee." Hanna responds, "to go."

"Cream? Sugar?"

"Um…"

"Is this for Sterling?"

"Yes!"

He laughs, breaking the awkwardness of the moment.

"She drinks hers black." He pours the coffee from a glass pot. "And for you?"

"Lots of cream and sugar."

"She usually sends in her employees."

"That's me. I'm the employee." Hanna musters a smile.

"You're married?" He says, pointing to her finger.

"Yeah, I am," she says casually.

"Are you a witch?" He looks puzzled.

"Yes. I mean we are hand-fasted."

"You tied the knot."

"We did. Literally."

"Congratulations."

"Thank you."

"My pleasure," he says, still observing the ring, "is that Celtic?"

"The Celtic woven band – a promise from my husband."

He collects the money and she places a tip into the jar.

"Thank you." He smiles. "My name's Bill. I'm the owner here."

"Hanna," she says, lifting her butt from the chair.

"We're having a gathering for the Sabbat," he says, "perhaps the two of you would like to come."

"Which two?"

He catches his mistake, "I meant you and Silver, but of course…"

"Of course," she says, and leaves the bar.

She enters the *Mystic Mountains* where the incense permeates her senses. In the next moment she turns subtly over her shoulder, the guest is not Goldie, she breathes deep, but they are a group of teenagers. There are four of them; two males and two females. Hanna senses they are couples. The blonde buys a *Craft Book for Teens* and Hanna rings her up. She sips from her coffee when they leave and she stares at the back door knowing Sterling must be back there but she does not dare to enter — because back there was where it all started. She thinks about The Lady back in Goldie's prison. No longer the Crone. Sterling must be preparing her altar for the Sabbat and Hanna peers at her coffee getting cold and as the hours idle by she thinks of Sterling who never got her coffee, wondering if she is still back there, but with that thought her attention turns to a journal and when she opens it she discovers her own neatly wrought hand and realizes those pages are the last of her two years.

The journal begins:

The Sisters of East Brunswick are not strangers to magic... but when she tries to read on she is interrupted by four witches who hover over the cauldrons, and she muses – *it's them!*

Chapter Two

"Sydney!" Hanna says and the warmth she's been feeling leaves the room.

"You do possess the spirit of the witch…" Sydney says.

"Not just because you work here…" Priscilla smiles her sweet smile.

"Well," Hanna speaks softly, "I learned a lot of what I know from you."

"I told you she was odd," Amber rolls her eyes.

"No, trust me," Hanna gasps, "…the time warp …"

"Would only happen in the most noble of circumstances," Sydney explains.

"Yes, the Goddess …"

"You're friends with the Goddess?" Amber huffs.

"Maybe she has…" Paisley interrupts when Sydney finishes her sentence.

"Met the Goddess…" Sydney says and she turns to Hanna who relates the story of the vision she had when Alysiah was a baby.

The Sister's Coven listens attentively as Hanna recounts the event as they happened when Sterling joins them.

"If the Goddess herself came to you then it must be a dire situation."

"We created a diversion by having another child so not only one child would possess the energies of the Goddess and the Prince of Peace."

"Then the situation was resolved?" Paisley asks.

"It was." Hanna still speaks gently when the clanging of the bells startles them.

"We have to work now, Hanna," Sterling opens the cash drawer and removes the one-hundred dollar bills and shuts the drawer.

"We'll be at *The Witches' Brew* this evening," Sydney says, appearing inquisitive when Hanna says, "do you have Rajah-Jade?"

"A what?" Sydney is further confused.

"The Magnificent Cat... an animal familiar." Then the customer pipes in, "Do you have a rose quartz chalice?"

An image of her grandmother's closet enters Hanna's mind and she thinks immediately – *duh, she lives at her grandmother's place*, but then she recalls those buildings have been demolished to make room for new construction then she has another vision of a quaint little cottage.

"Tully," she thinks that place must be a wreck – then she ponders how the home would be better than her old apartment or worse yet, Jace's.

Hanna's mind drifts again when she is brought back from her reverie – that locked closet and her grandmother's home are no more and her grandmother resides in that special place among the stars; she longs to see her again. Then she is distracted by the customers that now fill the shop. Hanna shows her guest the marble chalices they have in the store, but the customer only wants rose quartz. Hanna understands and she wants her grandmother's old chalice just the same.

"Let me check the basement." Hanna goes to the cellar where she takes her satchel; she finds all the things she may need: the talisman of the cat with the jade-colored eyes, the athame blade given to her by her husband, the orb that contains her memories and there in the bottom wrapped in an old cloth is the rose quartz chalice. Among her spiritual items is her grandmother's *Book of Shadows* and contained within are all the rituals of her life before she wed into a strict orthodox family. Hanna has never met Pratt other than the images in photographs and her memories of her grandmother's home only span five years. Alayna took Hanna away when the closet was discovered then Hanna, pregnant, was not forgiven by her mother for not being wed.

"That's too unorthodox under God," she said to her.

Hanna had never met Tristian either but she knows her grandmother is with them in the eternal life of the Celestial City.

"If I can order one for you…" Hanna says.

"Would you please?"

Hanna takes down her information.

"My grandmother preferred the rose quartz as well." She smiles and looks radiant.

The witch hands her a deposit; her hair looks frosty and her dimples are infectious; she is as radiant as Silver – they must be good friends Hanna thinks.

That evening *The Witches' Brew* interior décor looks medieval. The gargoyle on the entrance wall is unnerving; Hanna sees a flash of dark. The demon glares in her eyes and breathes into her as if to search her soul; she is alive, and he feels threatened momentarily then retreats, and her vision turns back to the wall. The gargoyle is an image of safety inside the bar; now, in the evening, they drink from glasses made of bronze and Hanna orders a mojito flavored with mango and mint. At this moment she is thankful for normalcy. Inside the walls are painted black and the sconces create a soft glow. There are skulls atop a shrine to honor the dead and Hanna is seated aside Lucius. He is modestly dressed in carpenter pants and a flannel shirt and heavy overcoat. Hanna dazzles in a long-sleeved dress and pumps. The charm of the magnificent cat adorns her neck. She is pale. Lucius takes notice but shrugs it off. The sisters gather together at a round table they reserved at the crowded bar. Popular contemporary music plays in the background. Sterling feels grounded there. She is calm and the atmosphere honors Pagans and is rich with tradition despite the music coming from the jukebox. The bartender approaches their table.

"You're still working?" Hanna says.

"I am. As the owner, I'm pretty much always here."

"What's the accent?" Amber asks without reproach.

"Aussie," he laughs.

"Charming." Sterling smiles and in walks a friend to take refuge from the cold.

"This is Elenor," she says, introducing Hanna, and Elenor is short, cute, and petite.

"We met today at the station." Sterling continues and Hanna simply says "Hello."

Her mind is on the sentient experiences and Reese; how long should Reese be with her kids? She had been away from Aly for long enough, she thinks. Her thoughts are then interrupted by Amber's intrusion.

"Tell us all about the great time warp," she says.

Hanna appears uneasy. The bar is silenced by the outburst. Hanna is greeted by Bill who is her strength at the moment. Hanna speaks calmly and casually as she explains to the lot of witches about her visions and the circumstances surrounding her past. Lucius remembers but his eyes peer at Hanna when a woman speaks…

"You gave birth to the baby of promise, honey." She says from the far corner.

The baby of promise? Hanna is confused.

"The Goddess… and the God," the older woman says… "they wish for a birth."

"The Goddess wanted my baby?"

"We only know there is a baby of promise, one that is birthed during the Solstice."

"So, now the Goddess, you know," Amber begins but Sydney stops her.

"No, she doesn't know," Sydney says, "and neither do the rest of us."

"Was my baby promised to the Goddess?" Hanna turns to Lucius who takes her by the hand, "just finish telling your story Hanna," and when she reaches the point of the time pause the room erupts in laughter. Elenor turns to Silver and Silver turns to Hanna…

"My sister could never be so cruel."

30

"I'm a witch and I find all this to be unbelievable," another woman says.

"Lucius?" Hanna turns to her husband, who can also remember.

"My memories are sparse, my love… not as deep and intimate as yours but I fully trust your experiences."

"The Lady of Brighton is just a legend," a male voice says.

"It's the truth," Hanna says, and she stands from her chair.

"No need to interrupt the lady," Bill says… "I'm sure she's not delusional. Let's give her a chance."

"Sure as shit she is," the man blurts out.

Hanna is feeling small. She stifles what she's really thinking and has a lot to digest – how can no one else remember? She wonders if she and Lucius still have a home at the lodge. Are the lodges of Vermont and Connecticut housing the Shamans? She feels disoriented when another thought pipes in – nothing has changed but one's

31

perception of the past. She excuses herself and enters the restroom. Her satchel containing magical tools is bound to her hip. She removes the crystal orb which glows subtly between her palms. Her grandmother's face is a blur but Hanna can hear her voice telepathically.

"Stay on your path," she assures her, "this is your journey," but Hanna is still feeling sullen and defeated. She feels robbed or cheated by the dark enemy as well as the light – they were not welcome to have her baby.

"You will understand," LaQuinta says and Hanna has a solid tear running down her cheek. She cradles the orb to her chest. She can feel the pain of her past. The pain of having her daughter taken away from her. She feels uncertain of her own future.

"The Lady is to bear a child," a strong masculine voice says and Hanna peers about the room with no vision and no one to be seen. The voice sounds like the God himself. She may bear a child to be used by the deities … or Goldie and the demon she created. She storms out of the restroom and into the bar, and they erupt in laughter once more. She is no longer perplexed but she is to some extent alone. She makes haste out the door and into the cold. Lucius follows behind.

"I only know that our children are safe," he says.

"But no one believes me." She whispers.

They embrace, "But you also cannot remember," she says.

"I remember, then, what I am supposed to do."

"I need Jace's help, Lucius." Her voice quivers. "Where do we live, Lucius?" Her thoughts are fleeting.

"We bought a little cottage about a month ago."

"And before that?"

"That's what I cannot remember. But you must understand that I do believe you."

"There is a lapse in your memory, and that cottage belonged to a witch named Tully."

Hanna finds a lone Raven perched on the roof of the *Mystic Mountain* and the moment she thinks… Sage also appears from a portal and Hanna extends her hand to her; the great bird of prey takes her arm and Clover takes flight.

"I still have my animal familiar," Hanna feels more confident. The bird takes flight and another portal opens; the bird disappears into it, and Hanna wants to know where she is going.

The portal is too small for a human to enter and it closes with Sage inside.

Lucius speaks, "No matter what … it doesn't matter who else …" and as he speaks, Sterling also enters the outdoors alongside Elenor.

"Elenor will be helping us at the shop," she explains, "she'll be a help as I take leave."

"On vacation," Elenor reiterates.

"Yes, that's right. I'll be leaving for two weeks."

Hanna nods, feeling awkward… This is the sister of the woman who stole her baby… and now she is merely an employee … Sterling must know nothing of her own sister. Hanna still forces a smile.

"My sister did not excel in the ways of magic," she insists and Hanna begins to speak, "but…" and Lucius walks away, kicks up stones with his feet, and huffs – a cue for her to stop speaking, and leave it alone.

"I'm sorry, I'll see you tomorrow…"

"To begin training Elenor."

Hanna waves them off. She pays her respect to her seniors – stifled by her husband. Lucius turns to her, "It's time to go, Hanna," he says.

"Where?" She seems baffled.

"Home." She envisions the quaint little cottage nestled in the mountains of the Appalachia; to the place where she met Tully when she experienced her first time warp in the way of a reverie.

Once home they burn a fire and Hanna has the gift of freely moving between worlds. She knows she can move within the portals – a sign from Sage and in the next moment Reese with Hanna's two children moves through the portal and Hanna senses déjà vu …

"How can we do that exactly?"

"By focusing on our energy centers, the chakras, and becoming one with the energy."

"Grandall?" She is saddened.

"He relinquished his powers onto you Hanna."

She senses a great deal of loss and a sense of guilt. Lucius takes notice and tells her not to worry. The fire is ablaze, "You'll understand all within time," Reese tries to reassure her. On a ledge overhead Sage sits quietly.

"You were meeting me here weren't you, you smart bird."

Hanna has heightened senses and keen awareness. She feels strong aside from feeling alone and she thinks she should go back to the sisters.

"They will be fine," Reese says, reading her mind. Hanna is reminded of Sydney, when they first met, and how she could finish her sentences. Hanna is tired and she is thankful to have Lucius.

Somewhere in the cavernous dwelling there is a man who is twenty years old. His hair is white. He peels the skin from his meat, feeding on the rats, with the force of his own nails. The occasional spider provides minimal water and the only company he had died there. He wears a burlap sack – the only possession they gave him. He was left there to be forgotten. He wants to live for only her – all he can think about.

And Jace, the overseer of the Underworld, is the balance of the duality that exists between the light and the dark – a torch to light the way. In her dreams she finds him in the Underworld where they walk a distance through the tunnel, "He cannot see us," Jace says.

"Maybe he can sense us." She takes notice.

"His energy is very low."

"And I don't think he was a witch… but maybe…"

He is seemingly sick, very cold, and covered in snot. There are feces – his own, and the rest from the rats.

"He is hanging on for her." Jace continues.

Hanna is startled from her sleep beside Lucius who is not awake. The dampness of the Underworld chills her bones, and she finds the bed sheet on the floor and pulls the covers over her head, but she doesn't feel the need for sleep because she knows he needs them.

Chapter Three

Hanna has unrelenting energy. She feels exuberant and enjoys the essence of her experience. At the back of the store engraved in stone is new inventory; the stone is a depiction of the Goddess, the God, the Prince and their unity in an embrace completing a full circle. Hanna reads the letters etched in stone:

Celtic tradition is rooted in the belief that there are places where humans can interact and communicate with the divine; Pagans go to these enchanting places where they can feel sacred energy, and while there, one might attain the Zen.

The thought comes to Hanna's mind: one must sacrifice a great deal of energy of extraordinary measure. Hanna immediately pulls a book of Zen from the shelf and flips through the pages. She comes to a concept of time and she stops. She reads:

What might cause a shift in the perception of time? The present moment, such as right now, has no duration of time, so the idea of now is already past.

The present moment breaks down in space and time having no concept of duration… as Hanna comprehends it. She thinks the past never happened or is always happening – perhaps that is the paradox. But she does feel she can conclude that time can cause a shift in awareness of time, hence, a lapse in memory. She focuses on the fact that the past is all a consideration in perception so now if one can no longer perceive the past in the same way then it's no matter if it occurred or not. She feels like grasping the otherwise perplexing state of déjà vu and she contemplates Mount Katahdin when Elenor enters the door.

"Good morning back there," she peeks around the corner.

"Hello," Hanna musters but she is preoccupied while contemplating a place to experience a profound mystical state of awareness and altered states of consciousness – the Shamanic Way, the way of the Zen Buddhist as described by the Celtic mystics – the way to the Warrior as taught by Grandall in the now ruins of the Hidden School of the Temples. As Hanna turns the page, she simply says, "How are you?" And removes a folded note where it is written: *in the end there's a little yellow bird that looks after us and keeps us on our path and to keep clear the way to becoming a Warrior.*

"Grandall," she says aloud when Elenor approaches her side, her voice chimes like a bell, "darkness seems like something that is difficult to defeat but the light is strong; it only takes a small amount of light to dispel the darkness."

"Perhaps to oblivion," Hanna huffs, "like for good this time. I know because Jace sent me…" when Sterling walks in they both stop talking. Sterling looks uneasy briefly and turns the sign to *open.*

"Sorry, I forgot." Hanna says.

41

"The lodges are now a School like the temples," a familiar voice says as Lucius steps through a portal. "All the lodges are fully restored."

"You spoke with your father?"

"He says we should come back to raise our children there…"

"Don't let us interrupt," Sterling says and she alongside Elenor make their way to the counter.

"The spirit place is where we need to go to communicate with a higher being …"

"Haven't we done that enough, Hanna?" His voice is pleading, but Hanna changes course.

"There is no end to a great circle, the circle, like life, is a perpetual motion that has no element attached to it …"

"The time warp again, Hanna?"

"Yes."

"What are you saying?"

"I feel the need to reclaim his great staff to have the strength to walk through trauma and feel the spirit of his presence."

"I felt the need to be behind you Hanna, but the words of my father… has me second guessing … what we need to do for the children…"

"Or the Lady of Brighton."

Hanna becomes engulfed in an aura of pure love – a state of being that she just cannot describe. Her grandmother, her grandfather and her uncle are like the color of indigo, like being shrouded in profound love and unity in her mind's eye. They embrace like the circle in stone when the moment only lasts for a few seconds and the mental image is gone. When the warmth fades Lucius can see a sparkle in her eye… "You would go without me wouldn't you?"

"Yes." She whispers knowing duty is of the highest good and Lucius walks out.

"Is everything okay in there?" Sterling asks.

Hanna simply replies, "We're okay," as she enters the store and Lucius walks out the door. She slides her card through the time clock and her shift has begun.

"Let me know when you want to conjure magic," Elenor giggles and Sterling wisps away and waves as she disappears from her spot.

"The portals are cooperating this season," Hanna says and Elenor wrinkles her brow.

"Haven't they always been working?"

"Not when there's a dark witch …"

"The energy here is rich," Elenor says, taking off her wool coat and slips her gloves into her purse.

"You mentioned Jace…" Elenor whispers.

"You know him?" Hanna is perplexed.

Elenor leans closer, "I have been where he is." She whispers, "But that is for another time and place… my life is better now."

"So you've been to the underworld?"

"I was in and out of consciousness…. I was taken to the other side to determine where I wanted to go… and I got another chance at life."

"A near death experience?"

"Yes. Drugs you see… but I am better now."

Hanna's mind wanders over the idea that her grandmother's sacred things were stored in a locked linen closet and how she might be able to do them more justice. She then has the intuitive thought; the message on the note, scribed within the *Book of Zen* says to be patient, to let events happen and not to force anything. In a meditative moment she has a vision: two crescents with a staff running down the center. The image stings a little. She ponders if the Goddess wanted a child as much as the dark had wanted.

"I'm sorry to hear that," she says, snapped out of her reverie.

"Have a lot on your mind?"

"I do."

Her mind comes fully to the present.

"His staff is calling me…" 'Elenor glances in her direction as she straightens the stones on the glass case.

"Perhaps it is …" Elenor says and Hanna takes the conversation into another direction… "Your astral body left your physical body and you explored the cosmos, too?"

"No, just to the Underworld where I met Jace. I had a life review, and a chance to go back to my physical body."

Then she surprises Hanna, "You see, Sterling would never conceive of her sister… being so evil…"

Hanna keeps her cool "Never in that regard."

"They are twins and should share that special bond."

"You saw the future."

"I did. I saw where I would be and some of the past."

"Do you see the symbolism?"

"Good and evil for sure."

"Yes. And the duty of the blessed one…"

"Do you mean the cursed one?"

"More symbolism… I see both…"

"Possibly as one perceives it…"

"The duty to balance the dark and the light."

"Hanna, it sounds as if you are intended to take a Shamanic journey and you may want to state an intention for it."

"I've had visions with Jace lately as well."

"I brought Jace's most trusted companion or rather Thor brought me to you, here, and then he returned I suppose."

"If your visions are like mine…"

"Visions of a solitary witch Hanna, remember, there is or can be great power in solitude."

"Like my grandmother."

"You'll have to tell me about her sometime."

"But I know nothing about you."

"I primarily practice alone."

"Why is that?"

"I was an only child, perhaps that's why…" she winks.

"I'm alone as well." Hanna thinks of the lapse in memory that she herself does not experience.

Hanna thinks that Elenor has a Mary Poppins flare to her and she chuckles to herself. She excuses herself for a break and there she clears her mind only to have a flashback and her arms feel bare again, robbed of the most precious thing. She yearns to be with her daughter as if she intuitively also feels the pain of another – she is the only one who can feel the pain of The Lady – the inherent pain. She turns to the scrying mirror to call upon Reese. When she reaches her she is giving Aly a bath which makes her smile.

"She made her way into the kitchen," Reese says from the scrying mirror reflecting back to Hanna. She then flashes Hanna an image of the peanut butter jar and the two children covered in the butter. She then sees Lucas aside his sister. Hanna feels relief and wishes them well. Her shift ends at three o'clock PM. The sensation of a glow, like warmth, engulfs her body again and she smells an aroma: lily of the valley. The scent permeates the room like a divine message and as Hanna steps away from the mirror all fades and she soon forgets because work duties overwhelm her; in preparation for Samhain, the shop is becoming crowded.

In the path of the divine sacred one must follow the path led by synchronicity, a customer says, her face in a book, and slams it shut and approaches Hanna.

"I'll take this one," she says, looking cheery.

"What path are you on?" Hanna is naturally curious.

"I'm a witch first, but I'm always looking for the path of ultimate enlightenment – the ultimate truth!"

"Well, what do you think it is?"

"What?" Her eyes get big.

"The truth?"

"Oh."

Hanna hands her a single for change and she continues to rummage in her hand bag.

"Better to ask the Goddess herself," she smiles and a silver tooth gleams from behind her red lipstick. Hanna gives her an inquisitive eye. The eccentric woman with purple hair takes the bag. Hanna feels contentment and smiles at the idea of going home to her two young ones; contentment in the back room.

In the after-hours, Hanna leaves Elenor to work the desk as she is comfortable with working the register. Hanna finds their stock in the back room and lays her eyes upon a bag of individually wrapped wands. She reaches for one but gravitates toward another as if its energy field connected with her own field of energy. She picks up the box and peers at the marble spiraling wand through the cellophane face. She slowly and deliberately breaks open the package because the energy she feels is splendid. When she holds the cool, smooth wand in her palm it vibrates subtly in her hand and she turns it over; there are initials engraved in the stone: *A.E.H* – her daughter's initials. She examines the package and finds it is not inventory but is addressed in her name, sitting among the store inventory. Hanna's mind stirs, thinking of the ruby studded wand of her adversary. She feels the power of such an eccentric wand in her hand – why marble? When most other wands are made from wood. The handle feels firm in her hand. Elenor enters her space; the credit card machine is out of paper. Hanna moves to the front and lifts the top piece and removes the jammed piece of paper. The receipt prints smoothly for the woman who buys a crystal. Just then, Sterling enters the store yielding a smile.

"We'll be closed for a week for renovation," she says, "I am making the store bigger." Hanna knows she's comfortable having the store closed during the week of festivities; the Wiccan community is having a fire festival to honor those who passed beyond the veil of physical existence. Hanna thinks immortality is a curse but wisps it away with a clear thought; the Way to Satori (bliss and enlightenment) was through the mind, the home of clairvoyance and sentient thinking. She feels her Mind is sharp, clear and somehow progressed beyond any comprehension - with the wand she feels super human.

"A wand made of stone is most precious," Sterling says, eyeing the wand behind her spectacles. The energy of that stone courses through her body. Sterling looks closely but she knows to never touch the sacred tools of another witch.

"How could you afford such a wand?" She questions out loud. "I've only seen such a wand at the *Two Black Cats & Sage* before it became owned by a follower of dark magic."

She places the wand into her satchel that is armed with the orb, the athame blade, *Book of Shadows* and around her neck are the jade-studded eyes of the magnificent cat. She steps out the door, into the cold and frigid air and there is Thor laying beside the door entrance and above on the rafters are Sage and Clover side by side. She is missing the sight of the white dove – a sign of balance – why is she armed with the full artillery of the witch? She does not know. She is late taking her lunch and as she enters *The Witches' Brew,* she finds Lucius there waiting for her.

"Did you send me a wand?" She asks against her better judgment.

"What? No. Hello to you too." He gestures for her to have a seat. "I cannot say that I have. "

Hanna tells her husband about the wand and about Sterling seeing one at the old store. She wonders who could have sent her such an expensive and prestigious wand...

"I'd ask to see it, but I am famished," he pats his stomach. She musters a smile. After filling their stomachs on nachos and sandwiches, Bill closes early to join the

Wiccans who have already gathered outside for the beginning of the fire festival. The air is calm for the celebration of Samhain to begin which is reassuring; Hanna and Lucius arrive to find that the bonfires are lit and the houses can be seen in the distance with pumpkins aglow. Festive skulls and bones adorn their front porches. Their altars are ready to perform a spell. They enchant crystal balls to see clearly into the future. But this night is also special because they call upon the Goddess of the Night to aid them in many blessings. Hanna removes her shoes and her stockings are thick. She is warmed by the fire. The chanting begins and Hanna cuts a door with her athame blade so that she may enter the sacred circle without disrupting the sphere of energy. She moves closer to the fire and sees that there are over one hundred Pagans among them. Many are members of the *Druid's Army*. Lucius does not search the parameters for his father, but instead he holds the hand of a beautiful woman who looks dazzling as her face searches the starry sky for a glint of hope that the Goddess of the Dark will emerge from them. Hanna still dazzles in his eyes and the woman dressed in a full cloak emerges from the circle and centers herself among the fire, "We are the star people," she says. Rocks have been laid upon the ground to form the sacred circle. The High Priestess whose pentacle shines upon her neck raises a wand toward the darkened sky and she sings in the name of the Goddess of the Night first and then to the Goddess of the *Celestial City* to merge as one upon the earth and she beckons…

"Oh' great Goddess we call upon your presence in this time to honor those who have passed beyond the veil and to see your wisdom to know your vision!"

As all is still there is a spark that erupts around them and from the smoke and emerges not either Goddess but Jace, Lord of the Dark Underworld.

He is an eternal spirit body who will never age from his youth and the Wiccans are bewildered but Jace speaks calmly and reassuringly…

"I am here on behalf of the divine…" he begins when a disgruntled gentleman with the cloak the color of walnut steps forward.

"On behalf of the divine? But you're just a boy…"

"Let the boy speak," the High Priestess says and Jace doesn't hesitate.

"There is a Universal Order, and in that order, there are laws to bring balance and harmony to the dark and the light! In that agreement, there is a Code of Ethics that sanctions us in a unity to bring peace to the chaos. As Prime Minister of the Dark I request this order to be delivered to the ones who seek power, control, and dominance; under the Universal Agreement we will all become one power."

The gentleman bursts with laughter and Jace flashes a piece of parchment engraved with the names of the Divine and rolls the scroll into his fist, and as it turns to light it erupts into particles of light. He then materializes and walks among them. The gentleman is stumped. A woman approaches him, "You are one of them…" She is elegant and aged. She speaks slowly and intently, "you have walked among them and have become one with them…you are on your path…" she is comfortable in her demeanor.

"One with who." The gentleman says.

She goes on… "The Coven of the Phoenix … my daughter…."

Hanna nods and takes a step toward the woman and offers her hand; when the woman reaches for her hand she is startled…

"Who is your daughter?" Hanna faces her.

"She planted the seed long ago," the woman says …

The man with the critical voice approaches, "Don't listen to that crazy old wife," he hollers, and his breath is full of booze… "she thinks she's a mother alright, to the legend herself," he bellows.

"The Goddess planted her seed aside my daughter." The woman is still calm. She flashes Hanna a bag of bones – she is aged sixty with pale skin and green eyes that are distant.

Hanna takes the bag from the woman, "Who are you?"

"I am Alexandra," she replies … "or I was once."

"Once?"

"Before she died," she whispers.

"She couldn't live without her…" another voice says. "The name is June," she speaks directly to the intoxicated man… "My friends call me June-Bug."

The young woman is sweet and reminds Hanna of Paisley and Priscilla. She looks for them but there are too many around.

"I remember." She whispers to Hanna.

Hanna is quiet.

"Who has died?" She turns back to Alexandra.

"It's just an old wives' tale." The man sniggers.

"The Lady of Brighton?" June says.

Alexandra scans the cold night with her eyes, "We had our rituals here too…"

"The Goddess wishes for a daughter," June continues.

"Old wives' tale…" the man continues.

"How do you know?" Hanna asks.

"How can you call yourself a witch?" June is flustered.

"I'm just here for the beer." He grins.

June rolls her eyes.

"He doesn't like women much," Hanna says as he belches.

"Don't mind him, ladies," a man says behind a thick red beard and plaid flannel cuffed at the sleeves.

"Can't believe no woman," the drunk sniggers before staggering off and the bearded man is polite, "Sorry, he's harmless."

"Harmless." Alexandra says.

Hanna is standing with a bag of bones and Lucius peeks inside. He sees what was once a dog but what he calls a coyote …. Alexandra corrects him. Then walks off.

"She's not dead." June says "but in her mind she has died."

Hanna is solemnly wondering about the bones.

Chapter Four

As the cold harshness of the darkest days ensues, the Fire Festival of All Hallow's Eve continues. As Lord of the Shadows, Jace returns to the Underworld and awaits his chance to find his queen; but Goldie has other plans, and so the darkness is in chaos beyond the foolishness of drunkenness.

Hanna darts her finger to her satchel – "You behold the curse so long as you keep those shadows among you…" but Hanna feels no fear; her grandmother's *Book of Shadows* has been blessed – she feels within her soul.

"A follower of the dark brought me to you in this vision…" Alexandra continues to speak, but her words are lost in the chorus of chatter; the Pagans sing, dance and chant the mantras of Hallow's Eve…

"Blessed be the Goddess…" they say and Hanna takes up her satchel to keep the troubled woman from prying any further.

Lucius hands her the bag of bones, but she refuses, "those are tainted by the curse," Alexandra says, and Hanna can see traces of tears upon her cheeks.

"My grandmother…" Hanna searches for words, but she is too choked up to think.

"She was in the dark…" Alexandra says but Hanna will hear none of it. She walks off, briskly, and Lucius drops the bag of bones and follows after.

"Don't mind what she says…" then he finds his father, Luther, convening with the Warlock's Coven among other men. One of them is smoking a cigar. He is aged and he flashes them a deck of cards; the people are enthralled by his magic. Another challenges him and they duel one another; Alexandra belts out a scream and June Bug finds Hanna. Hanna's attention steers away from them.

"She lost her daughter," June says… "then she adopted all of us girls." She tosses her hand into the air, and there are a dozen girls among them of various ages appearing in their twenties; Hanna is overwhelmed, but she gathers herself.

"How can they care about cards?" Alexandra says.

June Bug explains, "She told us how the loss forced her into hiding… the hex…"

"But she hexed my grandmother, too."

"She just doesn't know who else to believe…" then Luther interrupts them.

"Come back to the lodges," he says, but Hanna's mind is whirling.

"You can leave Virginia behind," he continues.

"Our place is vacant in Connecticut," Lucius says.

"And the lodges in Vermont," Luther adds.

Hanna enjoys the idea of being among the Shamans; Virginia has her feeling as though she is drowning. Hanna sees the magicians conversing with the woman – Alexandra appears to be screaming and pleading at the same time.

"She's the daughter of an evil witch," someone in the background says. "The Lady they call her…"

Hanna can take no more.

"She's the follower of Grandall," June Bug says.

Hanna sighs.

"Your grandmother's Coven…" another girl's voice is shaking and Hanna steps closer to the fire momentarily when she thinks of her babies – when they diverted the energy among two instead of one – she thinks – who else wanted her child? She shrugs the feeling.

She turns her attention back to June… "How is it that you can remember?"

"I was a student of Grandall before Alexandra found me alone on the hill… I was the only one with my memories, me and Malaki but Alexandra doesn't take in boys."

"What about my grandmother's Coven?"

"Alexandra has taught us the legend… your grandmother broke her ties to the Coven and hence the curse was placed upon her and her family."

"Where is Malaki?"

"To find his place among men; he was searching for an army, the Druid's Army, when he was found by a nomad."

"Bernard?"

"I'm not sure."

"No one understands you…" the other girl says.

"Who are you?" Hanna says, feeling overwhelmed.

"She means his position in the darkness…"

"You're associated with evil," the other girl cuts her off.

"His darkness is not evil…" Hanna tries to defend Jace.

Lucius steps in and places his hand upon her back, "We'd just be running away," he changes the subject.

"No," Hanna says softly…

The drunks sing loud, the Pagans ring bells, they clap, chant and dance. The two magicians are still entertaining them. Hanna feels out of focus, confused.

"We'll see you at camp," Luther says and walks away.

"Those men are in their eighties," the girl says, and June retorts, "only one of them… Mr. William Banks…"

Hanna is startled by the name, as if it means something to her.

"LaQuinta's father," June continues.

Hanna makes haste toward the two men; in her mind, he does not appear eighty, but Hanna pays no more attention to their ages; she notices the other gentleman must be ten years younger; the other man is Edgar as Alexandra shouts his name to scorn him.

"My dear," he says calmly, and the other woman slaps him across the shoulder; his new wife, Hanna assumes, and her intuition proves correct. "She's your ex wife," the woman scoffs.

"You left me … if I need to remind you," Edgar says and Alexandra throws up her hands, "because you cared more to be among men…"

"And you care more among girls."

Alexandra huffs, "Have you forgotten about Rose?" She scorns and takes his deck of cards into her hands when William grabs her by the wrist.

"What is this?" Luther says from afar.

"Family." Lucius says, and Hanna remains focused.

"One gave me Rose and the other raised her…" Alexandra says to the bystanders who have gathered among them; most are curious of the town legends surrounding them.

"We know," June Bug says casually and Hanna feels the satchel at her waist burn with intensity. She takes the orb into her hands and the commotion ceases.

"Does he even know you're dead?" Hanna says flatly into the orb.

But her grandmother's face is serene.

"I didn't …" she begins and her voice quivers a bit.

"She stopped speaking to the family," William Banks steps forward, "after her marriage…"

"To protect them…" her grandmother continues.

"The hex?" Hanna appears to understand.

"Magic is best left to a deck of cards…" Edgar says.

"Yes, because Magic is damaging to us all…" William contends.

"You're not a Warlock?" June asks.

"No, I'm no longer in the practice of magic and sorcery."

"Then what are you doing at a fire festival?" She asks.

"I'm an entertainer…" he says, and turns to Alexandra when Edgar takes a deep breath and begins to light a cigar. At age seventy-seven he still maintains his mannerisms. The crowd among them has moved on to a jousting competition. The rest drink from goblets, feast on turkey legs, and dine on cheese. Within a barn the area houses a large grand cottage that reminds Hanna of Connecticut and Vermont – a sign she takes as the future. Edgar secured Brighton as his own when Alexandra left to tend to an all-girl's home. The legend says that she was in exile as a witch - something the children outside of Brighton say because the wealthy live a different kind of life. Then it dawns on Hanna – Rose, The Lady of Brighton, is just like the legend says – she was possessed by evil as the Priestess of the Dark cursed her soul – Goldie that is, hexed Rose as she hexed her own grandmother. The words of the legend are imprinted in the minds of the town; the daughter of an illegitimate witch became in the possession of a demon. Hanna doesn't know if she should speak; she places the now dim orb back into her satchel. Alexandra leaves the men to squalor among themselves; their form of magic will never help her to find Rose.

Hanna has also been scolded as evil as she is in direct lineage to the cursed and her affiliation with the overseer of the dark – Jace – does not win her positive attention. June feels Alexandra is also lost, desperate, and still yearning to have her daughter back. Hanna thinks her grandmother never forgave her father for the affair she had with her mother. Hanna plans to consult the orb at a later time, but for now, the knowledge of her family's affiliations overwhelms her. She thinks her great-grandfather, Mr. William Banks, is lousy with magic and she storms off to enter the quiet. To meditate. To travel the cosmos and escape. She hears her husband's voice but she does not respond; she collects the bag of bones that was left on the ground and she does not know why, but she feels the need to give them a proper burial; in the place of Brighton – at least until she can lift the hex so she can think clearly among its grave.

"Duke," her mind says, "the protector."

She follows the river. She intuitively goes directly to the place where the bones were found and from the thick of mud she finds beads; the very source of the curse, and she knows not to disturb them. The material, the source, of a curse should never be startled; the curse had its victim and would be appropriately buried among the bones so the curse remains attached to it and not be bestowed onto any others. But what is the hex of her Grandmother? She wonders. What is she to find here?

Hanna moves the mud over the bones and packs it tight to keep with it the curse that took its life. Hanna returns that evening to the quaint little cottage that she temporarily calls home – knowing that she cannot continue to stay there. Reese is off duty and turns in to rest. Hanna finds her husband asleep and she lays down too. Rest – her mind quickly goes into dream mode and she enters the cosmos; her ethereal body forms like Jace. There, she finds her guide who takes her deep into the Underworld.

"Lakota," she says softly, and he smiles back at her.

"Hello Hanna."

"You're dead?" She responds.

"I was poisoned by the bite of a rattlesnake."

"Why are you in the darkness?"

"I was called upon by the Prince of the Dark… to guide you."

"Why can't Jace see me himself?"

"He is a ruler now… not a mere guide… he is one who gave his life for the protection of another."

"He was murdered by a dark entity."

"Yes. Professor Beecham is his name."

"Yes."

"Jace was granted his position by the Celestial Body."

"Who exactly?"

"The Council of Deceased Elders."

"And the Goddess?"

"She did much to approve."

"Jace gave himself to Aly, our daughter."

"And they did not keep their promise."

"What promise?"

"The High Priestess could have ruled like Jace but they decided to go into evil when they tried to sacrifice the blood of the most innocent child."

"My child was born on the eve of the Winter Solstice…"

"On the darkest day… part of the curse I'm afraid."

Lakota takes her to the depths of the Underworld. Hanna's ethereal body is not buoyant like she is in the presence of the Divine. She feels weighted, thick and salty, as if she is merely being preserved, rather than enhanced - how can Jace stand it here? Lakota breaks her concentration and they find before them graves with no names.

"These were prisoners," Lakota explains, "of an unknown tribe; Indians to the whites but no one knows how they got here when the tribal Shamans didn't bury their dead."

"Wouldn't it be the whites…"

"Who buries the bodies of an enemy?"

"Another tribe?"

"Some say that Grandall himself buried the dead you see here."

"Where is he now?"

"To be reborn. To grow again and become a great spirit."

"I don't understand."

"You will see… but first there is more to explain.

Lakota is calm and casual. His spirit body is opaque and shimmers despite its density of dark matter. Hanna grazes her palm across the erected stone with no name…

"These are the people of the Lakota tribe…"

"Your intuition is telling you this?"

"Yes."

"Good."

"I was deceitful to gain a sense of your strengths for the impending journey."

"Another journey?"

"I need to be specific here Hanna, you are cursed by the hex and are therefore disadvantaged."

"How?"

"You are not permitted to use magic like your grandmother was not."

"But how…"

"Exactly … you must use your senses, the mind, your intuition, and don't forget about tools…"

"Tools that are used for magic…"

"But they have many uses…"

"Just not for magical purposes?"

"Precisely."

"How then?"

"You will need to be creative."

"How can I…"

"The dark enemy hexed you, much like the Lakota tribe, so that you cannot achieve the Highest Order."

"Goddess?"

"No. High Priestess, an adept in magic, and then anything Divine would be included."

"How does the hex work?"

"When your grandmother passed the hex then was passed on to you – the next witch in your lineage."

"Then not my mother?"

"No. She is not a practicing witch and she has forsaken you."

"A contemptuous dark."

"But her dark is like his dark…" Lakota points toward a portal that is opening to gain access to the Underworld. Hanna sees in a vision a male youth who is face down on the floor. His spirit body enters the portal.

"His darkness," Lakota begins, "is full of grief, sorrow and fear…"

In the next moment, Hanna can see his life through a review; she sees a man, likely his father, scowling at him, close to his face; he raises a fist and strikes the boy. Hanna can see the subsequent years of his drug abuse; she understands his plight and then she realizes the fears within her own mother – how her mother is simply afraid because she does not understand that Wicca is a nature-based religion that accepts the Divine Mother, the Goddess, as overseer of all things that are light; Hanna's heart is full of empathy. She sees her mother who lost her father and brother and how she fears the Craft that got them there – she fears the dark magic and sees all of Witchcraft as dark. She knows that her mother cannot see the workings of the Craft for the highest good of all with no harm done. His darkness, the boy's, is not evil but is of pain. Hanna can also sense the pain that Jace feels; his own father abandoned him after he beat his mother – how Jace feared to be like his father – but he overcame the fear, grief and sorrow to save Aly's life.

"He wants a queen." Hanna whispers.

"Yes," Lakota laughs, "we all need someone."

"Who needs me?"

"Besides your children?"

"Yes."

"The Lady… the one the outsiders call The Lady of Brighton."

"But we already set her free…"

"But we are within a time lapse now…"

"Oh, yes…"

"She is no longer cursed, hexed into a wise Crone they use for the dark, like they use Mr. Beecham for demonic reasons… but she is of her own body now and hasn't aged over twenty years."

"She carries a child…"

"Pregnant. You are right."

"Then that is convenient…"

"As Goldie aims to sacrifice her child as she tried with your child."

"To shed the blood of the most innocent."

Hanna then has another vision as she sees Goldie in her youth and two girls who call each other Kamra and Victoria …

how Kamra is brutal and Goldie's face is forced into the earth; Kamra sits on top of her with the blonde, Victoria, laughing in the background. Hanna feels empathetic once more.

"So you see his darkness is unlike her darkness…"

"But their pasts are similar."

"Yes, indeed."

"One harms himself while the other seeks to harm others."

"And take power by possessing others."

Hanna learns, once again, that Jace is the Lord of the Darkness but also due to his courage, he has the blessing of the Goddess to show the deceased out of the dark and into the light. When her regard for prisoners of the dark is evident, her vision then shifts, and she can see a woman and a man in small quarters; she realizes that they are like prison cells. The woman is dead within the hole where she is being held.

"She is what you call a Guardian," Lakota explains, and Hanna gasps.

Lakota continues, "She is Alexis, Guardian of the North Coordinate…"

"No wonder Goldie is so powerful…"

"That's right. They took possession of the North when they found you…"

"And she stole my baby."

"But there is a reason there has not been total victory… light is a powerful source as well."

"There were many of us…"

"She's just more willing than most to find power."

"She seized Alexis's power.. the way she took from my grandmother."

"And now she has taken yours," he says before fading away and Hanna turns her attention to the man who is barely alive, but is emaciated and merely breathing… His hair and beard have grown long and his fingernails are like blades from his fingers; his teeth are tarnished.

"She refused to eat rats," the man says.

"You can see me?"

"I haven't seen another face since she died here."

The woman, Alexis, is shackled. In the cold her body has preserved. Hanna's central body flickers before the man as he shouts for her not to go…

"I am Michael," he coughs, and she fades away … and when she awakens she can smell breakfast. Reese is up early.

Chapter Five

They have not gone to Connecticut as that's been their argument for the past hour. They finish their meal in silence. The small cottage is comforting for Hanna. Her children play on the floor. The moon wanes. Hanna plops on the couch and takes a deep breath. She does not want to leave Virginia; she feels a connection with the area: the mountains, the river, and all she has known. Tully, she learns, had a cottage in Virginia before she moved to Connecticut; the witches there were solitary practitioners like herself but Hanna feels no connection with the area although she is fond of the Shamans; her senses tell her there is more within than without. She ponders over having magical tools if she is cursed by the darkness – how can she use tools without practicing magic? She thinks about Grandall and where he has gone when she hears a voice inside her that says, "Grandall relinquished his immortality – he aged and died naturally."

"June Bug," Hanna recognizes the voice.

"It's me. Just like Sydney but this time the sisters chose not to help you."

"But why?"

"It's not personal, they are just unable to help this time."

Hanna shakes it off – they must have their reasons. Alysiah and Lucas fill her heart and soul with love by the sound of their laughter. Her thoughts drift to Michael and back to June Bug. "Where are you?" Hanna thinks quietly and telepathically.

June responds, "Homeless."

"What?"

"I was a child of the temples, a student, then Alexandra found me. I stay in her group home, but it's just a place to stay. It's not like a home. I mean, not any that I know… I've always been an orphan."

"How do we connect?"

"We're both sensitive witches with a keen perception through our intuitive minds."

"I know," Hanna says softly and thinks momentarily that she wishes she could be normal and not be a witch; she shakes it off. She wants to help Michael; she wants to be with her babies. She is torn. Her soul yearns for redemption – to redeem her grandmother from the curse. But hasn't she already? But only through death. How does she lift the curse that has hexed her now – down through the generations. She now must, once again, protect Aly. Hanna wants to connect with her via the orb but a subtle thought keeps her from doing so; why does she feel she should not? What would Grandall do? Then she thinks she hears her husband who would say … "magical tools can be dangerous for you, Hanna." Hanna feels a chill move up her spine. Lucius impedes her concentration. She blinks. Then no sooner than June enters through a portal – "Let me get right to it," she says, "I'm here to help you… to help Alexandra."

"To do what?"

"To find Rose. And her baby."

"Alexandra sent you?"

"No. Grandall sent me."

Lucius does not want to go. She knows this. But the hex must leave her and to leave from exposing Aly to the curse. An hour later she leaves her home and enters the store; *Mystic Mountains* has a face lift; the interior is stunning. The walls are blue like the ocean and accents stream from the ceiling, crystals and orbs glow against the lighting. Hanna doesn't want to leave Virginia for Connecticut. Part of her is now yearning to be a solitary witch who can work remotely – but why can't she? She ponders the idea for a moment when her first customer walks in the door. No bells clamber against the glass; the woman's demeanor is friendly. The woman is heavy and walks with a crutch. Her hair is wild and frazzled. She wears eyeglasses like coke bottles: round and clear, but the rims are full of stars. Hanna feels that she is a woman who is in touch with the greater good of the people.

"Susan," Hanna says on a whim.

"Yes," the woman chuckles. "It's an anomaly, isn't it," she continues, "unless…"

"No, you're absolutely right," Hanna says, "I don't know you."

"Always a mystery…"

"Yes."

"I'm looking for a few items to give my daughter," Susan moves on.

"What can I help you find?"

"A satchel for magical tools… like that one there …" she points to Hanna's sack.

"I do have a few of those in the back room. The others have sold and I haven't gotten them out yet."

She moves to the back room to dig through a few boxes. She emerges, yielding a sack that looks like the Milky Way galaxy.

"Sold." The woman shouts very pleased.

"Can I get you anything else?"

"No. I think I can find the rest." Susan assures her and begins collecting oils, candles, incense and stones. She fills the bag as she goes.

Hanna has an inkling to ask, "Are you familiar with the Lady of Brighton?"

"Yes, I do hun," she frowns, "she is every witches' nightmare."

"Nightmare?"

"I don't mean her personally, but what happened to her…"

"To be hexed by an evil and sinister witch."

"Yes. Such a shame. So young, so beautiful and with a baby. It's a great legend … a great tragedy."

"Yes."

"A dark witch poisoned that young woman severely… Most other witches my age are familiar with the estate – their land was auctioned and it's a pride place for Pagans to celebrate in the festivities; at least it could stay in the ownership of a witch."

"Who is that?"

"He is an old man named Porter. From Europe many years ago."

"How old?"

"He's now over one hundred if you can believe that."

"That is hard to believe."

"I heard that the land will be going up for auction again… two magicians want it, one who wants it back and the other who wants it too … for the money they say. Brighton brings a lot of revenue… but he wants to develop the land and do away with the land that had his daughter so cursed. The curse they say that killed her."

"How exactly?"

"A broken heart – a heart so huge she choked on it. Lost her breath of life."

"The curse that says she can never practice magic and will be passed down for generations to come?"

"Then you know it too…"

"Well then I can still meditate." The words slip from her mouth.

"Thought the place had strange energy." She glares at Hanna briefly and places her items on the counter. Hanna rings up the total and Susan hands her a crisp one-hundred-dollar bill.

Hanna still feels magical. She doesn't feel cursed – like being a week pregnant – one doesn't know she is pregnant again with a third child. She is only twenty-three. Hanna places her hand to her abdomen - she relishes the idea that she still has her mind's eye – her keen sense of intuition – her telepathy and she can move through portals freely when the weather doesn't dampen transportation. But she cannot create a spell or evoke the Goddess. She takes a deep breath and tries to relax.

"I'm pregnant again," her mind jolts. She is still in the store but in her mind's eye she is taking a pregnancy test – and it's positive. This she knows; she knows it like she knew Susan by name, and she takes back what she said about the "not knowing one is pregnant," because a witch knows – a witch knows energy, energy like foresight and premonitions; a witch can move through space and time and her mind just left the present moment and glimpsed the future.

Her stomach grumbles after three hours of work and she enters *The Witches' Brew* and she finds Bill behind the counter.

"So what will it be?" He smiles.

"Load me up on caffeine," she jokes.

"Oh yeah? Any special brew?"

"As opposed to alcohol." She grimaces uncertain of her pregnancy this time.

"Ah," he says in his Australian accent. "You got a bun cooking in the oven?"

"My third. And my last."

He maintains his smile and she slaps a bill onto the counter.

"Give me the grilled cheese but hold the tomato soup, I don't need the heartburn."

"Chips it is."

The register chimes. He pours her a cup of hot coffee and a glass of water, "It's on the house," he winks and she leaves the bill for a tip as she takes her first sip.

"Thank you." She is charming.

"No problem." He knocks his knuckles onto the counter and moves to the next customer.

She squeezes the lemon into her glass. Lucius walks in and she forces a smile – uncertain how he will take the news. She feels he'll be happy but not so happy about another adventure to help a witch. He kisses her on the cheek as he takes a seat. He orders the mean veggie burger with a side of fries that he dips in ranch dressing.

"I always loved gravy on my fries," he says casually as his eyes meet Hanna's, "What is it babe?"

He notices her discomfort.

"I'm pregnant. Again."

He smiles like the Cheshire Cat.

"Oh, good. Nothing to be afraid of then."

He takes her by the hand and kisses her fingertips.

They are served their food when he says, "I've been offered another job…"

"Where?"

He pats her on the knee, "In Connecticut, honing my skills in building primarily and then there's always working the ski lifts."

"Building where?"

"They want to remodel some of the lodges. And I'll get paid well. I assure you."

"But I'm not ready to leave Virginia."

"Well we cannot live solely on the store salary and that was just a temporary job until you found something else … now I can work and you can stay home."

"Jobs are scarce I understand, but the cottage is paid for."

"So is the lodge." He takes another bite.

The next day is rain. She stands over the bathroom sink and peers at a second pregnancy test that confirms her initial results. She doesn't flinch. She is casual and feels good overall. She places the test strip in the plastic it came in – a keepsake she has come to love after Aly and Lucas. She heads into the living room to accompany her babies. The cottage is comfortable and Reese is there to watch over it if they must go anywhere. Tully is a blessing to Hanna and she feels a sense of attachment to the places that were owned by an adept solitary witch; the place has good vibes, a history worthy of energy.

Reese emerges from the kitchen, "I have a date," she says "I'm going home and later tonight I'm going out."

"You're off baby duty," Hanna gleams. And Reese gives her a hug.

She thinks about June Bug who now occupies the guest room; both women have sworn to help Hanna. Hanna feels certain she has it good where she is now. Her work hours at the store coincide with Reese's availability; she works during the day and is home with the children at night – certainly Lucius can find employment in Virginia.

She hopes Reese will tell her all about her date and in the coming week *Mystic Mountains* will be closed on Sunday and Monday, and Sterling has hired Elenor to work evenings and Saturdays.

Thor whines from the kitchen as she prepares his meal and pours water into his silver bowl. Her satchel hangs from the coat rack. She still does not know what to do with magical tools without being able to practice magic. Thor laps at his bowl at the chicken and rice leftovers she has given him when she hears June coming down the stairs.

"Thank you again for letting me stay."

"A friend of Grandall's is also a friend of mine."

And Hanna turns to find Lucius now standing behind her, "You were so quiet I did not hear you."

"Sorry love, didn't mean to startle you."

"He used a portal… he's been teaching me all day while you were at work."

June cannot wait and when Lucius leaves to shower she begins, "The Lady of Brighton…"

"Rose…" Hanna says.

"Yes, and Michael needs us."

"My husband can show you how to open a portal, but he cannot show you how to master a demon or his witch."

"I can move through a portal," she says defensively, "but I cannot move through space and time."

"The reason you have your memories."

"Grandall insisted it would be for the best."

"He has his reasons I'm sure."

"Think about it… you cannot perform magic… I don't have the hex over my shoulder the way that you do."

"Do you think we will need a coven?"

"No. But there is power in three."

"And who should be our third?"

"I don't know… but, maybe, Lucius?"

95

"I don't know either. He's really into family… but I need to make him see that the curse will be passed down…"

"And you must relieve the curse."

"Yes."

"A coven has too many ordinances… the reason your grandmother could be hexed by another witch."

"Unfortunately, yes."

Hanna hears a light tapping on the windowpane and she sees a lone Raven behind the glass. As she approaches, Clover takes flight and in the distance, Sage is in flight - a reminder they are near. Hanna feels a warm glow upon her neck; the talisman of the magnificent cat with the jade-colored eyes glows subtly. Tomorrow, she thinks they should visit Brighton, possibly to pick up the pieces and to hear the auction.

In the catacombs, Michael is chained to the wall, and covered in filth. He can only feed on rats that have expired by their own death and he gets water from the occasional spider that he places between his teeth to get nourishment from the juices. The body of Alexis bothers him because he thinks of Rose; they aged together – has she seen death? He longs to touch her, but the fire went dim long ago. His flesh is thin over his ribs and he wears only a dusty tunic - a garment that was used to haul potatoes. A burlap bag. He used to talk with Alexis; she told him of the years she spent as the Guardian of the North; how she was an honest-to-goodness witch and came to be prisoner by two deceitful women.

Her story entails how she was conjured to preside as a Guardian; about how Goldie told a lie with a stern face: *we are to evoke the Goddess for protection against those who do harm.* Leisha was behind her one-hundred-percent and so Alexis joined them to call upon the Guardians but instead they seized her arms and invoked a demon in place of the Goddess who she learned was Herschel Beecham – a man who had been burned a day prior and in his pain he felt no love for his God. He sided with Goldie and she felt fabulous; she thrilled him by enticing him with the powers of retribution. Herschel was promised a new life as a demonic entity; he however had to feed on the soul of another to gain his immortality; he had to feed on the blood of the most innocent. He would then become an immortal demon with immense power instead of immortal as the former Herschel Beecham.

He took the position as demon and Leisha stole the position as Guardian of the North. When the Goddess was to be evoked … Goldie would emerge and claim the body of the most innocent. Alexis was take to the catacombs, shackled, and held as prisoner while Goldie sought out her plan; after the death of her coven mate she would find her own daughter and the daughter of her daughter and find in them witches' blood; blood the demon would shed over the highest point North … but first he spilled the blood of Alexis to fuel his cravings, then she was tossed onto the catacombs, then, barely alive, and unwilling to live on the rats that abound them. Alexis died while Michael lives… hoping to see the light of day. To make it all right again and to see his beautiful bride… his forever Rose.

And Goldie sniggered before Alexis as she shut the door… "The key to freedom now lies in the body of a rat." And so the door closed. Shutting them both inside.

Chapter Six

Michael yearns for Alexis to be alive. He yearns heavily for his wife. He feels his cries go unheard. His lips are parched; he stifles himself from screaming. He thinks about the one who came to him...

When Hanna enters night she leaves her body to travel the cosmos. The astral plane exists between worlds and she once again finds herself in the Underworld. June takes her side; their ethereal body is transparent and unstable; the energy is low and they fade in and out. Jace cannot reach Michael like the shadows did for Alexis; he only finds himself in a labyrinth of obstacles: caves and doors with dead ends. That is Goldie's doing; Hanna assumes Goldie wants to lure her there but her body is back in Virginia asleep beside her husband – pregnant with her third child. Her astral body wavers in the dark. Michael cannot see them either; he snores faintly, his breath full of dirt.

Deep in the underground of the catacombs Goldie awaits Herschel; his transformation should be complete. As a demon he is strong, vile and desirable for her intentions. Every evening he changes form. Then he seeks to feed from flesh and blood; he has not had food for days; when he is hungry, he is more powerful, and on this night Goldie grazes the field for an old friend's grieving family. Goldie does not forgive or forget. Herschel hovers over an oval table made from massive wood where the food should be plentiful but is not. Goldie's' lair is lit with surrounding candles; the Underworld still smells; the rancid stench of socks and sweat goes unnoticed by Michael over the years he's breathed from the dusty bottom. Herschel Beecham stands on hind legs, with feathers of a bird, and a mane of a lion – Goldie pays homage to the Ravens that surround them like bats to a cave. His face is pointed in a sharp snout like the lion and his teeth are razors to the touch. As a demon he can be ruler of the dark and his animal characteristics give him keen sight; Goldie marvels over his yearning for a good feast.

"Now whatever you want done with them only after I'm finished is up to you." Herschel makes a flight to the entrance of the cave. Leisha follows behind; there is a grave marked for two beloved daughters at rest and he gently lays their bodies back upon it; he knows best to leave them there because her work is not truly done. He awaits the ripe flesh of the precious innocent to best fulfill the desires of his dark High Priestess of the Blackest Coven. Outside of the cave he sees the half-moon and he calls loudly into the night like a wolf that has finished its prey; Herschel Beecham is the demon, the monster, of the darkness who has begun his calling to rally all things evil – and he preys upon the dark ruler to overturn his status – but he cannot locate Jace either.

"Oh my God what is that?" A voice says as the beast moves toward them.

"Oh my God..." two stray teenage girls say in unison when another voice shouts, "run!"

And the two girls flee among the graves. Kamra and Victoria were buried together but Goldie hadn't known that until she sought after their family; she thinks the two birds analogy would be befitting if the birds were not her familiars of the darkness. Goldie knows that robbing their graves to bring them back to life will ache the poor souls of their mothers; Giving life back to them makes her ill but she broods in the thought for their dear mommy to see them so alive again, but owned by the dark, and that makes her heart sing. The girls were preserved by the curse; and she applauds herself for desiring them as followers of all things dark and possessed. Now there are two empty graves and the stray teens turn away for fear of the dead girls who have returned to life. Leisha thinks about how the catacombs are beneath the cemetery where her dear cousin made almost the entire family perish over time – a family that is cursed by the Black Death – death by choking. The survivors, their mothers, have been alone. Goldie is guile but evil and she does not care how dark she must become to gain a following of loyal shadows. If Jace could locate them he might have been able to help them into the light but their souls did not seek the shadows nor the light; the curse that kept them preserved harbored their souls within until Goldie could fulfill her evil deed.

The darkness in her runs deep – the feeling of hate and revenge runs in her veins and Hanna feels she has seen all she can handle of this vision when she and June return from sleep unable to reach Michael. She thinks about the store as she awakens – where there is literature because she has not stopped her from reading.

Hanna's first book: *Unlocking the Akashic Records* – to gain knowledge and to obtain all that she can about Goldie, about her life, and to learn her magic. Through Buddhism, Hanna learns that one must know his enemy before one can learn the art of war. This war between Hanna's family, and that of Kamra and Victoria, is grounded in the *Laws of a Witches' Creed* and black magic can be broken. But how to lift the spell that has cursed these two families? And without being able to perform magic? Hanna then opens a book on divination and reads:

The key is to understand that what may seem like a fatal moment is not necessarily the end result; then, through enlightenment, there is a means to understand the future. Existence is an illusion and a source from which one can tap into the higher realms; through the power of divination, the fortune teller, learning of death, seeks a higher meaning and purpose.

Hanna slams the book shut; she forgot about the auction; when Elenor enters the door she makes a swift exit out the door, forgetting to clock out and when she arrives she finds Mr. Edgar Worthington who is conversing with Alexandra; from afar Hanna can see their embrace when she feels a tap upon her shoulder.

"I hoped to find you here." A voice says, and when she turns, she finds Mr. William Banks who she barely got to know because he was always a man of business.

"You have her eyes." He says modestly. In his advanced age, he stands tall, lean and healthy.

"Why are you here?" She asks firmly.

"Don't hold it against me too…"

"My mother has done the same."

"I've tried talking to her…"

"But she thinks you're an infidel and a pig."

"Pretty much," he huffs. "Have you seen Rose?"

"No, I mean, well no I haven't."

"My wife is gone, my daughter, my granddaughter…"

"And your great-granddaughter hasn't spoken to you until now."

"Yes, but you see…"

"You don't want to be alone?"

"No. No I do not… I am getting old."

"Your son-in-law is gone?"

"Yes. Many years."

"LaQuinta…"

"Where is she?"

"How could you lose contact after all these years?"

"I went back to Europe. Back to banking. She was married and it changed her, you see… It was all very odd. That kind of magic is… or can be… ruthless. My magic is harmless you see?"

Hanna appears furious as the auctioneer begins to call out for the bids on Brighton; the premise is full of investors and many want to develop on the old estate. Tickets are being raised as the bid falls on the One Million and William Banks raises number 243 …

"What do you want with the estate?"

"How about making things right again?"

"No, really…"

"Really, Hanna, to raise horses for the races… for myself and …"

"And?"

"And for Edgar Worthington if he would be willing."

"Shouldn't you have found out first?"

"I couldn't…"

"Face her?"

"No. Alexandra has a heavy heart."

"This land is cursed." A feeble old woman says, "Haunted by the ghost of that girl… legend says a witch party burned her here … burned her alive."

"No," Hanna scowls, "no one was burned here."

William hears "sold to 243" from the auctioneer and the guests look impatient. Hanna does not feel he can make anything right by buying the land of the daughter he did not care to raise. She thinks about her satchel – she has left it inside the store. She dismisses the thought and approaches Alexandra who is distraught.

"I couldn't love after I lost her…" she confesses and Hanna feels awkward. Had she seen her as the Old Crone Hanna feels she might not stand the pain.

Then there is June at their side. Alexandra is beautiful but tired; she has dark circles around her vacant eyes and lines on her face.

"June Bug?" Hanna says, hoping she does not mention Rose, not yet, not at this time.

But June appears to be there to listen.

"We understand." Is all she can say.

"June is staying with me to learn magic." Hanna explains. "My husband has been teaching her …"

Alexandra sobs still. "My home has been sold to …" and she breaks down. "I also teach," she musters, "I teach the girls at my group home all that I know of the Craft… secretly, I suppose, I have always hoped their magic would find Rose… if that's not too awful to say."

"No, it isn't." Hanna assures her.

Hanna can feel her energy – the energy of a good and wholesome witch.

"That no good man bought my home," she says again, shaking her head. "Those bones…" she is in deep thought, "that was our beloved Duke," her voice is a whisper.

"You are both cursed," the feeble old woman finds them and points a crooked finger; there are men in suits giving her an inquisitive look; many shake their heads; they care for the money the property could make them – and none of them believe in anything of the Craft. The good magic of the highest good – even William Banks himself has lost that kind of magic – the kind of magic that would bring them all peace – the magic Hanna is cursed not to use against the dark.

Hanna thinks again about her satchel but she must shake it off. She does not know what she should not say – it seems that June has told her nothing of her daughter's brief escape, but chances are they have her again wherever that may be: dead or alive. She thinks if only her grandmother had told her more… Perhaps she could have brought Rose back to Brighton. But she left her to go her own way – she had Alysiah and she had not known. Hanna's thoughts are interrupted when Alexandra takes a deep breath, "my daughter was pregnant," and she lifts her eyes toward a pale blue sky… "there will be a New Moon on the Solstice," she says… "I'll be preparing a ritual … another attempt to invoke the Goddess and perhaps invoke the soul of my daughter."

"Do you have help?" June says.

"I'll have the girls, my students, and I'll call upon the Guardians."

"Do you want us to join you?"

"It's open to all my students in June. Even you. Even though you're gone."

Hanna explains that the Winter Solstice is the birth date of both her children…

"Twins?" Alexandra asks.

"No, exactly one year apart."

111

"Two babies born on the Winter Solstice?"

"Yes."

Hanna and Alexandra take a seat at a nearby bench by what is a lush garden in the spring and June accompanies them. Alexandra tells her all she experienced at Brighton with her oldest daughter and three younger sons. She doesn't quite know why she feels a connection with Hanna other than helping orphaned girls, but she likes her energy. When she speaks of Duke Hanna feels at the pit of her stomach that the poison of the berries were fed to him – enticed by a meal of tasty meat. In her mind's eyes, she sees a hand upon a wand, and the image fades; the wand is ruby-studded and looks sharp and sophisticated. Hanna's vision shifts to the single rose that was unearthed, but then she sees another – a Lily of the Valley deep in the heart of Brighton.

"What were those beads with the bones?" Hanna asks.

"Belong to the witch who killed him… my daughter made them, blessed them with a protection spell… thought she was a friend. Then she was counter-cursed just like our Duke."

Hanna's mind veers to Lakota: killed by the serpent – the snake has long been associated with black magic. One more thought comes to mind: the only permanent death is the death done by a demon, but re-birth is not an option for Hanna. She feels compelled to save her…

"My daughter was taken," she explains, "she was taken by the woman your daughter befriended…"

"Goldie?"

"Yes."

"She was a member of the same Coven as my grandmother. My grandmother is LaQuinta… your daughter's sister."

Alexandra nods subtly, "Go on…" she says.

Somehow Alexandra does not look surprised – but perhaps nothing can rattle her any more than the disappearance of her beloved daughter.

"Goldie hexed your daughter as well as my grandmother… if my grandmother dared to practice magic she would breathe her last breath and she forced your daughter to perform magic …. To tell her of the future."

"Wait a minute, you've seen Rose?"

"Yes."

"Alive?"

"Yes."

"We both have." June finally admits.

'Why didn't you tell me?"

"I didn't want to give you false hope…"

"We are not sure where she is now." Hanna confesses.

"Your daughter blessed the rose that contained her soul … and she lived… Goldie vanished, but no one knew to stay with her."

"We went separate ways." Hanna says.

Alexandra's voice cracks, "But you saw her alive." Her voice is barely a whisper.

"Yes." June is subtle.

Alexandra hugs them both.

"Thank you." She says, "You are my first ray of hope."

"To find your daughter this time, we may have to find Goldie first." Hanna sighs.

"Yes, and her cousin…" June adds.

"Leisha." Alexandra says.

"They were using Rose in the Cone of Power."

"Then we must become a Coven…" Alexandra ponders.

"But the hex is now against Hanna..." June continues…

"We will have to protect you." Alexandra is strong.

"But it's hard for me still… to leave my babies."

"Be with them… we'll get through this."

"Okay," Hanna says and Alexandra hugs her again like a mother would to a daughter.

115

Hanna returns home. When she enters night, she leaves her body once again to travel in the night while her body rests; June, asleep in the guest room, accompanies her; the Underworld is vast, dark, cold and empty. They are searching for Michael but they cannot discern where there is a cave in the vastness of space before them. Hanna feels she needs a guide – where is Lakota? Certainly she feels he cannot remain in the dark. But she needs him. June, becoming adept in the ways of magic, tries to intuit the direction to turn but her mind merely winds in circles and without a guide, they feel lost. Upon entering their bodies they both awaken and Hanna thinks to consult her grandmother's *Book of Shadows*.

Chapter Seven

Hanna searches frantically through the store; her satchel is missing. Elenor takes her by the shoulder. "Deep breath," she says, "try and relax and feel with your energy – use the powers of the mind." Hanna tries to relax, but her muscles are tense. She cannot feel her way through this one; her grandmother's chalice, *Book of Shadows*, the wand-- all gone. She feels numb as she works her shift; Sterling has not installed the anticipated security system, but a witch can get past such things. Hanna has her lunch at *The Witches' Brew*. She orders a grilled cheese with a slice of tomato and basil soup, kettle-cooked chips, and a cold vanilla latte from the new barista; his name is Kevin, and he's pleasing in looks with a dark complexion and pale gray eyes. Hanna experiences food aversion, and the tomato will likely give her heartburn, but she throws caution to the wind. Hanna's mind wanders; how can she be a witch when she cannot practice magic despite possessing any magical tools? She then thinks of Michael – of Rose – of their baby – and her own family. When can she just enjoy life? Hanna succumbs to the feeling of unease. She hurries to the restroom and vomits. She blows her nose with a paper napkin. Time is slowing down; she thinks of the ritual to call upon the Goddess; she feels she wants Helga – the dark still threatens the light; what were they to do to end the darkness? It was bound to happen again because they failed to make a permanent and lasting change. Hanna learned through her studies in the esoteric arts and through her practices in mysticism that change does not happen in a day when all that has been created is rooted in time – and the irony is a single moment can change everything – how then does one know what to do in all the contradictions?

Hanna is confused, and she knows she wants to walk away; she pays the bill and returns to work when she sees Susan again;

118

she is in the store browsing through Craft literature. Her heart is sullen, and she cannot speak; she just wants to enjoy being a mother and enjoy her family. She takes her place behind the counter while Elenor arranges books and other various merchandise. Sterling has the two of them working the busier day shift while she intends to work at night. Hanna feels she could use a mentor and she sighs thinking of Grandall who has begun his journey anew: rebirth is for the restless spirit, or so she thinks. Elenor burns some incense in the back room as Hanna takes a stack of books from the returning Susan.

"They're for my daughter," she says and she emanates in a soft glow. "She wants to be a witch… so I figured I forgot to get the books the last time I was here."

"That's really nice," Hanna musters a smile. She goes home with another thought; what will the night bring?

But the night brings nothing other than much needed sleep. June Bug must have too because she snores within the guest room. Come morning Hanna's day begins with sickness but she makes her way to get a drink of water.

"There's a ritual tonight," June says and Hanna accidentally drops her glass after being startled. After it shatters on the floor June is perplexed, "Are you all right?" She asks and Hanna looks pale.

"I'm fine." She says, "I just dropped a glass."

"The New Moon is tonight."

"Yes, I know, just before the Solstice and I haven't planned a party."

"A party?"

"For my children … who were born on the Eve of the Winter Solstice…"

"Yes, I'm sorry, I wasn't thinking."

"That's tonight. The same night as the ritual."

"Why hasn't Lucius mentioned anything?" Hanna says as Lucius rounds the corner.

"No worries," he says, "I've got it taken care of." He kisses his wife upon her head and she sighs in relief.

"What have you planned?"

Lucius grabs the orange juice from the fridge. "We'll have dinner and a party."

"Where?"

"I've made arrangements at the *Eagle's Nest* – a nice little Italian restaurant and right beside it is a *Live 2 Play.*"

"Oh wow," she kisses him again, thankful he already brushed his teeth.

"But the ritual…" June says and Lucius interrupts her.

"That we will not be able to attend tonight, June."

Hanna embraces him. "Thank you." She whispers in his ear. "It'll just be us."

"Maybe later we can also talk over going to Connecticut."

Hanna takes a step back.

"Don't try to be so manipulative." She slits her eyes.

He kisses her quickly on the lips and he leaves the kitchen to attend the children's room as they have awakened. The three room cottage is full; the siblings share a room. Hanna knows that is also a sign that going to Connecticut would be best for their family. If June continues to stay, she won't have the extra space for the baby. She also thinks that June is the only other witch who still has her memories alongside Jace and Lucius. Even the past is fragmented for Lucius but Hanna may prefer it that way – if only Goldie was not allowed to be free. She takes Lucas into her arms; today he is two and Aly is three. They are perfect as if in a divine plan, but Hanna shrugs – because she feels no connection with divinity or The Craft. She is three months into her pregnancy, and she has gone weeks without noticing; she has been distracted. She considers Alexandra and she speaks with June as she re-enters the living room. Lucius follows and their toddlers play with toy cars and plastic food.

"Maybe you could go back to Alexandra…" Hanna hesitates so her words are casual. Aly speaks in full sentences and Lucas imitates his sister: "Three," Aly says and Lucas responds.

"Are you asking me to leave?" June asks.

"With the baby coming…"

"I understand… but you must help…"

"Possibly. But after the baby this time, June."

"Rose needs us. Alexandra needs us."

"If Rose is still alive…"

"Don't say that."

"Okay, I won't… I just need some time."

"Because she is alive, Hanna."

"How do you know?"

"I just know."

"I just like to know how…"

"We all trust our intuition … Alexandra calls us her girls … and we can feel Roses' energy even if we cannot say anything to Alexandra."

"No false hope."

"We're just relying on instinct here."

"But she is my grandmother's sister…"

"Then you should feel her too."

"I do." Hanna admits.

"But?"

"But maybe only in spirit."

"No Hanna, she's too strong. And we did find Michael and Alexis once… we can find Rose too."

"It's not easy."

"No, it's never easy."

"Okay."

"Tonight at the ritual we'll invoke the Goddess."

"I will try to stop by but I cannot practice…"

"You don't have to. Just try to drop in."

"After my babies' birthday."

"Of course."

In the early afternoon, Hanna and Lucius go out for dinner with their two young children; their children enjoy pizza while they enjoy pasta dishes. Hanna tries a salad but her stomach turns. After their meals, they take their children to *Live 2 Play* where there are games, bounce houses and ball pits. Blue and white balls remind Hanna of the ocean. They build castles with fake sand.

"Good times," Lucius has a sparkle in his eye.

"Good times." Hanna is reassuring.

"Don't worry, my love," he places his arm around her.

He picks up his son and gently tosses him into the ball pit.

Tonight, Hanna is not just a witch but a mother, and tonight she doesn't miss *The Sister's Coven* because the day is plentiful.

Later that night, June is not home. Hanna lays upon her bed after putting children to sleep and intends to visit the ritual in a body double. Hanna quickly goes to sleep.

Alexandra, in her home for homeless girls, opens the sacred circle. She walks in a clockwise direction upon the floor and draws an imaginative circle with her athame blade. Her guests are assembled in the spacious kitchen; in the open living space her altar is decorated with evergreens and the home smells like pine. The home is warmed by a fire that she burns every morning and again in the early evening. She marks the boundaries of the circle with stones the girls have cleansed, consecrated and blessed. Above the fire she has placed a bubbling cauldron to be used during the ritual; she removes the cauldron and places it at the center of the circle. The girls assemble within the circle and Alexandra begins…

Guardian of the North, I call on thee to aid this magical rite.

June Bug lights the first candle, pointed North and the girls begin to chant:

Come to us

126

Dear Guardian

Of the North

To aid us

In this ritual

We call upon

With peace

A portal opens, and the Guardian of the North steps through: Juno looks beautiful in a pale blue dress.

Thank you

Dear Guardian

For aiding in this

Invocation

Of the Goddess

The next girl, Sarah, the one June and Hanna met at the property of Brighton, lights an anointed candle in the East coordinate.

Oh beloved

Guardian of

The East

Join us in

This ritual to

Invoke the Goddess

And from the East, Gladys enters the room from a portal of magnificent pale orange light.

"Happy to join you." She says cheerily.

Thank you

Dear Guardian

Alexandra moves to the next candle and Rebecca lights the candle before her and the girls speak in unison…

Oh dear Guardian

Of the South

Hear us and join

This ritual

To be blessed

By the Goddess

In the South, a light shimmers and from a portal Elusha comes through.

"Can she be trusted?" Sarah whispers to June Bug and the other girls hush her.

Alexandra is eager and she moves to the West and invokes the Guardian…

Guardian of the

East, join us

In his invocation

Of the Goddess

And in the West, Vicnna emerges looking pleased.

"We are all here just as you desired," Juno says.

"Thank you, sisters," Alexandra says and she moves to the center of the circle that is now defined with a pentacle as each Guardian serves as the points of the five pointed star: at one point June Bug fills in as the student who is most adept in magic. Alexandra stands over the bubbling cauldron; she ignites the alcohol rub and the cauldron erupts into a blazing fire.

Dear Goddess… she begins

And the girls chant in unison:

We call upon the energy

Of the Goddess of

Celestial light

We call upon thee

To aid us in

This journey

129

As followers
Of the light!

The Guardians begin to sing and clap – "come to us Dear Goddess…"

From the flames of the burning cauldron the Goddess emerges; around her form is a magnificent light; she has the body of a human, in long white drapes, her bronze skin and wings of the Phoenix. She is a divine angel but the most powerful being that exists.

"You have called upon me in the time of Yule when the Great God is reborn…"

"Oh, please," Alexandra says, "I call upon your generous graces to ask of you to help me find my daughter…" Alexandra is anxious.

At this time, Hanna has left her physical body and she is able to join them in the ethereal body. She observes the room from above; no one seems to be aware of her presence as they are in the presence of Helga, the Great Goddess of the Celestial City.

"I too have wished for a girl…" her voice rings like a bell. "I understand your plight…"

Hanna touches her abdomen – *not again* – she thinks and she returns to her body feeling disgruntled. She awakes from her sleep and sits up in her bed, and she turns on the light to her bedside table; Lucius awakes beside her.

"What is the concern, my love?"

Hanna hesitates to tell him… "The Goddess wishes for a girl." She whispers.

"How is that so wrong?" He is confused.

Hanna spills the beans, "I can't help but think she is going to inhabit this baby, like she did Aly…"

"No love," he assures her, "she protected Aly. Get some sleep."

He is quickly back to sleep, but Hanna is feeling unnerved.

Back at the girls' home the sacred circle still stands between the worlds, but the

Goddess has retreated, and Alexandra is in tears.

"It will take time," Juno tries to assure her and one at a time the Guardians leave the sacred circle because the Goddess has spoken.

The girls move in a counterclockwise motion to release the sacred circle; June Bug leads them with the white-handled athame blade. They each give her a hug; there are thirty girls at the group home where Alexandra runs the entire operation, but the funds are getting low. She doesn't know what she will do. She turned to Edgar who could not afford the estate and lost the battle to no one else but William Banks who has promised to help Alexandra have a redemption of the past.

Yule marks the turning of the wheel as does the waxing of the moon that is moving from new to full. And the great Yule festival is set three days from the present date on the 23rd. And the Goddess sowed the seeds long ago that are currently dormant, but the Wiccans assemble over the wishes of the Goddess and the people praise her, but Alexandra is left feeling alone.

Chapter Eight

Twelve nights into the Winter Solstice, on Thursday the 6th, Hanna's abdomen grows with the waxing of the moon. The landscape is quiet and the land is still. The sun begins its return to the Earth. The days begin to get longer and Hanna can feel her baby kicking.

"I want to go to Connecticut, Hanna says and Lucius beams in response.

"It makes sense Hanna, for me to work, while you have the baby."

"I know," she says and they eat breakfast quietly.

Later in the week, she cannot tell Sterling and it is when she goes through her belongings that she finds a diary her grandmother had given her. Her grandmother wrote her history on those pages and Hanna would give anything to feel her energy and her heart was broken over losing the orb – it was entrusted to her, but she could not keep it safe. Her grandmother's apartment was written as *123 Holiday Street* and she thinks about visiting one time again – if the apartment has not been completely demolished. She takes Lucius' car for a ride; all feels cold but normal. The snow blankets the streets and she doesn't have much time. When she arrives, she finds that the apartment complexes have in fact been remodeled. She knocks on the door softly and after a minute a man opens the door.

"Hello," she says, inches below his tall frame and she doesn't hesitate.

"I'm here because this apartment belonged to my grandmother…"

"Yes," he responds, "I'm sorry I don't recall her name, but she might be the same woman we met…"

"I wondered if anything she owned might have been left behind."

"It's funny that you ask that now, here, because there is a storage container in the basement … she left a great deal down

135

there and we were just about to clean it out this week."

"Do you mind if I take a look?"

"No, and perhaps you'd like to remove it?"

"Yes, I will try."

He takes her to the basement where there is a locked storage facility.

"I had the original lock removed," he says as he turns the key; he pops the lock and the gated door opens. Inside there are four large storage containers; Hanna opens one to find Christmas decorations. Feeling disappointed, she opens another and finds a dozen quilted blankets – she had no idea her grandmother could crochet, in another she kept fine China wrapped in paper and in the last are several family albums; she opens one to find her mother's baby album and in another is Tristian's obituary. Hanna feels her grandmother's loss; she wonders why these things were never taken by her mother but she realizes her grandmother kept them in her solitude. Her grandmother just waited and one day Hanna showed up – then being a witch could make sense again. Hanna thanks the new homeowner, David, and he helped her load the contents of four boxes into her small car – and she needs to leave before the snow gets heavy. Hanna drives off thinking she can feel a perspective that Goldie may have felt: a sense of abandonment toward Rose and her grandmother. In her diary, her grandmother makes it clear they both left her to live their own lives in marriage and Handfasting. In her *Book of Shadows*, her grandmother paid close attention to the Ordinance of the Coven; everyone in that Coven had their own place then one day she ran off with a boy she met. Hanna's epiphany gives her a sense of empathy. She wonders how different the past could have been if her grandmother hadn't forsaken the Laws of Ordinances of the Coven. She does not know how to contact her grandmother; she cannot practice magic – cast a spell – perform a ritual - or be a witch without experiencing death by choking.

She pulls into the dirt road that has turned to slush and turns off the engine. Lucius greets her at the door and reminds her of the upcoming medical appointment. She tells Lucius about her grandmother's belongings and how she found her diary. The diary tells the lore of the past while her *Book of Shadows* contains her personal spells, incantations and rituals. The diary is a glimpse into the abduction and hex done by Goldie against the Lady of Brighton. How her grandmother felt she could not help her and how she did not feel resentful of Rose but she could no longer be a witch. Hanna reads the remainder of the diary and learns more of her grandmother's love for the Craft that ran deep, but her love for Pratt was deeper still, and Hanna can feel her sorrow. In the morning hours, she wraps the diary and other belongings in a quilt and sends them in a box to her mother: Alayna Harp. She realizes her mother never broke the vows of her marriage and is a good person but her grandmother is not evil. Perhaps something can come of sending her the package. It has been over twenty years since her mother spoke to her grandmother. Hanna's father had an active role in the church, but he's a push over when it comes to her mother. She attaches the required postage to the box and sends it off with a farewell and an ounce of hope. She returns inside with the thought that she needs to tell Sterling … and as soon as the thought enters her mind she can smell her perfume.

"Hello Hanna," Sterling's soothing voice says.

"Hello…"

"Elenor has told me about your satchel."

"Yes…"

"Elenor says that you have mentioned my sister."

"I don't think anything," Hanna feels awkward – that time warp.

"My family has never practiced dark magic…"

"I understand…" She protects Sterling even if she is in denial. Hanna continues, "While I am here I need to tell you that I will be going to Connecticut …"

"When?"

"In two weeks."

"I'm sure Elenor can run the store and I'll work evenings until I find a replacement. Well congratulations and I hope you enjoy it there."

"Thank you."

"You're welcome."

Hanna partially wants to hide while the other half wants to fight. She is yet still conflicted. She wishes for the guidance from Grandall or the Elders, but they have fulfilled their mystical duties, and now it is time for her generation of witches and warlocks to make a difference.

Hanna packs their clothing; all else in the cottage is furnishings but then she cleans out the closets and finds layers of dust and rat droppings; she closes the door – nothing feels mystical anymore.

As humans they have a car; as witches they have portals. Hanna thinks they should teleport but Lucius wants to drive; he explains that portals are fickle in winter and Hanna argues their sports car isn't good for inclement weather.

"The weather may be too frigid for magic… and too dangerous in that car." Hanna is discouraged.

"Well I cannot risk losing my family." He gives her a hug… "I'll figure this out and just think that during a six and a half hour drive, there will be plenty of time for contemplation."

Lucius replaces the tires with winterized tread and they make the drive. A drive that was painless. When they arrive, they find that Luther has put together a welcoming committee; there, Hanna finds Archibald with his wife Diana, Herman and his wife Eva and members of the Druids army who she recognizes by face even if she

141

cannot remember a name. They greet Hanna and Lucius with open arms; the Shamans and the Druids are strong allies and Hanna can sense their energy. But she has a knot at the pit of her stomach; she forgot to tell June Bug that she has left already.

The lodge is beautiful and Eva invites them to breakfast at the diner the following day but the sickness and food aversion keeps Hanna at home. She writes June a letter and gets it sent out in the mail. Eva and Archibald have made Connecticut their permanent home and the Druids' Army primarily live in Vermont so they maintain close connections. Lucius works the ski resort aside Loki and adds a helping hand to the construction of the lodges as they are being updated. Hanna tends the babies and misses the store. She quickly phones Eva and discusses working at the gift shop at the resort and Eva pencils her into the schedule. Lucius excels in skiing and has signed up to begin courses as an EMT to help skiing casualties – Jack of all trades, Hanna thinks.

They are comfortable in their own home and Hanna doesn't mind leaving the cottage for a while after all. Lucius returns home for a quick lunch and Hanna hands him a dowsing necklace and smiles.

"You want me to practice magic over you?" He is concerned.

"Yes." She responds simply.

Lucius hesitates but takes the necklace into his hands; the dowsing pendant is made of silver and feels heavy like a nickel. She lays upon the sofa, and he drops the pendant and it begins to turn, and moving faster, it goes in a clockwise direction.

"A boy," he smiles, and she kisses him and he kisses her back, then takes to the kitchen to finish a sandwich. In three days, June receives the letter at Alexandra's group home. Alexandra is afraid she may have to close the doors to the group home because the bed and breakfast is slow and there is not enough revenue to run the facility. She needs to find a means to make another income – although the girls are her staff for the bed and breakfast she still doesn't make enough to keep the lights on. Times are tough. She considers asking Edgar as she has done in the past, but her guilt and mixed feelings won't allow her to forget him. When she lost her whole heart and that drove him away she found the girls without a home and a bed and breakfast that was cheaply priced. They come to her from various walks of life and most, if not all, are orphans like June.

June met Grandall as an eighteen year old runaway; she left foster care at seventeen. There is no more support from the state services beyond the age of eighteen. Hence, Alexandra took her in after the Hidden School of the Temples fell to the weight of all the pressure. Alexandra to date has taken in hundreds of girls and thirty of them still remain – she needs to find a way. The women and girls now range from age eighteen up to thirty, and many of them are victims of domestic violence – the thirty year old mother (Sharon) and her eighteen year old daughter (Melissa) are the oldest and the youngest. The girls share suites that were once a room for the bed and breakfast, but as her crew grew, there were not enough bedrooms and the bed and breakfast got smaller. Alexandra wishes to continue providing a roof over their head and continue care for the underprivileged youth. She instructs the girls in ways of The Craft and at times she has foretold their future: what jobs they find, husbands, when they find their way into another life, and some that give birth to babies. Currently only one of the girls is pregnant, and her name is Celia; she knows she is carrying a boy, and although she wants a girl she is pleased they are both healthy. In this modern era, Celia gets to see her baby in a sonogram and the image reveals the sex; she wishes to call him Will and she wishes to find a gentleman like Alexandra had once.

June is not upset that Hanna did not say goodbye and she decides to visit Sterling; all the girls need jobs to help

Alexandra and that is when June meets Sterling. At first sight Sterling is whimsical and full of character and light; she seems to have an almost naïve blind faith despite her age. June wants to continue learning the Craft under an adept like Alexandra and longs to be among items that are a depiction of the light; she enjoys the crystals that dangle from the walls and the sea blue color that paints a picture of being among water. It feels good there. Sterling provides her with a paper application and prefers not to use much technology. June is embarrassed this will be her first job.

"It doesn't matter," Sterling assures her, "we offer on the job training here."

June hands her the application...

"You feel like a good witch," she gives June a warm smile.

June cannot help but wonder how Sterling feels about her own sister.

Sterling looks through the application and stamps in red: hired.

June is pleased.

"You can start any time…" Sterling continues.

"I'm free now," June says as Elenor walks in.

"Good," you can begin training now then.

Elenor shows her how to use the register and they scan the barcode into the system; that much technology Sterling does have. Elenor learns of Alexandra through June; they chat and gossip. Hanna is a topic of conversation.

"That poor girl lost all her magical tools." Elenor says.

"She lost being a witch too."

"I hope she does not blame herself."

June agrees and she considers all the darkness and brokenness within the witch community when Susan enters the door.

"Who are you?" She gives June a wry look.

"I'm June…"

"She's taking over for Hanna." Elenor is polite.

"Hanna? Well I was just coming in to speak to her. Where is she?"

"Connecticut," June says.

"Oh, it's got to be so cold," Susan says.

"It's pretty cold here too," Elenor laughs.

"Yes, well, let Hanna know I was in to see her." Susan says as she makes her way out the door.

"We will." June says as Susan shuts the door.

June learns quickly; she is curious about the back room but Sterling does not allow the staff to roam. They now have a separate space where the boxes of inventory are kept and the room where Sterling performs her magic. June is guided to the shelves where the merchandise is stocked when she notices a lonely little Raven inside the warehouse-like room.

"Don't mind Clover," Sterling says, "that's my animal familiar."

"Don't they usually…"

"Signify the dark? "Well, yes, usually I suppose but Clover is a bird of the light."

June just agrees with a nod.

"Don't forget to stock the stones," Sterling says, tapping the top of a box.

"I won't forget." June looks grateful.

In the back room Clover provides some company. Elenor returns to the evening shift; she is also grateful to have the hours that coincide with her husband's schedule as he works security in the evenings.

June finds books on divination: runes, psychic awareness, the mind's eye (third eye), tarot cards, palmistry, fire scrying, crystal gazing and automatic writing and so on. She purchases the handbook on Astral Projection: *Traveling the Cosmos and Beyond.* She wishes to learn how portals work too and wants to align her energy for moving her physical body through space and time beyond the second more ethereal body. For now, she will have to comply with bi-location as an alternative means of transportation.

That evening she leaves her body; she focuses on the return address from Hanna. Hanna is battling insomnia and fatigue; her doctor has prescribed her a medication that won't hurt the baby. June is aware that all are still awake and so she takes to a quiet corner and Hanna does feel a presence within the room. She scans the area with her eyes but physically she sees nothing; she detects someone is in the room using radar; she can sense the energy vibration of another.

"June?" Hanna has an inkling it's her.

June focuses her attention on the wall; she makes a photo frame fall and crash to the ground.

"That's one way to be subtle." Hanna laughs.

Her medication enables her to sleep after an hour, and when she leaves her body, she enters the veil between worlds and wonders what June wishes to show her.

"I've brought you here because this is the place where Grandall says that all spirits go – a purgatory between the light and the dark; a place in between the world of the ethereal body of the light, and the shadows of the night."

Hanna takes June's lead; she feels she has seen all this before and that it is nothing new to her.

"This is where Lakota stays until you fulfill your destiny."

"I am bound to this destiny because I am my grandmother's granddaughter." She nods.

"You have to break your curse Hanna."

"Will it pass on to Aly? What if I do not teach them magic?"

"Then the dark succeeds."

In the place of purgatory the spirits there are neither of the dark nor the light. In the state of between Lakota acts as a guide

151

to assist spirits on their journey. Hanna watches in a panoramic view as a young teen, addicted to drugs, leaves his body and finds himself in the place of the between; the teen finds Lakota waiting there for him and the teen receives the message that it is not yet his time. The teen, named Allen, returns to his body with the memory of his journey to the other side and Hanna views his life review; she knows that in fifteen years his experience in the afterlife has a profound impact on his wife and the synchronicity makes for a change; he gains knowledge of his physical life while visiting the state of purgatory.

He heads home.

"What exactly does Grandall want me to do?"

"The only thing you can do… provoke change within."

"Or?"

"Or Goldie will pass down her status as Queen Bee – ruler of the dark!"

"Onto a child?"

"Yes."

"What child?"

"Onto a girl."

"Why a girl?"

"That's all part of the curse Hanna; a baby girl in your direct lineage will be sacrificed in the name of the darkness to become heir and gain great power."

"They just want to devour all that is light."

Hanna turns to the dark where she sees Lakota and he gives her a gentle wave …

"You see Hanna, there are many sacrifices."

Hanna thinks of Jace wondering what Lucius will sacrifice…

Thus far Jace and now Lakota have sacrificed their place in the Celestial City and so she wonders too, what will she do?

Chapter Nine

"Sometimes we all need reminders." Hanna tells Lucius in the morning. She thinks to herself: *did he want a baby to forget Aly, or did he actually want to create a distraction by splitting immortal power between them; did the Goddess bless her daughter – or want her for herself; what was the Prince's role and where was the God?*

Hanna has more questions than answers but she hopes Lucius was simply trying his best. Jace gave up his life; it seems now that the demon was onto them and he was a human deflection; the demon killed, but not his daughter. And how are the Celestial Ones involved this time? Her mind goes on: Grandall and all the Elders made the ultimate sacrifice to pass immortality to the next generation, but now, this generation has to earn it too. They all sacrifice. Those of the light sacrifice themselves, but the dark others want to commit cold-blooded murder in the name of power.

At the brink of night, the Shaman women, under the guidance of Eva, assemble at the home of Hanna and Lucius to de-possess the evil that plagues Hanna's family and her specifically. Eva does not have to knock; Lucius lets the women in, and he personally takes the babies to his father's where they are to stay the night while the women work to banish the negative energy that consumes her soul. Eva starts by explaining that energy can be measured and can be manipulated, or better, influenced.

"We are here with the intent to drive the negative forces out of you." Eva explains and she burns incense that she uses to cleanse and purify the space. The women assemble around her in a circle of love and compassion and they begin to sing, clap, and dance just as the witches do, but the Shamans do not call on the Goddess to aid them; they call upon each other and evoke the Spirit from within; the healing spirit is only

155

known by the great oracle in person, but the Shamans can find the healing Spirit of the Greatness within.

"It seems that black magic has been against you, and is threatening your life."

"Yes," Hanna lowers her vocabulary to match Eva's.

"Perhaps," she continues, "if we raise the energy high enough then the dark ones will not be able to practice their black magic."

A counter-curse, Hanna thinks.

Another Shaman woman uses a dowsing rod to measure the energy they have created within the room. In minutes the dowsing tool begins to swing wildly while making symbols in the air.

"Runes?" Hanna questions but the Shaman women are in a full meditative chant; Hanna can feel something happening but she did not know what... the Elder Shaman woman, named Rhoda, takes out a smoker, a device to smoke out unwanted pests and she fills the room with the smoke; the women do not budge; the smoke has no effect on them – surely they know she is pregnant so they keep the smoke outside the circle and move about from within the house. The energy level rises so Hanna feels light as a feather and she thinks she can almost levitate.

"We are here to change the energy field that plagues you…" Eva continues to explain to Hanna while the women work on the energy from within the home and within Hanna so that they are not visited by evil; the pendulum continues to swing wildly and Hanna knows the energy is good and she feels her abdomen like tiny kicks; like butterflies in her stomach. In the next moment, Hanna feels something cold leave her body, and that is when Eva speaks in her native language and she sings like piercing through a bell. The energy shift feels good within Hanna and she becomes elevated.

"What we have done here," Eva says, "is manipulate the present so there is a change in the future."

Eva goes quiet after that, and the assembly of women go outside where the wind is howling and the frigid air comes indoors.

"I felt a cold like that," Hanna says, "but it left my body."

"Yes," Eva assures her, "the negative energy that possessed you is outside that door."

Hanna watches the women as they walk into the night clapping, singing and chanting to drive off the negativity off their homeland and Hanna has the best night of rest she's had in months.

Alexandra however is restless and June cannot locate Hanna.

"Rose was a gift from the Spirit world," Alexandra tells the girls, "and so are all of you." And that makes them smile.

June has it in her heart to help her and she thinks momentarily that Grandall may have appointed the wrong girl to get the job done. She doesn't know how to find Rose and Hanna is distracted. The best June can do now is sit, pray, meditate and contemplate in hopes that a piece of Grandall may shine through her own soul.

Lucius returns home in the morning with the babies and Hanna is looking fresh. She tells him what transpired with the Shaman women.

"I felt something leave my body."

Lucius thinks deeply, "You know, you have a lot of power without being a witch."

"How is that?"

"They cannot stop your intuition, your foresight and hindsight… they cannot stop your humanness. Your consciousness."

"She turned Herschel Beecham into a Demon."

"Another connection to you Hanna." He shakes his head.

"That is why I am the one to stop all this?"

"You were the one they wanted because you had Aly.. so it's not exactly about you Hanna. Goldie wants power,

power because she was hurt terribly in her past, so she never wants to suffer again."

"Yes, she's pure bloody evil."

"It's her means of retribution. It makes her feel better. Powerful. At the top instead of the bottom."

"She seeks to see her own darkness prevail – and the death of the most innocent child will aid her in accomplishing that task."

"Completely selfish, Hanna. She flat out sucks."

"Yes she does."

Hanna manages a giggle.

"Do I have you by my side, Lucius?"

"I'm always on your side Hanna… but I think you need to manage your time wisely and consider how you can stop Goldie from harming Rose…"

"But how do you know…"

"I don't really know anything but I can feel it, like a wildfire, it burns at my core; she wants to hurt Rose the way she wished to harm Aly."

"Rose was pregnant."

"Then she wants another baby, she's at it again; all her tyranny is based on shedding the blood of the most innocent."

"Lucius, when will she do it this time?"

"Goldie needs the energy of the universe behind her; she needs the power of the darkness behind her… the next Solstice…"

"This summer?"

"No. After the baby is born…"

"Then again on the Winter Solstice?"

"I believe so."

"I wonder why she didn't …"

"Take the baby from the womb and make the sacrifice with Rose and the child… I can't say for sure… she's holding back for something."

"What is she holding onto? Or, what is she waiting for exactly?"

"For the birth… to make her intentions complete."

"Something is behind the birth…"

"Yes, and doesn't it seem so contradictory that we can influence the future but we cannot change or fix the past?"

"I see. So you're suggesting we can only fix Goldie by changing the past despite the contradictions?"

"Exactly."

The time warp Hanna thinks…

"The Shaman women neutralized the curse…"

"Maybe we can neutralize the past."

"It's worth a try."

Hanna locates some twine from the arts and crafts room of their home. She sits, crossed-legged and hums, then changes, to enter an altered state of consciousness. Lucius understands that she is performing a binding spell and she lights the candles, burns some incense, and plays melodious music. He takes their babies for a bath and she thinks of Jace wondering if she will be visiting Aly soon; he is not one to stay away, and both Hanna and Lucius condone their interactions.

Hanna ties the first knot from the twine:

On this night

I bid your

Black magic farewell

And she moves to the second knot:

I bid you not

To do us harm

Through this spell

That binds you well

So mote it be!

And she ties the third knot:

You are forever

Forbidden to do

Harm through

This spell that

Binds you now!

So mote it be!

Hanna ties the twine into a large loop so the spell will forever evolve and Goldie would find herself counter-cursed if she uses dark magic against them. Hanna anoints their skin with Dragon's Blood; the resin dispels negativity and she lathers the twine, as well as her husband, in an exorcism of evil hexes that threaten them. She ties a talisman into the twine: a crescent split down the middle to remain equal on both sides – a token she got from the store – an offering to the deities, and she ties the twine around her neck; the necklace is now a symbol of her freedom: the symbol of the God and the Goddess in unity ascribed to her daughter – the sacred symbol of enchantment – and Hanna has her answers.

We must seek the holy unity between the light and the dark.

"Maybe we should also make a love potion, stop by her lair, and put it in her drink," Lucius winks, while trying to lighten the situation.

Hanna is not amused. He simply cannot make light of the dark with jokes.

"Rose tried love magic... She blessed and anointed the rose petals with water; she made a secret pact with the deity and placed her love upon it. Goldie to this moment has not found love..."

"Through her parents Henry and Agnes certainly though…"

"One would think, but they were often distracted and she was overlooked."

"What pact has been made?"

"I don't know exactly. The information about the past is fragmented."

Hanna yawns. The babies are placed in bed. She retires to her bedroom and Lucius falls asleep on the couch where he can still hear the music he never turns off. Hanna dreams the nonsense of a mind that is searching through the ramblings of the subconscious mind. She dreams of the river and a white fluffy dog, and a white dove and a lone Raven; they play haphazardly in the breeze. The daylight is warm and the sun is vibrant; in her dream the sky is various shades of purple. The butterflies are plentiful and Hanna hears a voice knowing it is the voice of Grandall. He parks himself beside her, as human-like as she, seeing herself in the dream and his voice is piercing, strong and clear.

"This is a day in the past Hanna," he says "when you have asked or sought the right questions, the right answers can be told to you." He motions with his hand, his mighty staff in the other, and they walk together by the river; across the river they can see Brighton: horses, an estate as grand as a medieval castle, and Hanna feels in awe by the experience. They follow the river downstream; Hanna can see a flock of birds; they are dark but not menacing. Rose kneels beside Goldie during an initiation ritual.

"Listen intently," Grandall says, and the atmosphere is serene and quiet. Hanna taps into her thoughts; Goldie is especially distracted from the day's events: she is only half aware. The other half conjures magic with thoughts alone. She imagines two girls choking, and in Hanna's mind, she can see them grapple at their throats. Goldie imagines them turning blue as Rose pricks their finger and the moment their blood is shed Kamra and Victoria undergo death by choking. Then, Goldie did something menacing, just for the sake of doing it, she focuses on Rose's senior dog and imagines that hands squeeze around his neck and Duke goes down at the other end of the river, making his way toward Rose. During Goldie's walk home she finds Duke deceased, laying in a pool of saliva... her heart pounds upon seeing the intensity of her actions, and she knew then and there that Kamra and Victoria had suffered the same fate. Goldie then tossed her bracelet onto his body and made her way home, wondering how long she would have to wait for their death: is there a limitation to magic?

Hanna views the past like a 3D movie; a film she'd rather not be watching. Within the tunnel, the one she would walk to find Jace, she sees Goldie years later and she makes friends with the rats and through their sensitive noses they find Hanna and so her most powerful curse was put into creation: only one baby girl, born through the innocent, would be shed and she would anoint herself in the gifts of power and immortality – no one would ever be above her again and in her superiority she would cause harm. Goldie found a way to defeat her own inferiority – through the practice of dark and sinister magic.

"It was a moment of good versus evil," Hanna says.

"Go on..." Grandall's voice is smooth.

"The moment Rose initiated Goldie, and she shed her blood, Goldie was conjuring another magic in her own mind, dark magic and good magic were both happening simultaneously."

"That is right. So in essence it's like they were born at the same time while one goes to the light the other sways to the darkness. And why is that Hanna?"

"Experience?"

"Yes..."

"I'm not sure..."

"You have done good for the day." He smiles and then smoothly disappears like evanescence.

He dissipates into eternity she muses and awakens from her sleep to find Lucius is up early.

Chapter Ten

Hanna considers how she didn't leave her body willfully to travel the cosmos, but instead she got to visit the past where Grandall had once been – in her dream they were both there, like being suspended in time. In the weeks that ensue the Wiccans follow the waxing of the moon to prepare for their Sabbat: Imbolc. Although it is only February 2nd and winter is still evident, this festivity honors the coming of Spring: out with the old and in with the new.

Alexandra decorates her altar with precious baby items. She has learned that her oldest son Samuel and his wife Kyla are expecting their fourth child. Alexandra holds onto the pure thought that Rose was, is, out there with a baby somewhere. The stories of *The Lady of Brighton* are stirring and non-Wiccans like to share the folklore. On her altar is a photo of Rose and Alexandra is planning a festivity on the old estate; after being purchased by William Banks he collects money for anyone to enter who wants to share or hear stories concerning Witchcraft. Alexandra says he's a sell out and Samuel agrees. Samuel and his brothers David and John scheduled a meeting between family members. They dine at the local pub downtown along with Edgar as they wait for their mother. Alexandra is late but she takes a seat after four gentle hugs. They order burgers and fries except for Alexandra who prefers the vegetarian burger.

"William went to England, opened a few banks and now wants my estate…"

"You mean you have your estate." Alexandra reminds him.

"Well," Edgar huffs and throws down his napkin.

"I stayed for the auction and yes, he spoke to me."

"Then long story short I plan to buy it back."

"Why did we give it up to Edgar?"

"Really mom?" John says.

"Yes, I know, I gave it up after losing Rose…"

"We're lucky now to have you back." David says as he's being served his burger.

"Thank you, David. Thank all of you for having me."

"Thank you for coming, my dear," Edgar says.

My dear, Alexandra thinks about how long it has been since she has heard those words.

"How is your wife, Edgar?" She asks, and he looks up from his plate.

The burger is a mess with ketchup and mustard, but he tries to act normal.

"Divorced." He says. And changes the subject, "That man cannot outperform my magic with a deck of cards." He says, losing his modesty.

"However did the two of you both learn magic?" She laughs, "A nutty coincidence."

"That's right, it's just a coincidence, Mom," John says, and the other two agree.

"We both learned on our own," Edgar muses, "no teachers."

"We also talked to Dad about buying the bread and breakfast," John adds to the conversation.

"How can you?"

"With money my dear."

"He had a very large win, Mom," Samuel says.

"Well, how much?"

"I won some money." Edgar is casual.

"Don't be so modest, Dad," John says.

"I sold the tobacco fields that I took up after you left Alexandra and I used that money … well, it paid off."

"And you want the estate back?"

"Yes. But he is being unreasonable."

"How much?"

"2.3 million … half my earnings."

"I feel like it must be done."

"I do, too."

"Does that mean that you'll be back after all these years?"

"Yes, I think we can make things happen…"

"How is it the time of year that we can remember the seeds we planted, like our deepest aspirations that are deep within the earth… a preparation for new beginnings."

"You mean the time of year is Imbolc which is a time of year for planting the seeds to new beginnings?"

"Yes, just what I said dear."

And she laughs.

"I never got into all of your festivities, but the literal, as well as the figurative meaning, is most interesting."

She smiles and Edgar does all that he said he would. He purchases the bed and breakfast and Alexandra gives it a new name: *The Rose Diner* – a name that she wanted for so long but she did not have the money to invest when she was merely hanging on.

During Imbolc, a Wiccan pays respect to the God as they learn there is a promise of new opportunities and from his strength all guests and ventures can grow. Alexandra creates seating at the diner on one side of the house and on the other are the rooms for the guests and upstairs, the entire length of the bed and breakfast, are dorms for the girls. Alexandra feels hope. She has been hearing rumors that a young girl named Hanna Harp went on a quest and found Rose; the lore says that she was hexed into an ugly old Crone and Alexandra's heart sinks further as the story unfolds and she learns that Rose planted the seed to her youth and became young again. She remembers the attention her daughter gave to roses and how much she loved the color red. She wishes she could find the ruby-studded wands Rose had made, but a better part of her hopes that maybe Rose has it to use. Alexandra thinks of Edgar: how much he must have felt defeated when she left and he later lost the estate. She feels awful for leaving, for his need to sell Brighton, his need to leave too, and then his losing once again but this time to the one and only William Banks.

Alexandra quickly notifies the Pagan Community of the festivity she plans to host at the estate in the next three days to introduce them to the home they once shared with Rose. As word of mouth passes in those three days there is a line out the door. Among the guests are Bill, the owner of *The Witches' Brew,* Sterling, owner of *Mystic Mountains,* and her employee Elenor, and June – all who wish Hanna could join them. The guests enjoy wine and refreshments then they gather together at the diner for a country-fried dinner, and Alexandra welcomes them as they too wish for her to be the Lady of the great estate.

"She lost her daughter to the dark witch" some of them whisper.

"Might serve her right," one of the guests at the bed and breakfast says as she catches word of Alexandra's story – "that illegitimate daughter. Teenage lust," she snarls and returns to her room but before closing her door she hears Sterling who says, "Oh, what does she know?" As she makes her way to the powder room.

"The rest is just mere speculation," another woman says.

"Well, stick to what you know." Sterling says and enters the room. Upon closing the door, the woman huffs.

"My brother went missing too," another woman who is slightly younger says, "they took my brother who is likely to be dead."

June rounds the corner mid conversation, "Don't say that," she pipes in, "I mean, your brother Michael is alive!"

"How do you know this?"

"Because I am a witch and a former student to the greatest adept in magic – Grandall who taught me well and through magic I have seen him."

Lucy stands from her seat. They sit at the table nearest to the hall.

"Where is he?" She asks.

"Somewhere underground. In the catacombs, but we have not been able to find him again."

"But you saw him?"

"Yes. When I was in my sleep – but I could leave my body."

"Oh, you witches," Lucy says, "and your witchcraft, took my brother!" She tosses a cloth napkin onto the table. Joshua places a hand to her shoulder as she sobs.

"She was open-minded," Joshua reminds them, "but then all this happened."

The room is quiet. Some feel guilty. Most of them do not.

"We all thought there was no more black magic when they sold that store," another woman says.

"We all thought so." Bridget, from the girl's home, says.

Samuel also stands from his chair, "They took our sister," he says, "we can feel your pain Lucy but we are here tonight to call upon the God and the Goddess to get them back. Get them both back."

"That's right," Elenor says, easing the tension.

"If you want to proceed with us now," Alexandra says, "we will call upon deity to aid us in finding Rose and Michael, Lucy."

Lucy looks serene. She is sincere and decides to stay calm and allow the witches to work their magic.

In this ritual the Wiccans will be singing the song of the Goddess then of the God to create a positive atmosphere to charge their space with positive energy; Alexandra takes him to the reception hall where she always intended to host festivities, handfasting and ceremonies as the High Priestess of her Coven. As the bed and breakfast is now part of the expansive dining hall she has the space she needs to practice Witchcraft. As they assemble together, nearly eighty in the room, Alexandra lights candles and decorates with photos and as she burns incense, lit by the flame of a white candle, she sings:

> *Oh won't you come with me*
> *On this night to journey*
> *Complete with those*
> *Who we speak of…*

Bridget steps forward,

> *Oh won't you come*
> *With us Goddess*
> *Of the light,*
> *Won't you come*
> *To stay*

Next is Juno,

> *Oh, dear God*
> *Of the light*
> *Won't you come*
> *To stay on this*
> *Night*

In unison,

> *And be with us*
> *God and Goddess*
> *Of Celestial Light*
> *Be with us*

Then Alexandra speaks,

Dear God and Goddess

Of the Celestial City,

We call upon thee

In this rite

To ask of you

To help us find our

Dear loved ones

As Alexandra continues to purify the space with the light of the candle and the scent of incense she continues,

Oh dear Goddess

Hear us …

Won't you come

To us

And behind them they hear a voice speak, "I have come to you…"

And the Goddess appears in a human-like form with the wings of a great Phoenix, and she continues, "I am here with you always, for I have sowed the seeds for the birth of a daughter…"

They gasp, but the Goddess says no more. She bursts forth into a prism of thousands of grains like sand but in iridescent colors and then she is gone and they are speechless.

"That's some Goddess you have," Lucy shouts and she storms out the room as Joshua stands to follow after her. Alexandra goes down to her knees …

"Maybe the storm Goddess will take her out," a Warlock tries to lighten the mood.

Her sons go to her aid.

"I think we're on our own," Juno says, looking at Celia, Bridget and the other girls. Sharon and Melissa want to help so they pray but they do not possess the skills of a witch.

"We're sorry," Celia says, aside from Alexandra and her sons. Then Edgar approaches and takes her by the hand, "He's willing to sell the estate," he says, "I hope this news will help in some way." He hands her a tissue. She sobs. She feels lost.

"I need Hanna," June huffs, "she is having a third baby … but we are all still faced with Goldie." June turns away.

She cannot contain herself. She fidgets in her seat.

"I have the store covered," Elenor says to Sterling, "if you need to take some time off."

"Thank you." Sterling says, appearing sullen.

Outside the moon is a bit more than a crescent and Alexandra thinks of a cradle – she wants to hold a baby in her arms and Kyla takes her husband's head onto her shoulder and with Alexandra on the other they sob. The townsfolk talk. Alexandra is near humiliation – how can they believe in a Goddess who appears to only believe in herself? She is the widow of Brighton – one without a daughter. June returns to her room and she hopes that sleep will bring on something promising. When she leaves her body, she finds herself in a grove like a meadow nestled in the mountains. She finds Hanna – is she in the future? She wonders why the day is so bright and warm. She sees a housing development; beautiful log homes and lodges abound the landscape. There is a ski resort; she sees Lucius giving a guided tour – but the day is so hot and majestic. She wonders what month it is. Something tells her it is the Summer Solstice – but how far into the furniture? She also sees a young man approaching her – but can she be seen by him – "Yes" his voice says and they communicate telepathically. Then he uses his voice, "I am Malaki," he says.

"Yes," she responds, "student of Grandall – I remember."

"As were you," he responds. "The Shamans live and practice magic similar to the Wiccans…" his voice is magnificent and she feels drawn to him like a magnetic pull in his direction. She finds herself not wanting to leave that place.

"My mother Juno is a Guardian of the North quarter…"

"Then she must be magical…" June is in awe of them.

"Yes she is." His voice is captivating.

"The Crone used your body…" June is feeling a sense of clarity.

"To get close to the seeds she planted long ago."

"Yes…"

"And now my mother wishes to help…"

"Our work is not done…" June's thoughts are clear and she can sense his compassion.

She is more buoyant than when she is in her physical body. It's as if she has become separated from time. The sun shines behind him like a halo. She wonders how he has come from being a roaming, lost student to the form he is now. She does not ask – she simply wants to enjoy the moment. Some tourists are taking photos of the wildlife and they walk by without seeing them. It's a dream-like state of being. Everyone seems happy there. Vermont offers opportunity for a person who wants to align with nature. She never again wants to visit the Underworld. She wants to stay in the warm and loving

185

light. The entire experience only consists of minutes; *time is pure energy,* she thinks. She reaches for her bedside lamp; the light does not compare to her experience. She wishes to find Malaki and the place she had been. A piece of her mourns for the power and the light of Grandall but she feels she has experienced something more majestic that he had even achieved and why she was seeing this place is uncertain. June returns to the *Mystic Mountains* store thinking Sterling must have been to Vermont to give it such a name and she finds Elenor as they are both scheduled to work on this Saturday and June keeps with her the experience so she can remember the warmth she left with Malaki.

Chapter Eleven

The Wiccans follow the phases of the moon toward the beginning of the Spring Equinox; the Ostara festivity brings out the celebration of fertility and the last evocation of the Goddess weighs heavy on Alexandra's heart; she feels uneasy and plans to call on the Council of the Guardians to aid her in her quest to locate her daughter; she knows Juno will be looking for Malaki to bring back the peace they once shared. Malaki has been nomadic since his father robbed those banks and after being shot on a heist he was transported to prison. Juno knew and loved the other side of his double personality; the side Malaki knew and loved too. But he robbed whatever he could to get loot and that's what he kept hidden until the day he got caught; Juno was in shambles and at the time she couldn't hold it together for Malaki. They always believed he worked in the steel industry at the metal plant and at some point he did, but they have no knowledge of his leaving. Juno learned later he had been laid off. His first heist was a volt at the plant; he could sense when the lock jarred at the correct numbers; his fingers were that sensitive. But he did not survive that fatal shot, and he died in prison. By the time Juno got word and her son had already gone on an adventure to locate the hidden schools at The Temples – a place that sounded like Shangri La – he felt he could become the warrior he thought his father was to him. Juno became an adept witch and she took the place as Guardian when word passed that Leisha and Goldie had been sinister and had taken the rightful place Alexis once had. Malaki was making his way when he had been found, and his memory was lost; the word got to Juno, and although they all talked – Alexandra still needed to find Rose, Juno to find Malaki and Lucy to find her brother Michael.

Alexandra plans the Ostara festivity and slowly she and Edgar rekindle their passion as they both possess great earnestness for Rose. Edgar no longer entertains William Banks with card magic thinking it is too eerie they both exude similar characteristics with magic but William Banks also possesses the genetics of a witch and he then passed those magical talents onto LaQuinta and Rose earned her traits and skills from both her natural parents; that fact bothers Edgar to this day – the reason he always needed to excel against William at a deck of cards. Edgar has no qualities as a witch so of course he had taken to proving his superiority and status. William Banks at times defeated Edgar while knowing what card would land in a game of Black Jack – a trait of the witch. When William accused Edgar of cheating Edgar simply said it was the luck of the draw. His secrecy with his relations with William Banks left Alexandra feeling sour; she never knew of their relations until Michael let it slip. Now, Alexandra is picking up the pieces hoping that two men no longer have an affinity for showing off.

189

Alexandra heard around town about LaQuinta's daughter who vehemently had a disdain for magic – their spiritual mysticism often got convoluted by town folk and was criticized harshly as being the reason LaQuinta suffered. Alexandra still thinks about William Banks who is alive without his daughter the same as she and wonders if it is true – her legacy as a witch shines through Hanna who had to save her own daughter – can she help this time too?

Hanna and Lucius have made arrangements to visit Luther, the Druids and Archibald and Diana at their home in Vermont. Eva and Herman will look after their place in Connecticut. Hanna feels a slight separation from the Craft during family matters aside from her husband's telekinetic energy, and she finds herself enjoying the burning fires during the cold months, but they are nearing Spring and Hanna wishes to get away from home to visit the tranquil mountains of Vermont. Hanna tells Lucius for the first time that she has lost his athame blade he gave to her – the white marble blade that was his favorite and she tells him of the marble-made wand. Of that, he is not too sure about but he tells Hanna that all that matters is the kids are safe and they have Thor and Sage – both of which accompany them on this trip; although they are not opening portals they have used magic to gain speed like catching a worm hole through a vortex, "It's similar to opening portals," Lucius says, "but this way the whole car can move through it." Hanna is having fun, and Spring is what she needs to rekindle her love of nature apart from work; Vermont is a treasure.

Ostara marks the time for balance when both light and dark are equal. Alexandra says it is a time when seeds have been planted, enabling dreams to grow and flourish on the Earth. Like a young child, the Earth is young, fresh and anew. The buds of Spring begin to bloom and peek from the soil to grow toward the daylight that will gradually overcome the dark. New life will come from the old during Ostara; today Alexandra is greeted by a group of young women: "We are the witches of East Brunswick," the oldest says, "my name is Sydney..." and the remaining women follow suit.

"We are following the Legend of the Lady of Brighton," Amber says, sweetly.

"Oh?" Alexandra doesn't know what to say.

"We can help you get her back," Sydney says.

The word around town of the Lady of Brighton motivates a desire within. They cannot hold back.

"How can you do that?"

"Tonight when you call upon the Guardians we'll be there."

Alexandra is holding a festivity at the estate; the girls including Melissa and Sharon are decorating. Bridget places a vase of fresh lilies on the altar. Alexandra recognizes that these women have come together to grieve, and today they come together to initiate hope, change and to align their path by their will. The women assemble at the estate of Brighton to come together in a unity of one with the same purpose; they begin their rite by casting a circle; in a clockwise motion they walk and place stones at their feet; Alexandra carves an imaginary circle with an athame blade – once the circle is complete they hold yellow lilies and yellow roses in an offering to the Earth…

Overseers of nature, Alexandra begins…

We offer these flowers
A sample of Spring
For the seed of life
To grow and begin anew;
A symbol of rejuvenation
And of beauty.

The women begin to sing, hum and chant in a symphony of music:

Wherever my daughter
May be please bring
To her joy, love
And hope for
The future.

Alexandra moves to the North:

I call upon the Guardian of
The North to aid me in this
Consecration of the Roses
So that they may be blessed
With the memory of my
Daughter.

She then moves to the East:

I call upon the Guardian
Of the East; may your
Spirit of air bless
These Spring lilies
So that we may
Believe the best
Intentions and not
Look for the worst.

She moves to the South:

I call upon the blessings
Of fire to bless the
Practitioners with divine
Knowledge so that
My daughter may be
Found to help us all
Who is in need.

She moves to the West:

I call upon the Spirit

Of Water so that our

Spirits may be healed

And may we seek to heal

Others through compassion

And love.

She moves to the center of the circle:

These flowers are a gift to the divine

…

May the Goddess leads us to my

Daughter with the best of intentions –

For the highest good of all

So mote it be!

The women hold in their hearts that the Goddess of the Celestial City has the best of intentions (or so they pray); they sit down and visualize the radiance of positive energy flowing within the room and all around them. They chant, sing and praise the Spirits, the Goddess and the Guardians; from the energy Alexandra is lifted into the air and she levitates above them all; their heads are lowered as they continue to visualize radiant energy; Alexandra's head is gently tilted back and as her mouth opens she is filled with light – for the highest good, she is filled with positive energy and when she closes her mouth she is lowered to the ground and she can sense profound love emanating from the Guardians of the Watchtowers: *Bless Be,* they say in unison and the practitioners can feel the level and their souls are filled with hope to locate Rose for the highest good of all and with no harm done.

Hanna walks through nature feeling a stirring in her stomach – only a few months to go to give birth to another baby boy. She gains a sense of love all around her; the feeling is warm and bright. Goose bumps form on her arm and a sensation courses through her body – Hanna Intuit's she is being sent Divine Love; Lucius finds her among the first sprouts of Spring at their feet; he is with the children. Aly runs happily.

Lucas reaches to touch her; they too sense Divine Love.

"What do you think she is trying to tell us?" Lucius says and Hanna does not hesitate…

"She wants a baby."

"The Goddess wants a baby?"

"Yes." She punches him in the arm.

In the valley Luther trains an army but Hanna does not feel they will be fighting, but still, they train. Hanna begins her morning aside Diana; they practice baby yoga and Diana helps her along through her pregnancy. Hanna says this will be her last and Diana cannot say. She is the wife of a leader and she takes her role as a personal guide for Hanna who is a young mother of three – Diana believes that Divine Love is a blessing from the Goddess but Hanna believes the Goddess is sharing her own personal love – her personal need for a family.

She knows the Goddess planted the seed – the wish for a girl and Hanna wonders if Lily grows. Alexandra tends her garden as she Intuit's the same question: she searches by the river; she feels her way through the wild flowers that begin to bloom. Samuel calls: Kyla is in labor. Alexandra goes to the hospital to find that she has birthed a son. They give their son the name Eben Anthony. Alexandra holds her first grandson in her arms when Edgar walks into the room; "He looks like a proud Papa," Kyla says of Edgar and he looks at his new little grandson with adoring eyes. David and John join them. They ask the nurse to snap a photo. Alexandra is eager to have all of them at home. Samuel is a pilot and he talks of taking his new son a personal helicopter ride.

"That'll be a while babe." His wife jokes.

David and John changed course and went into business together; they built lavish homes and whole communities; David as the contractor and John as the real estate agent. They talk of buying historical buildings and making them new again. Alexandra is proud of all her son's successes.

"We wish Rose was here," Samuel says as a bird taps upon the window sill and scuttles off.

"One of those pesky Ravens?" Alexandra asks as Samuel looks out the window; on the ledge is a bracelet and Alexandra recognizes it as the same pendant that was found with Duke – did he not want to have it? Is this a sign? Did Clover bring it to them? As something made by Rose Alexandra wants them to retrieve it.

"We can't walk through walls, Mom," Samuel jokes but Alexandra looks uneasy. She calls on the janitor who they pay nicely and he responds, "Sure, no problem," as if it was as easy as walking through walls. The janitor returns an hour later …

"But how did you do it?" Alexandra begins but with that twinkle in his eye, she realizes he excels in magic too. He simply consults his familiar, a falcon, to find artifacts. He says that he is a collector of vintage items; he says that the falcon has been with him on journeys of majestic places.

"It keeps me busy," he says, and as the maintenance guy for the hospital he invites Edgar to join him for a smoke sometime. Alexandra then realizes that he is a Shaman.

"You are quick." He reads her mind and winks.

Alexandra cannot help but to speak of Rose and he listens intently.

"If she wants to be found then she will." He says reassuringly.

Alexandra explains that they thought they saved her once.

"She would have made her way back to you… but there is a reason she could not." His voice is smooth and warm.

"Maybe it's Michael mom." John says and something in Alexandra's mind clicks.

"She must have gone back for him. Hanna explained that Rose's memory had not been back until she was freed from the hex of the Crone" and that message was

200

received by word of mouth to reach Alexandra through June Bug.

"June has her memories intact," Alexandra says, "but the others…" she thinks for a moment, "she said the rest cannot remember – that they chose not to remember but why?"

Alexandra found it hard to believe June because she thought her daughter's things are finding a way to her – then perhaps Rose will too. Alexandra kisses her grandson and she places the bracelet with the pendant into her pocket.

"It was blessed by my daughter," Alexandra says, and the Shaman janitor looks her in the eye – his eyes are deep like an old adage, "I'm happy to have helped you today," he says and turns back to sweep the floor. He makes his way down the hall and when they look out the door there is no one there. She calls on the nurse who giggles.

"Oh, you too," she says, "that must have been Tribal… he's a legend around here… a Shaman and a Shapeshifter…

sounds like he helped you out." The nurse smiles.

"Yes," Alexandra says, and the rest of them are speechless.

"Thank you, Tribal," she whispers – knowing an old soul found his way into her heart – her wishes are being heard.

She takes the bracelet and wraps it around her wrist – because it's an insignia of her deepest desire to find her beloved Rose.

Chapter Twelve

Hanna finds an open field of new buds where she plants herself. The landscape is beautiful; nestled among the mountains of Vermont she meditates. Her journey is simple at first; Monarchs begin to spread their wings in her mind's eye. She can hear the birds chirping and the falling cascade of the waterfall over the mountain. She comes to a door, but she does not knock; the door opens and she is in a tunnel. The air is cool and the earth is thawing. She proceeds toward the light at the end of the tunnel and when there she is faced with a great chasm. She imagines she is able to fly; then, she feels a great wind as it blows the hair past her face. She knows the chasm is a bottomless fall into the void that is the Underworld. Hanna inhales and she takes a leap of faith; she moves backward in the tunnel and makes a great leap, lands on a small precipice, but she is on the other side.

Then the Earth begins to shake, and she hears a hum like a dissonant sound and her body rises; she becomes light like being suspended in the air and she is flying. A fairy scuttles by; it is Tia and she is leading the way further into the immensity of a bright light. She is in awe. In ecstasy. Hanna feels love all around her; she wants to be loved by the embrace; the light is hugging her. There are waterfalls or something like water cascading all around her when a prism of light explodes into thousands of shimmering colors and before her stands the most enigmatic presence her eyes have ever seen; the Goddess Helga, in full form, with wings that expand six feet on both sides and within her native home she is the most magnificent thing! Hanna does not want to approach her; momentarily, she does not feel worthy.

"Nonsense." Helga says, "Walk with me."

Hanna floats toward her; the buildings are made of billions of colors far beyond the spectrum of Earth. The City dazzles with castles among rolling hills. Hanna feels the witches have nothing compared to this place. How can anyone side with the dark? Jealousy is the dark way of seeing the light; she thinks this place is enchanting to say the least. She plants her feet on what looks like moving water; the landscape around her whirls and turns like pulsating beings of light like a great breathing womb. In the City there are angels and spirits dancing. Hanna sees babies and they are being birthed like wild flowers blooming. There are human forms and there are Pixies like Tia; her tiny wings are iridescent and her small frame flutters like a Monarch Butterfly. Hanna wants to touch everything, like being an infant again – like everything is in its newness. The Celestial City is made of light particles and when formed together structures look solid, but she knows that is deceiving. There are spirits at work to heal the sick; they respond to calls from the

205

Witches and the Warlocks who ask the Goddess and the Angels to aid them.

In the next moment, Helga walks Hanna through memory lane; Hanna sees a young child, a young girl, and she is standing on tippy toes. She is twirling in a princess dress. Hanna feels she is watching the Goddess as a human child; how she was human once and Hanna is in awe of her. The girl fast forwards into youth and then as a young woman. She meets a human man and they are together to consummate in love. Everything Hanna's eyes can see is moving rapidly, yet it feels like slow motion. Hanna sees Helga as she births a child and the child grows to the age of five then she becomes sick. Helga is unable to treat her; neither can the Shamans or the doctors. The little girl is laid to rest and Hanna can see the young woman's depression; she only grows spiritually upon her death. Helga blossoms as the blessed Goddess and realizes her loss made her grow spiritually. But the Goddess can remember the birth of her daughter; she longs for a daughter again and Hanna can feel her heart yearning. Hanna sees the seed she is planting: a Lily of the Valley. The seed has been planted with her wish to have a girl. Then Hanna can see Rose: she is handing over her child. The Goddess is in awe. Rose shivered; her tears were not happy. *What is the Goddess doing?* She thinks to herself and the Goddess responds, "My plan is the most divine." Hanna can see the Goddess in her glory. She can also see that Rose planted a solitary rose and within that rose is a soul and Hanna is forbidden to see more.

The Goddess grows in love and ecstasy as she surrounds the baby girl with love and Hanna feels torn between immense love and even more profound loss. Hanna does not fully comprehend the Divine Plan.

"Rose wishes to see her mother again," the Goddess explains, "and through our compromise …"

But Hanna stops listening; her own heart turns grave. The Goddess has taken to

Rose's baby – her baby girl – and Hanna's own body turns as she is nearing the birth of her third child – the birth of another son. Hanna feels herself leaving the Celestial City like moving backwards through time like a vortex that is backwards in motion. She does not side with the Goddess. She does not understand the Divine Plan. Hanna can only understand the loss of a baby; she cannot understand any compromise that involves a child. Hanna refuses to meditate any longer.

The people are being subdued by positive energy. Malaki has found June Bug.

"We have to help Alexandra find Rose," June says as they are approached by the Sister's Coven.

"We can help you," Sydney says.

"We can get her baby back," Amber adds.

"How, or why?" June begins.

"It's our calling," Priscilla chimes in.

Then Sydney explains, "Amber has the power of fire scrying… when she peered into the flames she saw a young baby girl being taken away…"

Then Paisley speaks, "Then Sydney intuited the name of Alexandra."

"It's her daughter's baby that is being taken away," Amber comments.

"So we are here to help," Sydney flashes a warm and reassuring smile.

Hanna tells Lucius all that she learned during her visit to the Celestial City.

"I was thinking," he interrupts her, "that we name him James Edgar, you know, to honor your Grandmother's half sister… I'm just saying."

"He is getting old…"

"But Hanna, it's okay, he is still alive."

"And we can get Rose to see her father again."

"And help Alexandra find Rose."

"I was wondering what you think…"

"I think you need to follow your instincts."

"My intuition tells me that no mother should lose her child… under no circumstances. None."

"Then it seems we are all in agreement," Malaki says, "we are going to help Alexandra locate her long lost daughter …"

"Yes," June Bug says.

"Then it's another adventure." Malaki assures her.

"But do realize there are risks," Sydney says.

"Of course." He nods.

The Wiccans follow the waxing of the moon to April thirteenth – a time of the Beltane Sabbat – a festivity that begins on the evening prior and lasts to the daylight of May first. They are prepared to officially celebrate the beginnings of Summer. The Wiccans celebrate in honor of love, maturity, creativity and nature among the landscape that is in its peak – when various shades of green are abundant and the flowers are in full bloom.

Hanna makes haste back to Virginia with Lucius, Thor and Sage in tow before they could tell Archibald or Diana of their leaving; Lucius worked the lifts and paid his respects before leaving but Hanna was on an early train. She too has a calling and as she connects with Sydney she feels there is a parallel of sorts – which she has not figured out yet; but with Luther in Connecticut he tends to their home as they gladly gave it away and Hanna returns to the store to work the day shift, and Sterling is pleased to have her back. Hanna simply needed the time away to soul search and find the way before her.

Alexandra is greeted by Amber at the estate and as they prepare to celebrate natural maturity and fertility, Amber lights the bonfire and as the eve of May is upon them – the Wiccans dance to the music of the outdoor band and the enjoyment of song can be heard throughout Brighton.

"May brings about the merry," Alexandra talks soothingly.

"The merry month," an unfamiliar and masculine voice says among the crowd.

"The end of winter's turmoil," Alexandra adds.

"But there is still turmoil," Hanna steps from the crowd and in her hands she holds two flowers that have been uprooted; in the left hand it's the rose and in the right is the Lily of the Valley.

"What?" Alexandra begins but Hanna steps closer. "The rose is the seed from your daughter and the other is the seed of the Goddess."

"But why…"

"I have uprooted these flowers so they may be kept alive for as long as we are searching for them."

Then another voice shines through, "We are here to help you," Sydney says and Alexandra looks to Edgar and back at them.

"I am getting too old," Alexandra says, "at age seventy-seven…"

"You can still practice magic," Sydney assures her.

"But the rest of us can go the distance." Hanna nods.

She places each flower into her hands, "For now," she says, "we must keep them alive in our thoughts, hearts, soul, and minds… These flowers attest to that."

"The warmth of the light has returned to us," Alexandra says, "the Goddess herself must help us."

Hanna refrains from telling her anything else that involves Rose aside from the fact that they are all there to help them.

"Plant the seeds where you know they can grow," Hanna says and the Wiccans gather around her. "Let's take them to the mountain," a friendly man says.

"Let's take them to the Valley," another says.

"Do what you feel is right darling," Edgar pipes in and takes her by the hand.

"We are all here as family again," he says, "but there is still one who is missing."

"Do what's in your heart," a woman speaks and the practitioners of magic agree in a chorus of love. Alexandra sniffs each one and she opens her heart to the possibility that she may see her beloved Rose again. She enjoys coming together in the greenery that is among them. She thinks for a moment and she takes up the earth with the soil beneath her feet and says, "We all happen to be standing where my daughter and my son-in-law fasted together as they tied the knot that bound them in love and unity. This is where I want the seeds of love to grow."

The Wiccans bow to their knees as a husky man leaves the crowd and with an athame blade he cuts for her deep into the earth and Alexandra plants the flowers back into the soil so that from them the wishes of her daughter can grow. She then plants the lily not knowing what wish the Goddess bestowed upon it. Hanna is merely following her instincts, although she cannot fully understand the Goddess' intentions.

Alexandra plants them feeling that there will be no harm done.

"The fertility of the Earth will bring their hopes and dreams to fruition," Hanna says as Sterling approaches them and she bows her head and helps to cover the roots with the Earth.

"May we be sisters," she smiles and Alexandra has a tear falling down her cheek, and she hugs her. Samuel steps forward and thanks them. Hanna hugs him and she can feel warmth in their embrace. David and John are there too and they wipe their eyes of the years Alexandra has also cried for her daughter. In a full circle, they embrace and after intermission the band plays again and the Wiccans return to song and dance to be in the warmth that is returning to Earth. The children dance around the maypole and Alexandra longs for her daughter but as she takes Eben into her arms she cannot help to wonder if Rose had a girl or a boy and as the day wanes to night the festivity ends on May first.

Hanna dreams she is awake and finds Jace, "I feel everything is waiting to explode," she says. She embraces him and although dreaming, he is still cold.

"You have the wisdom in your heart, Hanna," he says, "and so do you in this head of yours," he taps her upon the forehead.

"I came to you Hanna because I didn't think you could stand the stench of the Underworld any longer."

"You're probably right, Jace."

"I have to ask you – why haven't you been able to find Goldie?"

"Who says I haven't?"

"Well, have you?"

"Honestly I cannot find where they have been… I can only find where they are going."

"Do you have a hunch?"

"Not exactly…"

"I do have a hunch who took your magical tools."

"Who else can come in like a phantom of the night?"

216

"Goldie?"

"Not exactly, Hanna. Not this time. You need to be more careful – you do not know who you can trust."

"Then who else? Are you saying you took them?"

He touches a finger to his nose, "you hit it right on the nose."

"Why?"

"I kind of just explained that."

"Oh. Yeah, sorry."

"Don't apologize," he hands her a satchel that was tied behind his back.

She takes the satchel but her fingers go right through it. Her body is becoming a body of the mind.

"I'll deliver it to you, Hanna," he says.

"Okay, Jace."

"I want to see Aly."

"Can you come by in the morning?"

"It's not that easy."

"But isn't it?"

"The energy is shifting… the Goddess must be up to something."

217

"We are limited to our dreams?"

"But that should also slow down Goldie."

"Yes, being mortal."

"I don't know how you can see Aly if I cannot enter the Underworld…"

"I don't know either. For now I only know that the energy is changing. I cannot move freely among the worlds as I once could."

"The Goddess," she hesitates," wants Rose's baby."

"She wants her baby?"

"Yes."

"Well isn't that ironic?"

"She wants the baby they all seek her help to protect."

"She was mortal once?"

"She was."

"Then how did she become the Goddess of the Celestial City?"

"I guess we just have more to learn."

"Yeah, you know, I was thinking – I am the things the dark are made of."

"How?"

"My father…"

"It makes your dark a different kind of dark. There is a distinction."

"I guess." He ponders as she begins to wake from the dream without the satchel she could only dream of possessing again.

Later she finds that Sterling has changed the décor of the store as she enters for work; the place is decorated in bright tapestries on the walls and yellow along with hues of blue adorn the walls.

"They're new," she says, and Hanna has a look at the price tags: only twenty bucks for a tapestry.

Hanna takes down a yellow stained tie-dye with blue accents.

"I'll take this one," she says and Sterling rings her up on the register. Hanna has a thought she would like to ask of the twin sister to Goldie.

"How is Goldie?" She musters to say and Sterling gives her an inquisitive look.

"Word does travel through this town," Sterling says. "I have not spoken with my sister for many years now."

"She does not associate with the family?"

"No."

Sterling looks all the more stunned and she begins clipping the roses she places into a vase on the counter.

"I assume you have learned a great deal from Alexandra by this point."

"Some. Are the two of you friends?"

"We are not enemies."

"How do you suppose Goldie would become a Guardian?"

"A Guardian? Oh no, she mustn't - she has a dark soul." Sterling looks emotional. "But those girls…"

"What girls?"

"Their names were Kamra and Victoria. They were related cousins I believe. Victoria, a frail little blonde, was always protected by Kamra. They ganged up on Goldie any chance they got."

"What happened?"

"She beat the snot out of my sister."

"Why would they do that?"

"Why would anyone?"

"True."

"Goldie was harassed… but she never sought help… well, by anyone other than Leisha I suppose."

"She became closed off."

"Yes. I was so busy in my own world that I hadn't noticed."

"You two were never close then."

"No. Never."

Hanna thinks about Aly thankful she is back home with Lucius. She thinks about Luther and Reese and how they have come together – thankful too to have them.

"I am the things the dark are made of." She thinks out loud.

"What?" Sterling says.

"I'm sorry, just a bad movie I saw recently." She decides to shrug off the comment.

"Oh," Sterling says and she enters the back room.

Hanna officially clocks in and her work shift has started. She peers at the sun thinking of her baby wondering if she should speak of the Goddess but realizes she does not want to rob the Wiccans of their faith in the Goddess so she stays silent – sticking to her intuition when the door opens and she has the first customer for the start of her shift.

Chapter Thirteen

At lunch, Hanna finds Lucius behind the counter at *The Witches' Brew*.

"Lucius?" She doesn't have to ask any further.

"I figured I'm here every day for lunch … why not just apply to work here?" He says from behind the bar.

Hanna has a seat. They serve coffee during the day until they open at night for the after-hours. The pub is mostly busy during the daylight hours when the witches of all sorts come through. The area is known for the valley and tourists frequently visit its rich springs where they bathe to cleanse their bodies of impurities and rid themselves of negativity that affects their energy and therefore their magic. There is a castle nestled in the mountain that is open to the guests and the café of cats brings in enthusiasts who mingle in the company of felines. The mood overall is especially uplifting during the summer months. They can feel liberated of evil, at least in the moment. Hanna orders the veggie burger that is made from organic plants and she contemplates; going to the natural springs would help her relax, especially before birth.

Lucius is guided through the steps on how to make a café favorite: vanilla and hazelnut hot brewed latte. Hanna can see the steam brewing from the cup, and she has a vision: two young girls around the age of seven play by the river. They are running when one of them falls. There is suddenly a foot on her back and the other girl shies away. Hanna senses the girls are Goldie and Sterling. Her vision becomes more alert as Goldie struggles to get up when the hard fists of the other girl pound at her back – her face is in the mud. Hanna knows intuitively that nothing is private in the life of a witch. She thinks as she has forgotten about her burger when Lucius snaps her back to reality.

"What are you daydreaming about?" He smiles.

"A vision," she says but she wishes to tell him later.

When she returns to the store she is still aware of the Sterling experience, and she doesn't blame Goldie; the times were different back then when the children ran wild and there wasn't the parental guidance to shield them. Hanna assumes that her parents were unaware of the violence against her – or were they? She thinks that Sterling must have told them. Her mind drifts. She thinks of Michael – how he is on the brink of death from starvation – how long he has languished. She considers Rose too – she is a strong witch – she must know a way out. But as an aged Crone, Rose was guided by her senses even though her memories were not clear. Now she has her memories. Now she has the strength of a witch. Hanna thinks that if only they would meet in the middle – but how? Outside she spots Sage and Clover – even the animal familiars appear ready. The emotion sinks in: they must invoke her spirit, wherever she may be, and try communication. They must be able to contact her through strength in numbers. The witches shall come together over the same cause and Hanna feels immensely that she can reach them. Hanna isn't quite sure how to include Sterling or that she should. She quickly sends Sage with a message to be delivered to Alexandra. A séance will aid them in evoking Rose if they are able to find her.

Alexandra is at home when she receives the letter from the talons of the great bird of prey. Sage takes flight and she opens the letter – finally, she thinks they are coming together and she returns indoors to tend to Eben. She writes a letter in response to the wishes Hanna has proposed. She no longer has a familiar so she whistles and when Sage returns she hands over the letter to leathery talons.

As Hanna is leaving from her shift she retrieves the note and plans are set: they will evoke her spirit to accompany them in the séance. Witches are familiar with séances and in Alexandra's letter, she says she would like to perform the communion by the light of the full moon in three days. Hanna goes home to Lucius who is there waiting for her. His father is also present in the great room, and while Reese tends to the children, the men converse over the components of an engine and then onto pursuing new jobs. Hanna catches wind of the conversation and finds Reese who is packed and ready to go. She quickly invites her to attend to which Reese responds positively – she would not miss being there.

And she doesn't. They are eager to contact Rose. Hanna assumes Rose did not know where to find Alexandra, or, if she knows Alexandra is still alive. Alexandra has invited the *Sister's Coven* who introduce themselves as the *Witches of East Brunswick* – a sisterhood of benevolent women who aid other witches in times of great peril. Hanna relaxes, knowing that her past with the sisters are unknown by them.

She feels the sisters are the most legit coven of women whoever found her, and now, they have found Alexandra but it's no surprise; the legend of the *Lady of Brighton* spreads like wildfire. Non-witches know the story; Hanna thinks for a moment that her own mother likely knows Sterling too. She sighs over the thought of Alayna – that perhaps she just protects herself while being closed-minded.

They convene over iced beverages. They talk among themselves at the round table in Alexandra's home. Her place is lavish and Edgar settles in the great room; they have word that both David and John have found love. Samuel is happily married to a non-witch but Alexandra would never forsake him. They are family. And Alexandra needs her beloved Rose. Her hands shake as she first lights a black candle in the hand of the smiling Buddha that signifies warding off evil with positive energy and she lights a white candle in his other hand to allow positive energy to flow. They invite the energy of the positive light. The sisters,

Hanna and Reese, take a seat and at the head, -- Priestess of the table – Alexandra.

"I wish to invite the Guardians," she says and they light their individual candles of colors red and indigo for channeling and opening communication.

And so she begins:

"We convene at this great circle of life, light, and love, to call upon the daughter of the presiding Priestess who oversees this communion, who is I, Alexandra Worthington. I call upon the Guardian of the North Tower – bless us in this communion. Raise the powers within to aid thee!"

And the table vibrates to the beat of energy. The table lifts from the floor and elevates; from a portal Juno enters the room followed by a flowing stream of white light. She looks like a Goddess as the light emanates around her and as the light dissipates she speaks: "Sisters. I come to you in this evocation of your beloved daughter Rose."

229

"Thank you, dear Sister," Alexandra says and they move forward.

"Guardian of the East tower, I call upon you for this evocation of my beloved daughter Rose..."

And from the East coordinate energy emerges within the room as Gladys wears flowing garments that flow elegantly about the room.

"I am blessed to be here as your guide," Gladys says.

"We are blessed to have you dear Guardian," Alexandra says.

She continues: "Guardian of the South, will you give us the pleasure of your graces and join us for the evocation of my daughter Rose..."

And in the South, Elusha comes into view through a portal; she is the most provocative of witches and Hanna feels concern in her stomach as she takes a breath – she is unclear if Elusha can hold her place within the light.

"I am faithful to you," Elusha says.

"Thank you, Sister."

Alexandra lowers her gaze, "Guardian of the West, join me… I call upon your faithfulness to aid us in this evocation of my daughter."

Vienna shows in the West with tears rolling down her cheeks.

"I have been waiting for you," she says.

"Thank you, sister. As I have also been waiting for you."

"No need to thank me for being here, sister," Vienna says and they all lower their heads.

"In this time of unity we seek the soul of my beloved daughter – Rose Worthington!"

"Hear us!" The rest of them speak in unison.

"We have the presence of the *Storm Goddess*," Alexandra says as she feels the light in the room become more pronounced and they are buoyant from radiant energy that circles around them – the *Goddess of*

231

Storms raises the energy within the room with the wave of her hands and she blows and a surge emanates from her entire being.

"We call upon the soul of my daughter!" She shouts even more as her voice is carried through space and time from the breath of the *Storm Goddess*. They levitate as the energy within the room shifts; there is power behind her words, a blessing from the Storm Goddess and the Guardians.

A surge like lightning jolts them and the evocation of her soul appears to be working and they chant a mantra of *om* to elevate the energy further − they begin to make a connection metaphysically with her soul. At the center of the table is an opaque mist and she begins to take the shape of human form.

Alexandra breathes heavily. They stop the chant momentarily and Alexandra speaks softly, "Dear soul, come to us in peace in light and love…"

The shape of her daughter manifests and Alexandra can barely hold back as she gasps, "Rose!"

"Stay calm dear sister," Gladys says.

And they watch as Rose manifests as energy but materializes before them – twenty years old and pregnant. Her round stomach is most pronounced and Rose speaks, "She wants my baby," she cries.

Alexandra extends her arms toward her daughter, but Gladys holds her tight and they embrace there before Rose.

"Who is my daughter?"

"The Goddess Helga wants my baby!"

Hanna feels a surge like being crushed. She knows all too well when another wants to take a mortal child – but Goldie wanted to sacrifice her daughter – why would the Goddess want a mortal child? She thinks.

"Let's hear her," Juno says as if reading her mind.

"She will give me my life back, but I have to give her my baby…"

"How can she?" Vienna says.

"I don't know either," Elusha says.

Alexandra takes a step closer … "Where are you, Rose?"

"I can't tell you," Rose shutters.

"Why can't you?" Her voice is a whisper.

"The Goddess has plans for my baby."

Her image flickers as materialization is a precarious use of energy.

"We must give her what she wants?" Alexandra hears herself saying…

"I can't Momma." Rose bellows from behind tears.

The lightning crashes as the *Goddess of Storms* appears to explode before them.

Rose vanishes then and they sit there in silence. Disbelief.

"We will stay here for as long as we are needed." Gladys says.

"Yes." Juno agrees.

They hear a knock on the door and when Alexandra opens it they find June Bug and Malaki and Juno goes to them and they embrace.

"Finally my son," Juno says.

"Mother." He talks to her.

"We did not get word until it was too late." Malaki tells his mother.

"Tell me..." Alexandra is anxious.

She shivers with fear and Juno embraces her knowing how it feels to long for a   touch.

Hanna returns home to Lucius, and as the moon begins to wane, she has many sleepless nights until the daylight is strong and her contractions begin: the baby is born on the eve of the Summer Solstice. Their first day of life is the longest day and the shortest night. Hanna is four weeks early, but her baby boy is born healthy despite being a mere four pounds; upon his wrist, Hanna notices the birthmark: a crescent moon with a staff down the center. She quickly goes to Aly and upon her wrist is the half moon and when the two wrists are joined the combined half moons form complete circles.

"They are the image of the perfect balance between the darkness and the light." Lucius gazes over them.

"Yes," Hanna says, "but what does it mean?"

"They complete the balance..."

"But I still don't understand."

"This message is not from the light," he says, "the staff is Grandall..." he continues to ponder... "we are yet to balance the darkness among the light."

"Goldie wanted full power... the Goddess wants a baby... surely, she wouldn't sacrifice the innocent child to balance the dark and the light?" She questions.

Lucius looks earnestly at her, "if the dark sacrifices the child then her disembodied Spirit enters the Light."

"Something is definitely happening." Hanna's voice is a near whisper.

And when James Edgar cries, Hanna feeds the newborn boy and the night overcomes them so they can sleep.

Chapter Fourteen

It is a brisk, warm, sun filled day yet Alexandra is numb. She is outside hanging linens when she hears the phone ring; heading inside, she feels the caller must be a non-witch because, of course, witches are connected via the telepathic network when the energy is right. She is right, however, because the caller is a non-witch.

"Mrs. Worthington, we have your daughter." The male voice says but Alexandra is flustered.

"I don't have time for prank calls," she huffs but before she hangs up, she hears another voice.

"Mom." Alexandra is stunned. "They got rid of me after..." but her voice trails off when the medical professional's voice is back on the line.

"I have the deputy here who found her."

Then another voice responds, "We found her abandoned at the gas station. You may want to come down to the hospital."

Alexandra has already hung up the phone. She is gathering her bag when she shouts to Edgar, "Come on!" She says. "Rose is at the hospital!"

Edgar barely has enough time to process as he is running out the door as she is taking off and slams on her brakes when she lets him into the passenger seat. Out the side window she can see Sage and Clover and knows the witch community will get the word soon. When they arrive at the hospital, Rose is with the nurses, getting into her gown, when Alexandra sees her blood-stained clothing upon the floor.

"They cut her out of me." She can barely speak.

She sobs but she is numb from the pain medication. Word spreads fast throughout Virginia and the surrounding area makes its way to the hospital for support; crowds of people surround the area wanting to get a glimpse of the woman they have come to call *The Lady of Brighton*. Rose has not aged a day over twenty. They are all outside wondering if she has been bewitched because according to the police officers, she is still in her youth. They want to know if she was a lie or a fable and the police precinct patrons are as curious as the crowd outside.

"Does she age?" One woman says below and they can hear her from the window as Rose is transported for surgery. They clean and bandage her wound and the deputy gathers outdoors among them. They ask him questions.

"Is she alive?" One spectator says.

"She is." The deputy makes his way to the squad car that is parked out front. He cannot leave because they are crowding the streets so the precinct ushers them from the vehicle. They are mostly quiet standing there in awe of the great legend. Rose cannot recall how she got to the station, but the deputy took her to the hospital. She was seemingly left at the precinct to die.

Rose is given pain medication again through her port and her hand turns cold from the liquid after she awakens from the operation. Alexandra sits at her bedside and feels a slight coldness about the room when she sees Hanna walk through the walls. Hanna is outside her body – the ability to bi-locate gives her the ability to walk through dense objects as she is an energetic body.

"Goldie kidnapped my daughter once too." Hanna explains but knows she is not providing much comfort but she has to tell her…

"Goldie took my daughter Aly so that she could climb to the highest point to Mount Katahdin, the highest point North, where she wanted to sacrifice the most innocent and offer her blood to the Gods of the Darkness so she could become empowered. She aimed to become the High Priestess of the Darkness – the next level to a God."

"Humans cannot be a God nor a Goddess." Alexandra's voice is near a whisper.

But Hanna knows Alexandra is wrong. Helga had a human child once. She is Goddess for her unconditional love but now it seems that even love can be blinding when there is no longer enough heart and too much an empty soul – even for a Goddess.

"She had a demon who she also wished to fulfill all her desires. Now, I am afraid that the Goddess of the Light could…" Her voice trails off.

"That the Goddess could offer the child in an appeasement to the dark?"

"The baby has been taken from her…"

"How can you help us?"

"I am a witch with a past and I am hoping to take what I have learned to help you."

Alexandra needs all the help she can get and turns her face to Rose who is under the weather considering the medication and her condition. Hanna finally notices Edgar who has fallen asleep on the sofa, still unaware that Rose has returned from surgery.

Rose returns to her homestead after two and a half days in the intensive care unit – there is no more they can do for her at the hospital. She must have rest and medication. Reporters gather around the home and they marvel over the lavish estate as they feel the Lady makes a good story like a princess in the movies. She has long been a legend even for those who do not practice magic. She finds herself in the company of Samuel, his wife Kyla, their baby Eben, David and his girlfriend Isabella, and John with his fiancée Jasmine. Rose can feel their immense love like the warm blankets at the hospital. They all feel sorrow too. She mentions Michael and they all remain quiet when she is also met by Hanna, June, Malaki and Alexandra's close friend Bridget who are there to comfort and provide service as they are needed.

"He is alive," Hanna says. "I have seen him, during times of vision quests."

"How is he?" She asks with a glimmer of hope.

Hanna explains it all: how he has survived by feeding from the spiders that surround him and the rats that scurry within the cellar where he is kept shackled and where he has languished without Rose for twenty years.

She painstakingly describes how Alexis did not make it and she gives her a vivid picture of how Michael appears now that he has been hanging on.. Rose is not dismayed and she wants to take a journey with Hanna on a quest to find her husband if someone, somehow, can help her to advance to that level once she has healed and can maintain that kind of energy. Hanna describes the magical powers of Rhoda, the Shaman Elder, who can provide her with the right medicine – of tonic and herbs – that can aid her into the journey of the mind.

"That way," Hanna says, "you don't have to muster the energy of an ox, but of something more fragile…"

"Like a bird." Rose musters a smile and Alexandra places her hand on hers and they look at Hanna with hope.

Rose is familiar with the idea that the mind is not limited by space and time as the physical body is limited by density and as she gains her strength she asks that Hanna will take her to Rhoda who can help her to find her husband.

Back at the store, Sterling is faced with opposition.

"You," an aged woman points a crooked finger, "you and your family…" her voice is harsh and Sterling shivers from the coldness of her breath. She feels she should be used to confrontation.

"Ma'am , I'm not sure…"

"Your evil little family killed her and my sister's daughter."

Sterling knows this must be the family of Kamra and her cousin Victoria. The town folk speak of their fate as they both were choked to death on that same fatal day, and Goldie was not heard of or seen again.

Sterling understands her sister may be odd to others but she cannot conceive of the evil they have blamed her with.

"They took that woman's child," the woman continues.

"Who?"

"Oh don't be stupid," she glowers, "that young girl – and that sister of yours."

"She's just jealous," another woman says, and she stands among the other woman in front of the counter where Sterling maintains her composure from behind the register.

Elenor exits the back room, "I came by for my check."

"It's okay," Sterling tries to assure her, "you can leave now, everything is fine."

"Fine?" The woman huffs and the other spats.

Elenor leaves in a haste as the animosity is unsettling to her.

Sterling sets the clock on the window to *Will be back in an hour.*

"I have to leave for lunch." She is calm.

Hanna enters through the open door.

The two women snigger. Rose looks to her mother. She shakes standing aside Alexandra. Her will alone is helping her to muster beyond the pain. Alexandra is firm.

Rose looks at the women.

They glare at Alexandra.

"She's wearing one of those witchy things," the one on the left says.

"She is wearing the talisman - the one that is for blessing one during travels," Hanna says.

"Then you too found Duke." Rose realizes why they are glaring.

"Yes I did," Alexandra says. "I took it to feel close to you."

She turns to the women who spat, "Rose has survived great trauma; they used a dirty knife to remove the child from her swollen abdomen. We came by the store to buy some cleansing tools." Rose shows her wounds to the women to bring some kind of peace – that Kamra and Victoria are not the only victims. But perhaps she is doing more harm than good.

Samuel has followed them and he walks through the door. He is accompanied by Kyla. They are without Eben and Alexandra feels some relief.

"It's okay, Mom." Rose whispers to her mother.

Rose has always been intuitive like Hanna. In that way she is strong in mind. She collects herself enough to face her brother who is being protective.

"You see my sister has not aged!" He thinks he can lighten the mood considering the looks of the two women who have obviously been confrontational as he watched from behind the glass. He always felt his mother and his sister could defend themselves, but sometimes he thinks too they need the help of a brother.

"A blessing from the Goddess herself," Alexandra says to them.

But they cannot care so much about Rose when they are there to speak on behalf of the family.

Hanna can only think of the Goddess who blessed Rose only to plant a seed for birth. She fathoms then that Aly was chosen first. Then, she thinks too, that Lucius must be right – Aly was to balance the dark and the light; through her death she would birth an angelic soul. A birth and a death. The balance between the worlds. But her children have been born with the insignia of the birthmarks – the great staff is the insignia of balance – on the flesh of the mortal child – a reminder from Grandall. Hanna can reason how the girls' mothers feel being a mother herself. The way has become clear but none of it feels right to Hanna.

"Because you're a witch." The one spats again.

"Witches still age." Kyla looks suspiciously at the women.

Rose has to spend a lot more time with Samuel and Kyla to explain her experience as the *Crone* but they know enough momentarily to try to help them. She still has only partial memories intact.

"You want to explain why you have not aged?" The woman is overbearing, but Rose feels she can tell them all, now, while they are gathered there.

She explains how she was found in the Valley by Leisha who sensed she was pregnant and how Goldie took her that night into the deep expanse of the underground within the catacombs and how they told her of Michael's death caused by starvation.

Hanna tells them of Rhoda and her tonics – potions that aid the mind in making vision quests and how, on one of those quests, Lakota was there to guide them through the Underworld.

"So a Goddess Witch will save only a witch will she?" The woman takes a startling step toward them.

Hanna recognizes the two women in that moment as it has finally dawned on her – they are from the local magazine articles;

they have formed a revolt against Witchcraft, anything magical and wizardry. She recalls having read about the town folk who wish to close the shop, the café and the bar. She wonders if Sterling recognizes them too.

"I am Lucinda." The woman volunteers, "and this is my sister Danica."

She breathes heavily behind her large frame but she stands firm, "All your evil-doing…" she says.

"All that so-called magic," Danica pipes in, "killed our daughters."

Samuel looks quizzically aside Kyla as they all remain quiet knowing that only Goldie is capable of the wrongdoing they are blaming on the witch community.

The two women push their way through the door among them.

"We will let no witch live!" Lucinda shouts.

"If we can watch them burn!" Danica says.

Hanna retrieves her check and makes haste as well as she knows she is continuing her maternity leave and will need to help Rose all that she can. Alexandra hugs Sterling – one witch comforting another – despite that her sister has too done them harm.

When Hanna exits the door she is met by Rhoda who is bubbly, "Tastes like fruit punch," she smiles, unaware of the awkward situation. She is beautiful too. Her hair hangs past her shoulders, parted in the middle, sleek and dark. She yields a potion that is for vision-questing and Hanna feels she has shown when she is needed most and she looks to Rose who is smiling. Hoping.

"The Shamans are a blessing to the Wiccans." Hanna says, and they gather outside the store while Sterling locks the door behind her and she decides not to return after lunch because she has had enough for one day. She goes home to rest.

Danica and Lucinda are whispering and huffing as Sterling walks on by.

Rhoda can move through portals and is part witch and part sorcerer. She takes the cap from the potion and moves them along to the side of the alley and they follow her lead. They come together in a circle, "Now just breathe," she says…

"We might want to be sitting for this," Alexandra says, and they sit comfortably and bow their heads when Hanna hears her exhale as the smoking potion ignites their senses and like the sound of a bell, their minds leave them to begin a journey.

They are greeted by Lakota who is fully dressed in ceremonial clothing and Hanna gives him a warm embrace in his mind's eye while Kyla and Samuel wonder if the potion is working because among them they can only see the physical and the mind's eye is not in their blood.

Chapter Fifteen

"Can you show me the way to my husband?" Rose says to Lakota. She wastes no time. The way in which he moves is mysterious. He guides them with his hand extended and they move close to a closed door. Then there is a stench that is sordid and horrendous. Rose gags.

"They have left him to die," a voice says and Hanna finds Jace who emerges beside them. Alexandra is quiet so as to not disturb the energy between them. He opens the door for them and Rose steps through.

"It was easy," Jace says, and they stand at the foot of a hospital bed, "she has the baby she longs to sacrifice and the demon to kill her with. He was discarded like trash. Nearly dead though. I got to him in the moment I needed to thanks to Lakota here."

Hanna shakes her head. With her finger she tells him to watch what he says.

Lakota bows his head. "There was a shift in the field of energy. I could feel his soul leaving then I remembered there was a way through the catacombs from the Underworld. The tunnel was right this time."

The gossip throughout Brighton leaves the hospital staff and circulates around town. Lucy and her husband Joshua, their son Jericho and his younger sister Allison, all receive word and they endeavor to locate their missing brother who had been stolen by an evil witch. In the meantime the women cast a circle around his body. They lay their hands upon him and sing, chant and clap to summon positive, radiant energy. The hospital staff look quizzically at hospital room number seven; he feels the intensity of their good vibes as he is taking a bath for the first time in twenty years. Feeling energetic he asks the women if they can clean up his appearance. The nurse named Samantha studies folklore in college and she is particularly mesmerized by him and the women. She especially likes Rhoda who

255

attends in traditional ceremonial attire. She is embellished with jewelry and a long tunic. Jace appears momentarily at the foot of his bed and then quickly dissipates like water vapor. Michael is washed, his hair is cut, his long beard is shaved, he tastes toothpaste for the first time since he disappeared and his nails are trimmed. His skin glows. The women are in awe of him. He is a glimmer of hope amid the insipid flavor of a bad hex. The women converse and speculate that Goldie left him to die, to never be found again, not knowing he would feed on the blood of rats to live. He has a meal served to his bedside when his family walks in.

In the other room Rose has a clean incision that is being monitored in a post-surgical follow-up. She cannot tell the scar remains where their baby had once been. The experience is etched in her mind and she shakes from the painful thought of it. She is released from the examination and given another supply of pain medication. She knows the Shamans and the Witches will do their work on her. She enters the room and Lucy is now stooped over the bed attached to his shoulders. They surround him and appear at the beautiful older man he has become as Rose still appears to be twenty. Lucy is exasperated.

"Rose!" She says and those within the room are moved to tears.

Lucy embraces her warmly and Alexandra is seated in a nearby chair. A lot of them are in awe among the sorrow – the sorrow that is also hope. Samuel and Kyla, David and Isabella, and John and Jasmine, are still within the waiting room. Rose approaches her husband and quickly takes his body into her arms and the appearance between them is a twenty year difference. She bellows in a loud and curdling scream "They took her!"

For the next hour, she speaks of how she returned to her body with her memories intact, at least in part, and how she felt movement from the baby within her womb. Alexandra has tears streaming down her cheeks and the Guardians exit the room allowing for the others to gather within the room now that they too have cleansed, consecrated and blessed his body.

"Eben is with Edgar," Kyla tells Alexandra who nods among the reunion that is both intense and sweet.

"I am not so young anymore." Michael looks to his wife.

She kisses him. He glows evermore and the nurses take notice. They cannot help but to peer at the legend of the *Lady of Brighton* appearing before them.

Infants are the insignia of sustaining life on all planes of life; even the Goddess herself wishes to hold the new life; life in its newness breeds immortality. The darkness of evil wants to shed the blood of the most innocent to proclaim a relationship to the dark arts; the Goddess wishes for a child and they are left with not understanding how her baby could be used for such practices; the nurses do not sympathize entirely with the witch community – such things as infant and child abduction happen too often in the human population. Hanna was hexed by the darkest witch because her grandmother had ties with Goldie. Now Hanna feels betrayed despite the insignia of balance and harmony depicted on her children's wrists. She believes the Great Staff is a depiction of the Wizard Grandall – a sign of trying to establish the balance and boundaries of the light and the darkness.

Hanna peers subtly among them. She yearns for Grandall when in that moment there is a special glow in the room and she follows the light of an aura to a now empty waiting room. She sees the face of Tully from the orb-like light and she grows brighter into an etheric body that emanates in a spectrum of light.

"It has been a long journey," she says, in earnest wisdom.

"Yes." Hanna's word is a near whisper.

"Now you have seen for yourself the bind Grandall found himself in when…"

"When he found out the Goddess wished to possess my daughter too…"

"Possess her?"

"To take possession of course…" Hanna is candid.

"No, he did not know…"

"Well the Goddess is now clear in her words."

"Rose does not deserve this…"

"Does not deserve this like I did not deserve to have my baby stolen?"

"No one does."

"You have that right." Hanna feels the anguish return to the pit of her stomach.

"Some have experienced loss as you have but the Goddess has her place in the light and the light would…"

"Bless the child? Keep the baby for herself?"

"There is a time and a place for everything."

"It isn't for stealing a baby from the natural mother." She turns away.

Hanna concedes that Tully sides with the light no matter what disagreements she may have. Her spirit body moves toward Michael's room and she stretches her hand above his abdomen and moves it up and then down and over his entire body. Hanna sends a mental note: they have already laid their hands upon him. He has been blessed.

Tully responds telepathically, "Just trying to speed things up." The heat from her aura permeates his body. He smiles but he cannot see her. The only one in the room who is permitted to see her is Hanna but the sensation can be felt, and he smiles. She is working his body to cleanse his system of the rat blood he consumed and his own immune system was compromised from the twenty years he had been in the dampness of the dark. Tully's words stick with Hanna as she watches her create a portal where she enters to return to the outer world. Hanna says nothing of her. There is a faint cough from the hallway that veers Hanna's attention and she finds a being in the hallway.

"Tia." Hanna is delighted to see her little fairy friend.

There is a faint glow from her iridescent wings.

"You need to be in the Celestial City," Hanna says, always concerned about Tia.

"The portals and all things telepathic are working well this time of year." Tia tries to provide hope.

"But why are you here?"

Hanna cups her hands and Tia rests gently within them. Hanna moves them to the vacant waiting room out of the view of the nursing staff.

"To tell you…" Tia whispers and then coughs again, "they have stolen your magical tools…"

"Who has?"

"The dark ones."

"You mean Jace?"

"No." She coughs again. "The others."

"But how do you know this?"

"The wand of ancient marble stone can transform anything dull into something magical…"

"Go on…" Hanna is anxious.

"It was used in ancient Peru by the Inca … their civilization no longer exists because they moved on to the mystical realm and left the physical world. The wand had been buried among the other artifacts and placed within a museum until it was stolen. The thief who stole the wand abused its magic because he wished for all power…"

"Like Goldie."

"Yes. The thief buried the wand for safe keeping but died before being transformed into pure light energy, as that's what it's intended to do, and when it was found again, it was sent to you."

"By who?"

"Someone who looks after you. But its radiant energy is in the presence of the dark others, and now they stand a chance to invade the Celestial City."

"By impersonating the light?"

"By impersonating the light." She confirms.

"Jace's plan went awry?"

"He did not know."

"What happened?"

"Goldie transformed into a mere shadow – a lost soul – those he is to help transform. They tricked him, and when he turned away they froze his body into a cold, stone of ice."

"Where is he now?"

"Freezing is only temporary, and I must say, they don't feel threatened by him…"

"Especially without having such an exceptional wand."

"Yes." Tia coughs. "He still checks on you, after returning Michael's body, where he left him at the door of the hospital – to be on the same day as his beloved Rose – but now they are making advances toward the light."

Hanna sighs. She feels temporarily at a loss. That's when they begin to move Michael.

"He's been discharged," Alexandra finds Hanna and they steer him down the hall.

"Healthy as an ox," one nurse says, "other than that cough," not realizing there was a mere Pixie among them.

Alexandra and the boys head back to the estate while Rose and Michael get comfortable.

"I felt your energy," Michael looks her in the eyes, "and Jace moved my body… it was surreal… like you were there with me."

"I was with you." She whispers.

"I felt you. I became so light, like a God must feel, and Jace found me there – a glimmer of light at the end of a dark tunnel – he would not have found me if it was not for you."

"He stayed with you until you were safe." Hanna says of seeing Jace frozen in her mind's eye. He always risks himself against magic from others.

Within their own room at the estate they lay within the sheets. He has gone gray and she shines brightly over him. They are lovers. No amount of time could stop that. Lucy and Joshua say goodbye to Allison and Jericho; Jericho joins the Navy and is to head back to base since the family emergency has subsided. Being stationed in Virginia, he is able to visit often. Allison is eighteen and she plans to attend the University of Virginia.

Alexandra falls to her knees at the light of the waxing moon. She prays to the Goddess; this year there is to be the light of a full moon during the Solstice. She prays to the Goddess to find her granddaughter while the tears still flow from her face. There is movement from within the room as Jace appears in the form of a shadow and Alexandra is startled. He puts up a ghostly hand.

"I'm not going to hurt you." He says as he moves across the room.

The light from the moon is cast between them like a metaphor between the dark and the light.

"They did not get this." He dangles a talisman from what would be a finger and Alexandra squints her eyes to view the jade-colored eyes of the magnificent cat.

Thor whimpers from outside the door.

"He, I mean Rajah-Jade and Thor there, can be your Guardians." He says as a disembodied voice. His breath is frost but the hex is aging and he is becoming a mere chill. "Hanna will know what to do but I wanted to show you so that you can feel some sense of security and safety during the times of tremendous peril."

"But how to find my grand baby?" She is hopeful.

Jace slowly fades away leaving the talisman of the magnificent Rajah and Thor who cries behind the door until Alexandra lets him in.

She now has the protection she needed because a journey is before them.

Alexandra walks toward the window; Sage is perched on a nearby tree branch; she is nesting this season but Alexandra also senses that the Familiars are gathering at the time of tumultuous happenings. There is a white Dove aside a single Raven on another nearby branch as Hanna peers out the window in grandmother's cottage. She feeds James Edgar from a bottle. She ponders her feelings of significant connections to Rose and Alexandra and considers how they do not make her feel unwelcome or awkward regarding the fact that she is her grandmother's grandchild. They are related, Hanna muses, and she thinks they are also a part of her.

Sterling does not feel the closeness. She is most uncomfortable since being confronted and brandished by the town community as "one of those evil witches." She cannot dissuade them of the comparison as she is Goldie's sister. They protest outside her store; signs are held yielding the words to keep the community from entering or being cursed by the witch within. The town folk do not understand Rose's youth, and the gossip about her baby being taken from her womb spreads like a raging fire. Sterling does not feel safe. Jace does not appear there because he knows they would become frantic, so he must remain cautious. Despite that, Sterling does not sell relics of the Dark Arts; the town people do not know there's a difference between the dark and the light because they have not studied magic. Items from *Black Cats and Sage* are stored away in a closet, but she intends to throw them out – if only they would not fall into the wrong hands. She thinks that the dark one would know what to do with those items but for the time being they remain stored where no one has access to them.

The catacombs are full of wonder; beautiful jutted rock formations create a kind of another universe beneath the surface. Then there is the dark underworld where

269

decay creates the rancid stank of deep peril. Carnage is housed there and Jace is the overseer of the dark – but even he can be tricked by those who are far more sinister and dangerous. The dark is so immense there are levels where Jace cannot go and while he feels sorrow amid the deep – the dark ones feel ominous and more forbidding. Those facts separate him from the dealings with evil, and he wonders how long he can aid the light from the dark.

Like the catacombs, a place of refuge, Sterling's store was her respite from the happenings of dark lore, but her place of refuge has become a menace to her well-being, and she wonders how long she can go there – how long they will go there. And she has those things to consider.

Lucinda and Danica wait for her after-hours and they still protest. "They died on the same day," Lucinda says.

"Death by choking." Danica is fuming.

Sterling wonders of the wrong-doings of the Goddess herself and ponders if she will be praying at all to the light above, and feels at the time the depths of being alone within her refuge while the fire rages from the outside.

She takes a deep breath and goes to them. She locks the door to her store and they shout in a fury...

"That evil witch!"

"That sister of yours!"

She wishes momentarily for the comfort of family but her parents Agnes and Henry moved on in the Spirit Realm and when she made contact with them all they could say was "I'm sorry" and she felt alone and deeply crushed. They had already blamed themselves for not being as close to Goldie as they were with Sterling.

"We plan to shut you down!" They scorn in unison.

"All magic should be banned!" They protest.

Sterling turns to the waning of the day and walks away; she waits for the morning light to gather together where she calls for

271

Hanna, who along with Rose and Alexandra, meet her at the door.

"You are not alone," Alexandra says.

And the protestors are not there. All is quiet at the moment and Rose thinks she can simply talk to the protesters – that she can just inform them that the light plans to aid them. But Alexandra feels it is no use and they have to be cautious of exactly how to proceed.

Chapter Sixteen

The following day the protest is on the front page of the *Daily* paper. The Sisters' Coven initiates sip on lattes over the *Daily.* Adjacent from them are the Guardians who have not left Virginia. Lucius walks through the front door and peers at the boarded window.

"Some bloke smashed the glass," Bill says from the bar table.

The customers notice that Bill is still happy as he maintains composure. Hanna meets with Reese at her home this time. At age twenty-three she has aged by ten years but revels in her wisdom. She knows the Sisters' path is similar to the first time she met them; they will stick together and help Rose. She feels the need to formulate a plan, however. Time is idling but she knows the baby girl is in great danger just as Aly had been when in the possession of Goldie as the vessel to great power. The wrong kind of power. Goldie wishes to sanctify the dark occult and would soak themselves in a blood bath if it entailed eliciting intense power. The most heinous of crimes is to sacrifice the blood of an innocent child. Hanna contemplates what the Goddess herself would do with the child she yearns for and thinks the only place for the baby is with her natural mother regardless of the intention. Still, the baby has been robbed from her mother's womb and she knows Goldie has made an enemy of a friend. Hanna wonders why she can't turn her back on her cousin – about the only soul she bestows. But that is her weakness – she is therefore not completely or entirely evil if there is still a glimmer of room in her heart. That may be the door they need to enter.

Reese speaks about having wanted children and interrupts Hanna's mental wondering.

"I enjoy having them," she says, "I still want a baby." Her face is serene and Hanna considers how she has three before the age of twenty-four and how Reese, being twenty-eight, has none of her own. But it certainly is not too late. Again, she contemplates how to help Rose as her mind wanders and she feels distracted.

"There's still time." She says softly but her gaze tells Reese that she is lost in her thought processes.

Only the most sick and vile can commit infanticide. She reasserts her earlier thought on there being a hole in Goldie's heart. But she loves one and that is her own dear cousin, that much is true. There is a minute speck of light in that idea. Hanna feels that by finding one she can find the other. Without Rose their sorcery is limited. They do not have the wisdom of the Crone. Their Cone of Power is one less – or is it?

Goldie used the wisdom of the Crone to lead them – they must be a broken force. Perhaps, then, they are looking for their third. There is power in threes. But who? Who would rekindle the spark of the power of three? Hanna kisses her babies as Reese gets them ready for a bath; she takes her current role as surrogate seriously. Hanna makes her way to *The Witches' Brew* where she finds Warlocks and Wiccans convening over coffee and the *Daily*. She knows that the protests are in earnest because the use of dark magic was used to murder two women. She takes a seat at the table as Alexandra and Rose both enter and they too take a seat at her table. The followers of Witchcraft and Magic wish to know when they will cast a spell – put her in her place – but that kind of power is given to the dark. Hanna feels they must remember there is, there must be, another way. Hanna must recall the memories of the others as only she and June Bug have the most memories intact and then there is Malaki who ironically didn't know then – but he knows now. The rest are living a kind of daydream. Silver is back; Grandall gave his own life and returned to her a life through re-birth. Hanna tosses the idea out there: one must entertain shapeshifting to find Goldie's lair, and to find their way to the innocent child.

"Into the Crone?" The voice says among them.

The voice belongs to June who is accompanied by Malaki.

"I don't think that will work Hanna," Malaki says.

"She'll be expecting that…" June is certain.

The lot of them have their memories and Hanna regains her thoughts over the fact that they do not know if the wisdom of the Crone has been reinforced among them. The Crone is the eye of the witch. If she is not Rose, then perhaps they have invested into another.

Bridget and Sharon walk through the open door and a subtle wind blows about the room making the air crisp with a feeling of hope.

"It's a full house," Bill says and Lucius takes their order from behind the bar.

"Can Sterling get to her own sister?" June is trying to help.

If not through the eye of the Crone then perhaps the mind of sisters can be the gateway into their plans, into their hiding place.

Hanna shakes her head.

"That's a bad idea." She considers that Grandall took with him Sterling's memories and they have been given their own memories of the previous events to protect Sterling from those experiences.

"They barely spoke as children." Hanna does not know what else to say. "They do not have that kind of connection."

Her goal is to leave Sterling out of the context of locating Goldie.

"Perhaps we need the guidance of the Goddess," Malaki says and Hanna knows he is proposing a ritual to aid them in the process of locating the dark ones.

Alexandra pipes in, "I'm afraid we may have no other choice."

It seems logical but Hanna is in disbelief.

"What does she want with a human child?" June is trying to be sensitive in the time of great distress.

The bar and restaurant are at full capacity.

"She wishes for a daughter of her own." Hanna thinks of Reese too. She considers the love a mother feels for a child – the natural birthright of any woman is to carry a child.

"But she would never take her." Alexandra protests – certainly the Goddess must be on their side.

"We don't know unless we seek to find out." June is still soft but confident they can get to the bottom of this.

Michael is the last to enter the café and all turn quiet.

"Don't let me interrupt," he says casually. As if the last twenty years were not full of hell and anguish – he also maintains composure because there sits his wife who had a child taken from her abdomen and he knows they must fully consider her position.

But the Wiccans do not feel the safety and warmth of the Goddess.

Hanna yields a new satchel where Tia is tucked safely within as she is comforted with men's safety gloves that somewhat mock the warmth of Divine Light temporarily. But Hanna knows she must reside in the Celestial City and must return soon. Tia is fragile. All fairies are, and Hanna feels she could have the answers they seek when she notices a pair of eyes from the talisman that is around Alexandra's neck.

"Where did you get that?" She tucks away her satchel at that moment.

Lucius serves them warm chips and salsa to lighten the mood and bring some normalcy to the table.

"On the house," Bill says.

The Wiccans and Warlocks that congregate within know to exude their confidence as the emotions are necessary for positive energy to flourish within.

Michael reaches for Rose's hand and she smiles faintly as he kisses her.

She does not have to suffer alone.

"Jace came to me from the Underworld…" Alexandra says.

"He brought my body to them." Rose's voice is a faint whisper.

"Then it is yours." Sydney says entering from the door alongside her Coven.

Hanna is startled. "You remember?"

"That talisman has been in many hands." Sydney does not look concerned.

"It always finds its way back to her." Amber adds.

"I see." Hanna says and she considers that the talisman must have found another owner at a time before she met the *Sisters' Coven.* Possibly before there was a coven – when there was only a Sydney without the sisters.

Sydney smiles while Amber looks annoyed. Hanna cannot help to think that Amber has a hunch from intuition from the past and that it must be nagging at her – like having that word at the tip of the tongue but not finding the word.

"Shapeshifting is a valuable tool." They hear from across the café, "don't waste it." The feminine voice says.

The voice continues and Hanna believes she recognizes the voice as Tully. She frowns. The intentions of the Goddess makes her nervous. She also feels naked without the use of her magical tools.

"You have Thor." An unmistakable voice says.

"Jace?" Hanna speaks telepathically.

There are others among them from the Underworld and the Outer Realm and she looks around to see if others can sense them too.

Does Tully know Tia has left the Celestial City? Hanna thinks.

Suddenly, Hanna can hear music and she intuitively knows that the gate to the Outer Realm has opened. Someone has died. His or her spirit body has emerged. She is momentarily being reminded of the light.

She can hear bells and she feels in awe of the experience. There is a grand welcoming committee within the light and she can feel them. Her whole body tingles: the Celestial City is the realm of the good. The light. She hears a cough and it is over. She can no longer sense the departure of a spirit from a body she cannot see. The gate has closed and the light body has ascended. Hanna feels the absence of the light as if the room becomes stale and stagnant in comparison. When the gate of the Underworld opens she can feel the void of the Light – the lack of the warm, radiant energy that engulfs the spirit body. That is the realm of her Jace – reduced to a shadow of his former self. She feels the emptiness shroud her being.

Jace keeps Goldie out of the Underworld to the best of his ability so she cannot gain the power of feeding from their lost souls – their energy. Goldie's scars are deeper where the depth of sorrow is long forgotten and is replaced with immense hatred. Hatred breathes evil. Goldie has long

283

resorted to evil and Hanna begins to feel Rose's thoughts. She focuses intently to see into her mind's eye and Hanna has the vision of bones. Duke's bones. Like Alexis's bones. Their death had been the result of the child turning evil, from sorrow to hatred, and into the vortex of complete darkness.

The light provides an opportunity for the dead to survive in the Glory of the Celestial City whereas the Underworld is home of the void for the lost soul. Goldie is none of those things and to protect a lost soul from becoming an evil soul, and worst, a demon, Jace presides over them. In finding Michael Jace had to enter the catacombs and could not leave before being hexed but the frost of the night could not stop him. Hanna connects with Rose at the level of the psyche that is troubled. Torn, and lost. In essence, a mind and spirit that would find itself within the void, not ready to pass into the light out of concern for someone who is of the physical realm: her baby.

She also intuits the death of the child. Rose's child. Who then becomes a child of the light. This notion feels inevitable; is the Goddess herself awaiting the sacrifice of the child who, upon its death, will have a spirit body that enters the light, all-the-while the bloodshed anoints the mortal into immortality and complete control of the dark?

"Hanna?" June snaps her back to reality.

She does not speak of the child's death. She considers that her own thoughts are not being perceived by Rose as she had received her thoughts.

Hanna feels there might be a Divine Plan to keep the child's spirit amid the plan of the beasts. The dark witches of imminent hell and demonology. The dark ones keep the body and the Celestial Light takes the Soul. No longer a child of a natural mother at all.

"The protestors are wrong," Hanna says, not exactly sure what else to say.

They have all long put the paper away, but a lot of them listen to what she has to say.

The clock turns to noon. Bridget takes Alexandra's hand into hers and Rose's into her other hand.

"The protestors blame Sterling while their deaths were the result of her sister."

"A sister who was tortured by others…" June says.

"More like taunts…" Rose discerns.

"She was physically abused" Hanna reminds her.

"So we must consider her feelings amid all this" June continues.

Alexandra sighs but takes a deep breath. "We would never kill the messenger so-to-speak…" She breathes mildly while trying to remain calm amid June-Bug's words.

"We acknowledge she is not guilty by association alone.

"The public isn't exactly wrong in their outcries. We understand." Rose says softly and gazes at them with eyes that convey hope and love.

"I will continue to help you all…" Hanna wonders if she is even a good enough witch to offer such a suggestion…"

"We are all here for you…" Sydney beckons… and the rest follow suit.

In unison they stand to offer their expertise; the men touch upon her shoulder, the women give her a hug; they are sensitive of her circumstance and they all question their ability to add resolve – but as Wiccans and Warlocks they feel it is their duty to aid another Witch.

Hanna smiles toward her husband in tender affection and she leaves to get her children from Reese as she stops by the store first; she knows now that the Witches and the Warlocks are also sensitive to her innocence and she offers Sterling her regard.

"When will you be back?" Sterling musters a smile.

"Next week." Hanna's voice is soft.

"That soon?"

"We're busy."

"I am extending the back room to accommodate more books."

"The ritual retreat?"

"I am moving that back to my own home and not within the store."

"Desperate times call for desperate measures."

"Yes, it certainly does."

They too embrace as Hanna steps into the afternoon light and is filled with the warmth of the sun where the Ravens are gathered.

"I think that means there is movement." Sterling looks at them.

"Of what kind?" Hanna is modest in her approach to magical things. These women are adepts in their field and she feels humble.

June Bug enters the daylight from a portal to gaze at the trees beyond them – and they are filling the branches in numbers.

"They are the eyes of the dark." Sterling continues.

She feels a chill down her spine.

Malaki follows June outside.

"We need to keep the things of the witches quiet," Hanna says, "because the general public just doesn't understand."

"No, they don't." Sterling says, "Perhaps they shouldn't really, I guess, because it was one of them, and not one of us who died."

And Hanna thinks two who died, and almost her own, but she lets the thought rest and turns away toward her children while saying goodbye and she retreats toward home to ponder again how she can be the one to save them this time.

Chapter Seventeen

"Elizabeth Coral Rose," Lucius says the following morning and Hanna walks groggily into their kitchen.

"What?" She asks.

"That's her name." Lucius pours her milk.

"Who?"

"Rose and Michael's baby."

Hanna feels like a heel. She doesn't know how asking for the child's name has slipped her mind. But then again she has been lost in thought lately.

"I had a dream last night. I was in the underworld with Jace."

"What happened?"

"He told me someone has been luring. Not Goldie, but far more horrid."

"The Demon?"

"Herschel Beecham, and he thinks they are punishing him."

"Defying her."

"Only Leisha has never done so."

"Done what?"

"Not defied her."

"Then that is making her bitter."

"She's resentful for sure."

"Then Jace asked me to take Lakota home."

"Did you?"

"Yes."

"Then you were bi-locating and not dreaming."

"This one felt like a dream though."

"You're tired. Try to rest today. "I also need to take Tia home." She drinks from her cup.

"You have Tia?"

"In my satchel."

The air turns to a cold mist as they see the shadow-like presence appear subtly before them and they know it is Jace who is appearing like a dark vapor to show them the portals can be opened. When he dissipates, she thinks of Tia but he leaves the portal open and she realizes the portal is for her to follow Jace into the Underworld. She turns to her husband who waves her off and silently holds his hand to his heart to let her know that she has his blessing. In the Underworld, Hanna feels drawn to the sound of an infant's cry. She wonders if Goldie is near when she hears her voice too.

"We have to quiet the little brat." Her voice is morose.

Hanna feels nauseous and thinks of Aly having been in the possession of such monsters.

"She feels no mother's love," Jace says and Hanna nods.

The Underworld is dark, dense, and freezing. Goldie aims to freeze him out through her Hex because if there is no Prince of the Dark so-to-speak then there is no overseer or bridge between the Dark and the Light; the dark ones can never find their way home within the Celestial City.

"We need to find our way to Elizabeth." She is concerned.

Then there is a loud disturbance and Hanna's eyes peer at the flash of light produced by an electrical storm and she is surged back to where she came. She is back home and Lucius looks both relieved and concerned.

"That didn't take you long." He says quizzically when another flash appears out the window.

"The storm."

"The storm brings my father," he says, and he leads her to the main room when Jace appears before them.

"Can I see Aly?" He says and Hanna believes the infant's cry has made him miss his own daughter.

They notice that Luther has brought wine and Hanna takes Jace to his daughter.

She is suspicious of the arrangements brought about by her husband.

"My father needs to date." He says coyly.

When Jace emerges in full form he is still cold to touch but his love for Aly brings warmth.

Hanna relates to both Lucius and Luther that she heard cries from somewhere in the Underworld. As Aly plays in the arms of her father, he soothes her gently while running his fingers through her long hair. She is almost three and she speaks well.

"I heard the baby last night," Aly tells him.

He peers at her, "You mean your brother James?"

"No, Daddy," she says, "the baby girl Summer."

"Who is Summer?" He is perplexed.

Hanna looks quizzically at her as does Lucius. Luther is patiently waiting for them by the gas-lit fire.

"Summer was taken from her mommy…"

"Aly, how do you know," she thinks for a moment, "Where did you see… Summer?"

"The craft is strong in her," a voice says and Hanna finds that Lucius has opened the front door for Reese and Hanna knows that Lucius is playing match-maker.

"She was blessed by the Goddess." Aly says firmly and Hanna does not understand how her daughter could know.

"Jace?" She is suspicious.

"I haven't brought her to the Underworld Hanna." Jace is firm.

"Do you think the Goddess wants her?" Hanna really doesn't know what to say.

"The Goddess wants a daughter." Reese speaks gently as she enters the conversation.

"But not you…" Hanna says.

"No, Mommy," she laughs a little, "she wants the baby girl she named Summer."

Hanna is not impressed – why has the Goddess given her own name to Elizabeth?

"Perhaps we have a lot to learn about why the Goddess is seeking a child," Reese says and Hanna smiles warmly at her daughter.

They focus on Lucas who is playing at Luther's feet and Hanna wonders if James is still asleep. He cannot be heard from down the hall.

"But the Goddess inhabited Aly, to protect her," she explains casually.

"Yes," Reese says, "so we do not know the intentions of the Goddess until we hear from her directly."

Hanna then believes that Aly has seen baby Summer (Elizabeth).

"I just don't understand…"

Then a voice interrupts her, "Maybe it's their problem, Hanna, you know," Luther says, and she thinks he is being selfish over his engagements with Reese.

"We are all the Witches and the Warlocks of this city and it is our obligation…" Reese says.

"Our duty," Lucius taps his fist to his father's shoulder.

Luther stays quiet and nods to affirm his understanding.

"We stand together as the magicians and the sorcerer's magic," Reese affirms.

"But this is the Goddess we are talking about." He tries to affirm.

"Are you all afraid?" Hanna cannot help her suspicion.

"Not afraid, Hanna," Reese is calm, "but maybe the fate of the baby is in her hands." She tries to remediate the situation for all to feel comfortable and secure to some degree.

"Or maybe it is not." She says of the baby's fate being in Helga's hands because she knows it took hundreds of active Wiccans to save baby Alysiah.

James startles from his bassinet.

Lucius knows now why Hanna cannot feel at rest or at peace – last night she dreamed so lucidly of being in the Underworld which turned out to be a vision of foreboding and a premonition… he wonders if she feels at all rested.

"The Celestial City is a place of pure radiant light and I know why anyone would want to go there..." her mind veers to Tia again... "but Summer is Rose's child. Michael's daughter." She feels frustrated, "And her name is not Summer." Hanna hears herself get louder.

"Yes it is," Aly, going on thirty, says.

Hanna decides not to speak of the baby in front of her daughter.

She comes out of contemplation to find Jace rocking her to sleep because she is tired. Hanna wonders if her daughter was up all night. She thinks that her daughter may have found herself in the Underworld, playing with a baby. Did the Goddess find her there?

Lucas is being entertained with dinosaurs by Luther and Reese; despite their age difference of twelve years they look happy together. Hanna thinks of the symbolism on her children's' wrists – like dinosaurs and princesses – the Goddess and the dark ages. She wonders, who will win? Does everyone side with the Goddess who wants a human child?

Into the night there is a purple twilight outside after the storm. It is the eve of the Lammas on July 31st when the God lays down his life to provide for the great harvest and so his seeds may grow. Rose long ago laid down her seeds in the form of a rose when she also wished for a daughter. Hanna's mind is fresh with the image of the Goddess and the Demon yearning for her baby Aly; she ponders the confusion and wishes for Rose to have her Elizabeth back but she is also burdened with the fact that the Goddess wants this child and has gone so far as to give her a name. Hanna doesn't feel confused; she feels the Goddess wanted Aly for herself and was not inhabiting her baby to protect her for her birth mother's sake. She fumes but maintains her cool.

Back at her job Sterling prepares the store for the festivity as most Wiccans are enjoying the outdoors and planting seeds of their own. Alexandra though would rather say they will host a festivity during Mabon during the Fall Equinox when the moon continues to wane. This however is the time of the year when God and his son stand on the threshold of the Underworld. It is the time when darkness looms and the Earth prepares for longer nights. She senses a great movement taking place that rattled her nerves during last night's storm, but she stands still until the following morning when the sun is plentiful and the night is an afterthought. Edgar is pleased to be at home but there is a constant dampness where a child should be. Kyla and Samuel have baby Eben for a visit however and that warms his soul. John and Jasmine bring them fruit baskets and David with his wife Isabella have brought the wine. This is a time when the families are together and many Wiccans take a vacation. Rose and Michael hold onto one another in the way they do hope. Lucy and Joshua stop by and bring the potluck brunch and the family enjoys the company of one another while they know there is one of them missing. Although Alexandra is in no mood for the festivity, she feels some blessings when Jericho and Allison have returned to Brighton to feast with the family. Alexandra meets Jericho's partner Anna and Allison has brought her significant other Maverick. The family has heard a great deal about him. It is on this day that Maverick asks Edgar if he can have his daughter someday as his wife and he presents to her, in the presence of the family, a ring as a token of his devotion to her.

Over the course of days, they get to know more of one another as Maverick hopes to show that he is an earnest man with an equally earnest heart. There are girls from the group home who stop in to share their wealth of fruits from the season: Sharon, Melissa, and Bridget are with Celia who has a baby boy who she has named Cameron. Alexandra is like a mother to Celia and Rose feels in awe of the years Celia had with

Alexandra as she herself missed those years. She understands too that Celia, like herself, had a father who abandoned her as a baby. She thinks about how much Celia's circumstances were like her own with the big-time banker William Banks. They all take their seats at the oval table and delight in food and company.

Back at home, Hanna has her table plentiful from the Harvest as well, and Hanna learns that Luther and Reese have been talking for quite some time and have engaged in a relationship. Lucius brought them together for dinner and wine before the Lammas festivity so Hanna would not feel kept in the dark. She is pleased and does not feel slighted in the least.

"I hope you don't mind," Reese says casually.

"Might as well," Luther winks, "I'll get to see the grandkids more."

Hanna then feels a bit slighted about the fact that Reese has the children more often than she does.

They share a laugh and Hanna forces a chuckle when she finds Sage perched outside her window. Lammas is the grand finale of the mating season and Hanna believes she has raised her young. The harvest has been plentiful and Hanna is curious if Clover's absence has meant that she is doing the same.

Jace has returned to the Underworld and Hanna's little cottage is full. Alexandra's home is full and Hanna thinks of Sterling who was decorating the store – has the public left her alone? She wonders too if Jace is alone since Lakota has passed into the Celestial City. The pervasive feeling of loss and grief overwhelms her and she knows this moment is being felt by Rose and Michael as they might be attending in body but are broken in spirit. Her thoughts race some more regarding the Sisters' of East Brunswick – the Sisters' Coven … how they helped her

303

and how she needs to form an alliance with a Coven to become a sisterhood of magic and sorcery that will get Elizabeth back!

In the Underworld, Jace finds Goldie deep within the Earth – hidden in the depths of her lair – a fortress beneath mud and stone. The Old Crone, Rose (The Lady of Brighton) cared for Aly – even if she cannot remember and that fact also resides with Hanna. She discerns that Rose had a deeper maternal instinct even within the façade of an Old Crone, an evil sorcerer, and with Hanna's constant thinking and reminiscing Jace forms into a mist like water vapor; he transcends time and space outside of the Underworld where there is the land of the dead – and at this time when the darkness will pervade the Earth he summons the deceased to be alive again. He calls upon Phoenix, the prize winning horse, the pup named Duke – the most loyal companion – and together they plan to locate the newborn infant who cries from deep within the Catacombs.

"If I can locate Michael, then I can locate Elizabeth." He says with a cold breath.

Chapter Eighteen

The bones of Phoenix and the bones of Duke turn to flesh and their flesh to a ghost as they arise from the dead. They leave their graves and shake off the dampness of the underground to ride the night like phantoms as the moon shines bright and Sage takes notice.

That following morning Hanna receives a visit from the Sisters' Coven.

"Hello Hanna," Sydney says as she peers through the crack in the door.

"We've been waiting," Amber says.

"So, you do know?"

"I told you I sensed something was off."

Hanna spends the day re-counting for their time together. She tells the story of her first born during the Winter Solstice. She speaks of their harrowing adventures, of Sterling's death, how the time warp turned them backwards and they listen intently. She tells of the birth of her third child James and how the symbol on his wrist and the mark on her daughter Aly signify the balance of the two worlds – the light and the dark. Her three children bare the birthmark as they have been marked by Goldie, heirs to LaQuinta, leaving Hanna to aid them with Witchcraft.

"So another child has been born?" Sydney says and Hanna knows she speaks of the baby that has the Goddess's interest. Now things make more sense to them and they can relate how Aly's birth is similar to Rose's daughter and that fact explains the constant state of déjà vu they've been experiencing. They hear a knock on Hanna's door and when Amber opens it she is repulsed by the stench of decay only death can bring.

"I've brought the dead to help us." He says aside Phoenix and Duke who are grizzly and ghostly at the same time. Despite the stench Amber is compelled to go to him when Sydney grabs her by the arm and they shut the door.

"Not yet," she says.

Paisley puts tea in the kettle.

For a while they sit in silence to absorb all they have been told.

The Worthington home estate is nearly complete but Rose leaves her room to go by the river. There are some campers scattered about and she is suddenly subdued by the heat. Jace could not bring the Sisters' Coven as they apparently were not ready and so he shows himself to Rose as he appears in physical form.

He appears to her as he is attached to something that is shrouded in white light when she recognizes Snow and she feels peace and serenity in the moment.

"I didn't want my true identity to scare you." He says as he brings Snow in the light.

"I'm not scared," she says casually.

He knows her beloved Snow aids him.

They are shrouded together in a warm light that is not perceived by anyone but them.

"Death has many forms," he says, "and my physical self, a cold body, is just one of them."

"Who are you?"

"I am the overseer of the Underworld. I protect the lost ones from the demonic ones."

"Oh…"

"Don't be alarmed, I'm the image of sorrow and grief."

He knows she can relate and so she too stays calm.

"How can you help me?"

"I gave my physical life to the demon. To lure him away from Aly."

"Aly? Hanna's Aly?"

"Yes, also my daughter."

"I'm sorry." She whispers, realizing he gave his mortal life to save her.

He then feels safe to bring Phoenix and Duke back from the deep.

Rose sees them and is in both awe, subdued again, and in horror by the smell of them. By this time the vision of Snow has cleared.

"I have brought them to aid you."

"Phoenix and Duke." She crouches to one knee.

"I hope I'm not being too forward."

"No." She says softly trying not to be aghast.

Jace would be moved to tears if he could cry.

She wants to touch them, but they are the undead and would not be the same to her but the sight of them brings nostalgia.

"We will get to her."

"I'm giving my trust to you," she says, standing to her feet.

"I'm here to help you."

"But the light wants my daughter…"

"No one but you can have her," he is certain and calm.

He can feel her still sullen and in deep remorse.

Back on the physical plane it is the day after Lammas when Sterling is cleaning after the festivity when she hears a loud thud from the door that has slammed shut.

"You have some Dragon Root and Toad's Foot somewhere in this vicinity?" A woman's voice says.

Sterling faces her. "Sister," she says, "but you always said magic never worked for you."

"Oh come off it buttercup, I can do magic with the best of them." Goldie's voice is severe.

"Buttercup?" Sterling looks her over, "I am your sister."

"Yes. I know."

"What brings you here?"

"I need the ingredients to make a potion."

Sterling looks concerned.

"I need the potion to keep some pesky old school friends away."

Sterling knows they are no friends at all and she thinks too that despite her familiarity with said pesky school girls she herself would not concoct a dreadful tonic.

"I tried to help you..." her voice shakes a little.

"You did no such thing."

"But you wouldn't let me in."

"No need." She huffs, "I'll just have to look elsewhere since your establishment cannot hold up to it."

Outside there is a Raven pecking upon another Raven.

"Call your bird away." Sterling is adamant.

Goldie is already outside.

She is then startled by a voice from behind, "I guess one of us is bound to be better at magic."

Sterling looks through the glass to see Goldie's physical body outdoors while her ethereal body is poking over her shoulder – a nice play at bilocation from an adept.

"Yes." Sterling is candid. "It seems you do have a way with magic."

Sterling is assuredly being given the one-up by her own sister, but she does not play the game of what sister can do better. Goldie blinks and her ethereal body is bound by the physical body. Sterling looks outside again and Goldie is gone. So is her bird. Only Clover is left with ruffled wings. She goes out to her and lifts the bird's petite body frame onto her finger and takes her indoors where she rests while perched on the rafter. She goes to sleep with her head tucked beneath her crooked little wing. Sterling keeps her sister's appearance to herself so as not to alarm anyone unnecessarily. She hopes that no   one   will   notice.

"How many more dead are you going to bring back to life, Jace?" Hanna asks.

Jace is mildly curious wondering how she must know – or is it because she is a witch?

"Kamra and Victoria haven't made amends with the past."

"Can they do that?"

313

"Am I dead?"

"Right."

"In the end there is a little white bird that looks after us and keeps our way clear."

He dodges her question.

"Did Lakota tell you that?"

"I can't remember."

"Perhaps if we get this right then it'll be for the good this time."

"Where do you think Goldie is heading?"

"It won't be to the summit of Mount Katahdin this time. We crushed that mountain to oblivion."

"But possibly Connecticut or Vermont?"

"She won't be visiting the ski slopes, Hanna."

"Right?"

"She'll wish to be a little more inconspicuous but I don't know if her plot is to sacrifice the blood of the most innocent at the highest point North."

"The highest point North is gone."

"We need to fix the past in order to change the future."

"The lodges are the Shamans' Temple."

"Okay?" Jace is confused.

"Perhaps I need to take the Coven there and enter a place deep within my consciousness…"

"And?"

"I need to get to Goldie."

"Through the mind could be a good route."

"That's what we need to be working on."

"You and the Sisters' Coven."

"Yes."

"Lakota did tell me a story once."

"What story?"

"When the Sun (God) and the Moon (Goddess) wed there will be the birth of the Morning Star – the most beautiful star among the many."

"Our goal is to open her up – not to all the details of her past - but for introspection."

Hanna cannot seem to focus on the story at the moment.

"Hanna.."

"Yes?"

"I feel like we've had this conversation before."

"We had many great teachers."

"So now we're starting to sound like them."

"The Goddess still wishes to balance the two worlds of the light and the dark."

"Where have I heard this before?"

"Think hard."

"Leisha."

"Yes, and Elusha once."

"Well then maybe there is a glimmer of hope that they may not be as dreadfully vile as Goldie."

"Perhaps Jace. But I need to find a place where I, all of us, can have a profound mystical experience."

"Why not Brighton?"

"No. I want to go to Vermont."

"To the Shamans… then that is where you need to go."

"I am going to seek Rhoda and Eva."

"You'll be able to get them all on board. I'm sure of it."

"Thanks."

"Glad to help."

Hanna wakes from her deep contemplation in the realm of the mind where she communes with Jace upon the couch.

"Our son was born on the Summer Solstice." She tells a groggy Lucius who has been watching her on the couch.

"He represents the time of new beginnings."

"We represent the Universal Agreement."

"You remember it because it has come to the moment when it is important."

"Yes. Of spiritual significance."

"To go see the Shamans."

"Was I talking out loud?"

"You always do."

"Yes…"

"This time Archibald and Diana will miss you."

"We will all go to Connecticut…"

"But from there you go to Vermont…"

"Does that make sense?"

"If it does to you, I support you, but there's a risk Hanna and I don't want to lose you."

"I have to find a way to carry out the Universal Order."

"But Goldie has a very dark heart."

"I know."

"She is the only one who can change her own state of mind."

"We must get her to listen to us."

"Maybe she feels no one ever did anything nice for her."

"Her needs were not met as a child. Then she went dark."

As the day gives way to night, Hanna contemplates how Goldie's soul went dark and how perhaps she can return to a state of total   innocence.

Alexandra gives lessons to the girls of her group home who wish to pursue magic. Sharon, Melissa and Bridget help Celia to care for her child, Cameron, and she has invited Allison and Anna to join them. Jericho spoke about the magic of sorcery and witchcraft to Anna in the past year to pique her interest. Michael is pleased when his own family wishes to take up magic. He and Rose still sit upon a dark cloud and it fills their heart to have the family committed to them to aid them in getting their baby back.

"I want to call her Summer if that means the Goddess will ascertain her safe return," Rose tells him.

"If it brings you hope." Alexandra is trying to be tender.

She is surprised when she sees Kyla, Isabella and Jasmine show to learn the workings of magic for themselves. She feels beyond blessed to have such a great family. Michael wonders if Lucy will show when he hears a car pull into the driveway. He sees Lucy emerging from her Sedan thinking that being a Warlock has its perks – but the way needs to take him to Elizabeth. To Summer.

"She wasn't impressed with Helga that last time," Alexandra explains.

Rose appears concerned.

"Never mind the Goddess for now," Alexandra just wants to soothe her daughter.

"Today we learn the basics of Witchcraft." She tells Lucy who musters a smile.

Alexandra covers her altar which is still decorated for Lammas and she moves to opening a circle, calling the four quadrants for the positive energy of the Guardians. She asks out loud for the blessing from the Goddess and Lucy appears put off by that statement.

Oh great Mother of Earth and beyond, bless us this day on becoming one with the Earth – may we use its energy to bless us and to carry out our intentions – we wish for what is respectfully ours – a daughter who has been named Summer so that she will be returned to us unharmed! So Mote It Be!

Alexandra lowers a pendant into the water of a bubbling cauldron that is scented with chamomile and when the sun has fully set the heat from the cauldron is used to bless the child's mother and she feels the warmth of blessings from the Guardians, the Earth but the Goddess is afar and she wonders yet what the Goddess has in store for the baby girl she calls Summer.

After the ritual is complete, they feast on platters of cheese and sip their wine. But Rose does not have the stomach to eat and so she thanks all of them for being there and she turns in for the night to stare into the cosmos hoping that it will reveal to her the whereabouts of her most precious daughter.

Alexandra teaches her students about the upcoming Mabon festivity when the God stands on the threshold of the Underworld, and Hanna thinks about Jace who can bring the dead to life hoping the impending darkness will guide them on their journey.

Chapter Nineteen

Jace is among the dead of the Underworld when he brings back the bodies of Kamra and Victoria, and June Bug is the first to know. Their bodies are stone cold like a perfectly preserved and mummified body. It is cold deep in the catacombs and even deeper still – the Underworld is like a permafrost to the skin. Jace is like an invisible cloak to Goldie as he maneuvers the Underworld in search of anything and anyone Goldie must be hiding. His findings are clever and he builds an army while knowing Goldie is still in the company of her Demon and Leisha who never leaves her side. Rising Kamra and Victoria from the dead only meant she could toy with them all-the-while she could care less if Michael survived or died – she has the child, the Demon and her best confidant. Jace can break barriers into the expanse of the Underground but Goldie is Queen Seer of the Catacombs – but the dead are his for ruling. He steals from her what are rightfully his.

"But why?" June feels concern about this. "Why would Goldie rise them from the dead?"

"To see that they never make it to the Celestial City – where they would be dead forever but not as children of the light."

"So now they are alive to you?" Malaki is behind them.

Jace is firm. "Alive in the Underworld."

They have completely undermined that Jace is alive in the Underworld too.

"Yes." June tells a startled Malaki, "What can we take back to Hanna?"

"Tell her to begin looking for the great staff…"

"Grandall…" Malaki says.

"And the Perfect Wand." Jace is formal.

"The wand made from marble?"

"Yes."

"A great conductor of magic."

Malaki understands and with their tasks at hand, they find themselves in the study of Alexandra's estate, the only home June knows, and now Malaki can rest because he can sense the safety there.

Alexandra opens the banquet hall of the estate where all Wiccans convene in the ensuing week when they have reached the Autumn equinox given the name Mabon by a fellow Witch in the time of her youth when Rose was still an infant. Edgar smokes on a pipe in his parlor room as the Wiccan community comes together to support Rose. Alexandra's roster is full and not a seat in the banquet hall is empty; all family, friends, guardians and the community gather together: Sterling and Elenor, June Bug and Malaki, The Sisters' Coven, Reese and Luther, Lucy and Joshua, Allison, Jericho and Anna, Bridget, Sharon, Melissa and Celia, Samuel and Kyla, John and Jasmine, David and Isabella – and in the back corner – Chris the reporter.

"This is a private matter," Elenor says to Sterling, concerned for her friend.

"Never mind him." She says of Chris being at the gathering.

She places her faith in the working of The Craft that will guide them to see the light. The babies, Alysiah, Lucas, James, Eben and Cameron are quietly watching the birds – the familiars that seem to subdue them. There is an ambience of peace and tranquility among them. They are transfixed as if the birds themselves can cast spells.

"Hello all," Alexandra announces, and she looks to Edgar who has stepped into the banquet hall, making a sound with the door.

"Hello." They say in unison as their eyes turn from the sound of the door.

Hanna and Lucius motion for Edgar to have a seat at their table.

"We are all here together to help one another in times of happiness and in times of great peril."

The guests look to Rose and they remain quiet.

"Yes, we are." A distant voice chimes among them.

"What can we do to help?" Another voice says from the crowd, this time, Bridget.

She is sweet, only two years younger than Rose, but Alexandra took her in after she had suffered a miscarriage at the hands of her husband, much like Alexandra's mother, and they have become great friends.

Rose and Michael stand to accompany their mother at the front of the large room.

June speaks softly to Hanna, informing her of their trip to the Underworld.

"We have gone to Jace," she whispers.

"Just like before…" Hanna thinks of her time with Aly.

"But different." June keeps her voice low.

This time, Hanna wonders if Goldie's closest, has her heart.

327

"Thank you all for coming." Alexandra says, who is still pondering what to say in response to Bridget…

"You all know why you are here…"

"To fight an evil witch!" Chris clicks the top of his pen, eager for the story.

"…but I am not yet certain exactly how you can help…"

Sterling looks uneasy but remains quiet and observant.

"I'm not sure that we are fighting…" Alexandra is cautious… "but I want to find my granddaughter."

Hanna no longer feels alone but she feels the remorse in the pit of her stomach; the sadness is close to her heart. She hears a scratching sound at the door from her left, adjacent to their table, where Edgar had entered, and Edgar pulls the door open to find Thor as he enters the room. He finds Rose by sniffing at their legs and he gives her hand a gentle nudge.

"Who is this?" Rose asks.

"That is Thor," Hanna says. "He is a guide for the Underworld."

"The Underworld?"

"Yes. He is here to help us."

"How do you believe he can help?" Rose asks and Alexandra hopes she has the answer.

Chris is now on the edge of his seat with suspense.

"We have to deliver the Universal Order to Goldie," Hanna explains.

"What order are you talking about?" She has Alexandra's attention.

"The basic order. The law is to balance the dark and the light."

"Where do you suppose we can find her?"

"We only know that she is, or was, deep within the catacombs," Hanna explains, feeling that she may not appear optimistic, then she thinks of her dream, "but I have heard her voice emerge much closer to where we are."

Sterling looks uneasy and doesn't speak.

"Where? How close?" Alexandra is hopeful but her face alludes to doubt.

"In the Underworld with Jace."

"Who is he?" Bridget chimes from the table. She is eager to help Rose.

"He is the Prime Minister of the Underworld. He gave his life to save his daughter. My daughter, Alysiah," she is not certain how to explain this, "he maintains peace and order and helps lost souls find their way to the Celestial City."

Alexandra is listening attentively.

"Tell us… what you mean about your daughter…" Bridget speaks on behalf of Rose, the only family she has ever known.

"He is my daughter's father. He gave his life to protect her. Now he oversees the Underworld as the guide for those who need to find the light." Hanna feels she has told them enough without the need for details because she does not want to alarm them and at the same time she does not want to facilitate false hope. "He also bridges the gap between the living and the dead." She's not sure how they would feel about bringing the dead back to life, but Hanna concedes that the thought of beloved pets sway them to believe in Jace and his good intentions.

In the other room, the babies have become restless, and Melissa and Celia go to them and they believe that Alexandra can fill them in with what is learned at the banquet.

"Then our duty is to find Goldie, find my granddaughter, and deliver to her the Universal Order."

Hanna feels the tension and the yearning.

Their guests feel strong amid the intention, yet no one is for sure where Goldie is hiding.

"Yes," Hanna says, and Luther raises his glass, "Everyone in your favor here will drink to that." He says, wanting to bring the energy to the guests. The optimism spreads as they all raise their glasses and they drink the wine that serves to fill their stomachs with the need to succeed for Rose. For Alexandra. For Michael.

"We are all with you," Bridget says and they nourish their bodies with food and water because magic takes great strength and good energy. The guests speak quietly among themselves at each table. The atmosphere, although positive and hopeful, is at the same time awkward and uncertain. Chris takes the opportunity to interview the guests but he is disgruntled when no one can say exactly how to locate this evil witch.

"Can they bring the infant back to safety?" He questions, anticipating for a variety of responses that would make for a good story in the *Daily* by tomorrow morning.

"We only know that is exactly what we must do." Luther is bold. Frank.

"Exactly what we will be learning," Reese explains.

They certainly don't want to give the reporter the know-how anyway, especially if that means getting the information out there and to Goldie.

"But it's important to know that we are all here to begin solving this problem and all matters with the dark others," Lucius adds.

"The dark others…" Chris likes the language. He looks pleased.

"How do you feel about the recent protests?" His attention turns to Sterling who he knows owns the store that houses the paraphernalia of Witchcraft and Magical Sorcery.

"They mean well," Reese helps her.

"I don't have any further comments." Sterling's voice is soothing. In control.

"We are working on helping them too," Hanna says but feels even that is too much as Chris appears absorbed by the idea.

"Can you help the dead?" He's anticipating the magical arts will be revealed to him.

"No," Hanna ascertains, ""we hope to help all who need to heal from loss."

That was not what he was looking for.

When they all begin to leave he takes for the door to get more from them – specifically for the secrets of magic.

Hanna enters a deep sleep that evening in her home that is like a meditative trance and she finds herself deep in the Underworld where time and space is vast, dark, and so expansive that Jace feels out-of-reach. And Jace is nowhere to be found.

She wonders if his ethereal body freezing is bringing down his abilities between the worlds.

Lakota, who was acting as guide, has moved into the Celestial City and she wonders why she cannot locate Jace but then she thinks about Thor. How he must have been sent directly to Rose, perhaps because he would be gone: but gone where?

He sent in his place his long beloved friend and Hanna feels both comfort and dread in that.

The Underworld is a vast place with dense air, kind of like the thick of fog, and

Hanna is not used to not being able to take the latest news to Jace. Now, she feels deep concern without him. She cannot locate a glimmer of hope in trying to reach him. She does not want to become lost in time and space and so she returns to her body feeling disgruntled as she awakens and Lucius is holding her hand.

"What is it, Hanna?" He looks into her eyes.

"I can't find Jace."

Lucius just nods, "So we'll head to Vermont." He aims to reassure her.

She returns to her sleep knowing the Shamans can take her there.

"It seems Jace can locate all but Goldie." She drifts back to sleep.

Hanna knows her husband is quick to her aid and wants to remedy anything of doubt; certainly, the Shamans can enter the caves.

In the ensuing week, the Wiccans are ready for Mabon; although the air is warm, they prepare for the end of the great harvest

335

as they approach the time of darkness. This is the time when one can cross the threshold of the dark. The seeds of the harvest are the promise of life to come in a continuation of the seasons when the leaves turn their colors of magnificent variety. At her altar, Hanna prays to the Goddess – to please give to them the infant that Rose carried to full term – the child that was cut from her abdomen and taken from her so violently. Hanna contemplates if the God will be reborn and feels his presence upon them; the feeling comes to her as a deep kind of knowing, but she wishes she could understand the Divine Plan – the intentions of the Goddess Helga who wishes for a mortal child. She prays. She meditates. She leaves her body at night to seek Jace in the Underworld. She does all that she can as she chants and sings at her altar to prepare her body for the ensuing darkness that will be ever pervasive and when the day falls in September she believes it is time to go to Vermont.

"Hello, Mom." Rose stays at home in the estate of Brighton.

It is officially the Fall Equinox when the balance of light and dark is subtle before the wheel of the cycle moves to winter.

"Hello my daughter." Alexandra opens her arms to bring her daughter in.

Rose speaks softly. Gently.

"I hope this is not going to harm anyone," Rose begins, "but Michael and I are expecting…"

"A baby?" Alexandra whispers.

"Yes. Another baby… and at the Summer Solstice."

"Elizabeth might have a brother…"

"Or a sister." She almost has tears in her eyes.

"We must get her back," Alexandra whispers.

"I want to…" Rose is looking for her words, "I will never forget her."

Alexandra believes she sees the doubt in her daughter that they will ever find her.

Within Alexandra's room her altar is decorated in dedication to her granddaughter; there is a shrine with tokens from the Harvest to bring them peace and justice. Her altar bares sweet sentiments in written words upon candlesticks and photos of birth to bring her back.

Hanna, Lucius, the babies, Luther and Reese go to Vermont where Lucius will earn their wages working for the resort while Hanna can remain at home. Sterling continues to run her shop alongside Elenor and Lucius' temporary placement at the café is over so it works in their favor to move on for the winter where they can aim at two birds with one stone – to work and to live but also to seek justice for another baby that has been stolen from the good witch community. The air in Vermont is cool and at night is frigid. Hanna imagines Rose with her daughter. She feels lost without Jace; her nighttime trips of leaving her body takes her into the abyss it seems but nothing, and no one, shows up. The silence is deafening. She trembles in the breeze of the day; the baby James is nestled to her chest. He is asleep. Hanna doesn't know how to feel about Jace's absence with respect to finding Goldie – and one thing is certain – Goldie is not looking for them. Or is she?

Hanna has sent word throughout the Shaman community that she is seeking Rhoda and Hanna meets Eva for brunch at her home while Herman works on the lifts. She motions to her wrist that it is time to go and Lucius gathers the tots and they head out to her lodge.

"I hope you all feel at home here in Vermont," Eva says while preparing the eggs.

"We are comfortable here," Hanna says and she doesn't have to ask…

"Rhoda will be here this morning," Eva says.

She serves them plates of eggs, pancakes, bacon and sausage.

"She will be here then?" Hanna says, as she takes a bite of crispy bacon not to addenda Eva.

"Yes…" Eva laughs as there is a knock on the door, "any minute," and she opens the door as Rhoda hands over a basket of edible fruits shaped into flowers.

"Shall we eat first?" She says, "I was just serving the plates…"

"Knowing that I would be here I'm sure…" Rhoda is sweet and she removes her wool coat.

"Certainly." Eva places her coat onto the coat rack and they have a seat together at the table after exchanging hugs of gratitude. Rhoda removes the *Daily* from her purse and on the front page are the words: *Out to Find the Dark Witch*

"Chris…" Hanna says.

"Yes." Rhoda is familiar.

Hanna speaks of Goldie but Rhoda knows all-to-well of the dark ones' ordinance to sacrifice the blood of the most innocent to obtain absolute power and Hanna realizes she does not have to explain the terror they are up against; Rhoda nods in the affirmative and they hope she can deliver something to them – even if in the form of a vision.

Chapter Twenty

"I have seen the Demon," Rhoda says, peering over her shoulder at the babies who play in the living room but cannot hear them, "and they are starving him."

"So he will feed on the blood of the most innocent?" Hanna is feeling the déjà vu. Rhoda wonders if they should be communicating telepathically so as not to bring the dark one's energy into the room when Hanna receives the thought.

The child is alive, Rhoda channels her.

Hanna affirms she receives the message when she nods.

The Demon is weeping.

"You can see them then?" Hanna asks, breaking Rhoda's concentration… "You can see them right now?"

Lucius wishes he could say that they should have killed her when they had the chance but Rhoda receives the thought.

"That would be the energy of the dark ones."

"I know," Lucius understands.

"The power she seeks is otherworldly."

"We have guests…" they hear the voice.

"Leisha," Hanna whispers.

Rhoda leaves her mind's eye and steadies her concentration entirely on the room to bring her awareness back to the physical space.

"She could sense our presence." Hanna is frustrated – Rhoda is the gate to the dark others.

"There was a satchel on the table they seemed to be protecting."

But Goldie stands in the catacombs yielding a ruby-studded wand and they hear her voice hover like a dark cloud…

Be gone!

Your time is done!

And the room turns dark.

"I told you I didn't want to bring the darkness here," Rhoda whispers.

"They are also gone," Eva assures them.

"That must be my satchel," Hanna says.

"There are a few things we must get her back," Rhoda is firm.

"These things are in the hands of a dark witch…" Eva contends.

And their breakfast has turned cold. The light over the range flickers and the bulb dies out.

"Their energy has created a surge in their power," Lucius explains.

"It's unnerving how easily they can find us…" Hanna says.

"We are not hiding." Rhoda reminds her.

"No, I guess not," she says and she cannot help but to feel how Goldie still seems to be the more powerful among them. The thought makes her uneasy.

When the first snow falls, Rose is feeling guilty about her pregnancy. She tells her mother that she feels she has lost her loyalty to her daughter but Alexandra disagrees. She wishes to form an extension to their family by creating an extended Coven; she believes the Coven will ignite the energy they need to stop something evil from happening.

Sterling dissipates and reappears in the room she designated in her mind. She is fluid like water and can easily move between worlds; if she is to defend herself then she must be the best witch possible. She chants to raise the energy from her own soul and she focuses using her third eye on the destination and slowly her body dissolves into the molecules the cells are made of and becomes an essence like vapor as the cells turn to radiant energy. Despite the weather, the energy in the atmosphere is strong enough to sustain her wishes.

Word has passed with Alexandra's intention to form a Coven within the hours she speaks to Rose; the mental energy among them is equally strong. The protests have relaxed as if the cool in the air has everyone staying at home – which allows for the witch to do her work. Without the distraction of negative energy they can plan while meditating on what action is the best method to take back baby Elizabeth who is rightfully Rose's and Michael's first child.

In a pool of crystal clear water Sterling collects in a basin, she focuses on Hanna and as she tries to reach her, Clover flutters her wings because the energy is contagious. She imagines Hanna's strong and beautiful face and she calls to her in a whisper: *Hanna* her soft voice moves through the atmosphere and through the fields and into her mind's eye – traveling telepathically has never felt so breathless. Hanna pauses; the call from an adept witch startles her. Initially she doesn't recognize the voice; she turns off the spigot in the kitchen and listens intently.

"Hanna, it's Sterling," she is more forward this time.

Hanna takes a seat at the kitchen table thinking that Sterling, like Rhoda, is able to use the mind's third eye more robustly these days. She concentrates on her voice and in her own mind she imagines Sterling's face as she communicates in thought form, "Sterling, yes," she says, "What is the reason for this mental intrusion?" She jokes, sensing the lack of suspense.

"I am practicing connecting in this way."

"The energy in the atmosphere is strong."

"There are more hopeful witches than there are rioters."

"Yes, I can feel the difference."

"When will you be back to work?"

Hanna is a little surprised by the candid question, "Next season." She says but omitting to say *if all goes well.*

"I'll get right to it..." Sterling seems rushed all of a sudden.

Hanna feels the suspense.

"Alexandra is putting together a Coven to form an alliance among the witch community and I thought you might want to be here."

"Of course... but when do I need to be there?"

"There will be a festival for friends in the community around the start of the Summer Solstice..."

"That is when I proposed to be back at work."

"Sounds like I have the right timing then."

"There needs to be a lot of things happening before the start of the next season."

"Yes, when the baby is born."

Hanna, once again, senses the déjà vu.

348

"There's one more thing…" Sterling interrupts her discourse… "I realize I hadn't told you that Rose is expecting a child."

"I see. You're thinking so fast that I didn't have to ask."

"We all want to come together to be sure that she is protected."

"Let me know what I can do."

"What have you done from your end?"

"I have Rhoda, an adept witch – she can find the mind of…" she hesitates…

"Go on…" Sterling is not taking this personally.

"Your sister…"

"What else?"

"And I have Eva, a strong Shaman."

"Any plans or intentions?"

Hanna isn't certain exactly how much she is willing to share with Sterling – not knowing precisely if she is protecting herself more or Goldie at all.

"Keep her in your thoughts and imagine her being protected." Sterling speaks of Rose.

"I will." Hanna feels that is the least she can do.

Hanging up is not like placing the receiver onto a cradle; the mind just goes blank. Hanna feels Sterling has communicated all that she knows but she wonders too how intensively Sterling would oppose her sister Goldie. She puts the thought away as she is defending any more mental intrusion from telepathy.

In that moment of silence, Hanna believes she can find, faintly hear, the whispering of voices as she steadies herself further to pry and she realizes that she is still very much connected in the psychological realm. She breathes. Then she hears nothing. She sighs and returns to the dishes. She believes that a ceremony for the Coven is a good time to summon a lot of energy as a way to focus on the birth of another child – a warm thought in the midst of a cold winter.

Sterling empties her water basin into a sink; she uses the water vapor to aid her in mental telepathy as the vapor helps her see into the mind of another. She lives aside her store and can see Elenor within as she begins the evening shift while Sharon is leaving the day shift. The shifts change over at the one o'clock hour. Sterling checks on Sharon as she is leaving her home and stops by the store on her way toward Alexandra's estate.

Rhoda finds Hanna within her home at the lodge; they have a hike and their destination is the summit of a small mountain. As Reese stops in to take over the care of her children, she puts on her hiking boots and grabs her satchel; Tia to this day still coughs from within; she makes her way into the frigid air. She peeks inside her satchel and says a short vigil over her rail little body *keep holding on Tia* she says; Hanna thinks about Jace; his deathly body is all she has left of him. She doesn't even know where he is or what he is up to doing.

She feels strong and hopes her strength alone will see them through.

Lucius works the lifts but is working toward working as Ski Patrol as an Emergency Medical Team. He has courses to study and has the duty of providing for the family all-the-while Hanna is immersed in helping a fellow witch with her tragedy. She is happy that Luther has arrived too and he has brought pizza for them. She heads out for the journey that Rhoda has planned for them.

"This tree root provides great medicine," Rhoda explains as Hanna emerges from the trail and they go off-course. Rhoda picks up her walking stick and proceeds into the forest they feel a kind of wind as if the Storm Goddess is pushing them forward. Hanna feels chills as she also feels a sense of urgency. Then Hanna sees him – Bernard is sitting by the tree. He has Magpie beneath his shirt and a mighty staff at his side. Hanna rushes up the steep slope to aid him.

"Bernard," she says and he opens his eyes.

"Hanna?" He barely recognizes her.

"What are you doing?"

"I'm just taking my time…" he says to her and pulls Magpie from under his shirt; they have both aged which is apparent beneath the white and the gray.

Hanna looks her over and she realizes that Magpie has nearly passed.

Rhoda places her hands over his body; her hands radiate heat energy.

"He has a sickness all over his body," she says. "It compromises his immune system… this one, I'm afraid, he won't be able to fight."

Bernard places his head back against the tree, realizing that he too is dying.

"This staff," he says, "is from the Elder Simon … you are here, now, on this journey so with this kind of synchronicity I believe it's now meant for you." Then his voice is ever more faint, "but the one you are looking for, Grandall's great staff, is close by. Just follow the little yellow bird."

Hanna looks all around her and she finds a golden yellow finch sitting upon a tree branch that is emanating in a golden hue. She can feel radiant energy coming from the little bird and finally, she realizes, is the time that she can return Tia home; she looks within her satchel and cups her little body into her hands and Tia coughs some more; Hanna extends her hands toward the golden bird, realizing that she opens a portal between the worlds, and Tia is lifted up and into the golden light as she disappears… Bernard speaks again.

"The Elder passed on his legend and that is how I have come to find his mighty staff and the little yellow bird."

The staff falls from his arms. His pupils dilate to an immense amount of black and Hanna catches his head into her embrace as Rhoda kneels before them; she takes Magpie into her arms.

"This is why we were called into the forest," Rhoda says.

"Just in time for Tia, too." She looks to Bernard knowing that the Storm Goddess used her wind to steer them toward Bernard who deserves a proper burial alongside his trusty companion. Rhoda moves her hands up and down his body to radiate warm, healing energy, "If by the grace of the Goddess," she says.

But there is a divine essence to his death; he looks peaceful and Hanna knows he would rather die aside his beloved Magpie. They lay his body into the earth and cover him with twigs and foliage that can be found in mounds beneath the trees, just below the layer of frost.

"That is the best burial we can give him." Rhoda feels respect toward them.

Hanna is not appeased. She feels the rodents can get to them.

She calls upon Eva and the Shamans to give him a burial worthy of a ritual, and they gather there to burn them so their ashes may rest; their energy ascends to the clouds and Rhoda nods in favor of the ritual. They spend the day seated by the burning brush as they pray over him and hope the Storm Goddess may direct them on where to go next.

"There is a great deal of sadness when a beloved warrior is laid to rest," Rhoda says when they ascend into night and the golden finch takes flight.

"I think we are to follow him," Hanna says, and she takes up the heavy staff, and Rhoda takes up her walking stick. They casually walk, led by the goldfinch, where up ahead there is a clearing.

"That would ordinarily be the meadow covered with wild flowers," Rhoda says, peering at the layer of snow that now covers the ground and they trudge through the expanse of the open area. They follow the little bird to a hollow tree that still stands despite being made of a now thin layer of bark. Snow fills the cavity but the finch rests upon it.

Hanna is uncertain what she is to do. Rhoda climbs to the top where the hollow shell can support her body and she feels for the surface with the length of the staff as the snow gives beneath her weight and the hollow tree sends them into the underground – Hanna follows behind them.

On the ground, covered in snow, Rhoda speaks, "If you can't tell, this tree is a passage to the Temples."

But Hanna did not know the tree would lead to the Temples.

"But I thought they were gone." She says aloud.

"Yes," Rhoda affirms, "but something has been left here."

She jumps on the hollow tree that has landed in a heap beside them and she finds nothing inside.

"Nope," she says, "nothing else is inside here." Rhoda is perplexed.

Hanna takes a match from her satchel and the yellow finch joins them when Hanna notices a kind of Sanskrit etched into the cavern's walls. Together they find a peculiar drawing too and realize it's a warrior yielding a mighty staff.

"Is that Grandall?" She asks.

"Much older." Rhoda replies, "but the Elders who you came to know certainly follow the direction and legends of these ancient ones."

The cave walls are like a map when Hanna turns her body the finch flickers like light on the match when the match too goes out; Hanna lights another, realizing that was the last they would see of the friendly little bird, and she wonders what they must do next.

"Let's keep going then." Rhoda is optimistic.

They go beyond the opening of the cave when Rhoda removes her overcoat and from an undershirt she ravels the material into a ball; when she lights it, the fabric sends off a fire of immense light, and Hanna can see a bubbling hot spring before them; the area is protected from the outside elements and they are warm.

"This spring is why it is so hot down here," Rhoda says and sits on a rock overlooking the water. She is clearly hot and tired from walking.

Hanna removes her heavy parka too. She takes a seat beside Rhoda and feels the water with her hand. "It's about eighty degrees," she says.

"This is where the Warriors upon those walls would bathe before a ritual," Rhoda says, "that's what I saw ascribed in those legends."

They both go into the water and become submerged in water so pure that they feel nourished like a mother to a child – like the water is hugging them and they feel even more hope; they fill their minds with the essence of warrior-like energy.

Hanna closes her eyes and inhales deeply so that her mind and her body can relax. Then she finds herself walking a path that is led by the Elders.

Chapter Twenty-One

She is using her mind's eye, and she has reached a place that is equal to a deep trance like a place of immense meditation and the Elders are guiding her. She concentrates on her breath so that she can withhold the energy-state that has her subdued in euphoria. Her mind tells her to naturally feel her way to her soul. She is in a Zen-like state, a state so pure that she has never been before – and aside from the Elders she finds a child before them which is radiant with enigmatic beauty; the baby girl is nestled in a blanket and the light emanates from her body. Hanna recognizes that she is a Celestial Child, and feels the little yellow bird is connected to this child. Hanna wants to reach out to touch the child, but her beauty is too captivating. She watches in awe as the psyche of the child seems to mature rapidly and the enigmatic child blooms into an adult woman in a vision taking place with beauty all around her; all this happening feels surreal and she wonders why the child is growing so rapidly before her when the child becomes engulfed in expansive wings with feathers like a bird and Hanna realizes this child was the bird.

"Maintain the vision," Rhoda says and Hanna understands that Rhoda's mind is an important component to this experience. The white light with a golden hue courses through the radiant child's, woman's body, and Hanna can no longer differentiate a child from a woman because the being before her is more like a Goddess – the wings of a great bird, body of a woman and a face like a child – she is the most magnificent of creatures.

To Hanna she is seeing the birth of the Goddess Helga. The experience is ineffable but Hanna ponders that this being is more than she can comprehend and Hanna wants to hold her, embrace her. Then the being grows a great womb, and from the womb, another child is born, and Hanna can

361

feel the love the angelic being feels for the child; a love like a mother to a child. As Hanna is engulfed in Celestial Light she can feel with all of her senses that the light being wishes for this child and Hanna begins to withdrawal. She no longer feels she wants to stay in the Celestial Being's company. The child is not hers to have and Hanna feels the warmth as it turns back to a colder temperature and the darkness ensues. *The child is in the dark,* she thinks to herself, and she shrieks with a remote amount of terror; she cannot find Jace and the panic overtakes her. She trembles but feels that she must find her way back to the light – to dutifully return the child to her mortal mother – and let the light continue to shine without the Golden Child. But Hanna's mind shutters with the fear and tension as if there is a Dark Presence behind her – a presence like a cold mother – and she turns around to find a dark Maiden and behind her too is the Demon – who has been starving and who is ready to ravish the Celestial Child and then Hanna awakens from the vision she has before her.

"The vision is subsiding," Rhoda tells her.

It is with Rhoda that Hanna's senses are so strong. Rhoda is the adept with the knack for telepathy and maintaining the third eye sense of vision questing.

"They all want the child." Hanna's spirit is down.

"But first, let's examine your child before now."

"Because of the curse of my grandmother."

"And now why this child?"

"She is a blessed child, a child of the light, and now they want to possess the child and bring her into the dark realm."

"The dark needs the blood of the child to pour down upon them and make them immensely immortal and very powerful."

"The light yearns for a child…"

Hanna takes a deep breath.

"Goldie chose us; she chose the one who befriended her. A witch that is evil doesn't want friends."

"We must find Rose's daughter."

"To somehow create a balance between them and their wishes and desires … to restore the Universal Order."

"Some of us have gotten too greedy."

"No matter what form it takes."

Rhoda steps out from the hot spring and lays her head on her satchel, "For now we must get some rest."

Hanna dries herself as best she can with a small towelette she keeps in her satchel that had just wrapped Tia's frail body, and she lays upon the ground, thinking of her. She feels drained – even mental energy is an exhausting way to extend oneself. It is not much like sleeping however when through her mind she begins dreaming where she sees the Demon and his demise; he is starving just as he had been in their lucid vision – they starve him like Michael had and she finds Goldie in this dream where she dines on hot tea and pastries. The Demon, once again, needs fed in mortal blood; her mind calls to Herschel Beecham when she feels a *pop* and her energetic body leaves her physical body and her dream has evolved into a quest where she explores the cavern and comes across a fat rat – she thinks that she must be getting close. Her physical body lays restfully while her ethereal body moves swiftly without the much denser weight of the physical shell. The Demon howls in hunger; the rat follows Hanna while she hovers, suspended in the air, not in need of feet; his demise makes her flutter. He is ever more grotesque than before with a sickly body where the wax-like flesh is stretched like silicone over bone, and the smell of him is insipid like rancid meat. He squeals in a high pitch tone and Hanna wants to go back to her body – even the ethereal body can smell and she feels sick. The odor is unbearable as the Demon is at a kind of decay like a rotting corpse. But Hanna cannot get back to her body and she is found by Goldie when her mortal body begins to choke and Goldie has a deathly grip around her neck; she protrudes from the portal with only her torso visible and she holds tightly onto Hanna; Goldie has eyes that flush with hatred; they are dilated black, puffy and almost hollow like seeing eye sockets in place of eye balls as she hasn't been in the warmth of the sun; she is tired looking but her grip is strong and Hanna chokes.

Rhoda is asleep and Hanna cannot scream from being prohibited by the intensity of the bony hands; in the deep of the dark Bernard shines as his soul becomes a streak of light and Goldie's eyes become etched upon him; with her gaze she tries to intimidate her opponent. Hanna has turned blue and is close to death.

"The staff," he says telepathically to her ethereal body and he creates an image in her mind's eye of searing through her hands that are forcefully grappling at her neck; from the ordeal Rhoda awakens and takes up the mighty staff and brings the heavy wood oak onto her knuckles that bleed and Goldle recedes like a phantom from the portal and the dark impedes on them.

Rhoda takes Hanna's head into her arms and shakes her to bring her back into her body. Hanna coughs and breathes mildly.

"Bernard." She tries to say.

"It's a good thing we are so mentally connected," Rhoda says softly.

"That is how she killed those girls… Hanna's eyes are still wide and transfixed, "and my grandmother."

"But not you Hanna. She did not get you."

"This time."

"We must keep going on."

"Bernard was passing through the dark to get to the light."

"It was a matter of right timing I am sure."

"Yes. The legend says the girls died at the same time."

"She used a body double, as you are yourself an adept."

"I don't understand Leisha's devotion."

"Maybe one day we'll understand."

"I don't know…"

"It might be best if we move along from here." Rhoda helps Hanna to stand.

"To go where?"

"To the Village of Indigenous people. Where there will be greater and more powerful energy. I'm afraid that one came too close."

"Why is she so powerful?"

"The dark ones feel no sense of restraint."

"They have an immense amount of power," Rhoda goes back to speaking about the Indigenous people, "and they have a great sorcerer – one who has no name."

"Why no name?"

"They just call her Lorde and you'll see why."

When they get to the expanse beyond the hollow cavity where they emerge into the light of day, they find the remote village of Shamanic people, one that Hanna has never seen before. The coldness provokes a sense of foreboding as the beginning of winter means that the veil between the worlds is becoming thin and the people surrounding Lorde wear ceremonial attire to honor the dead. The one dressed entirely in black represents the Goddess of the Underworld as their culture is also much like the Wiccans. The woman Shaman, who they call Lorde, is a powerful leader among the tribe and as she draws pictures amid the snowy plains that are surrounded by the jutted mountainous terrain. Rhoda relates what Hanna needs to see from the lessons; Hanna must first embrace her dark side if she is to bring order among the worlds. Rhoda explains that the Shamanic tribe has been expecting them and their leader brings their lore together in images for Hanna to see.

"To connect with the Goddess of the Underworld, one must embrace their dark side," Rhoda explains while Hanna listens intently. Hanna has only met the Celestial Queen Helga and the Goddess of Storms but she is instructed to close her eyes, inhale softly, and to imagine that she is protected in a soft light of indigo – a hue of power in the subtleties of being mildly dark. Hanna falls into a deep trance led by Lorde who blows from a pipe into her face, and Hanna is surrounded by tribal people who form a circle around her; the elders also blow smoke from pipes and the atmosphere is a kind of quiet, yet a powerful vigil. The atmosphere turns gray around them and Hanna beholds a vision amid the smoke where she can see an aged woman, hunched over a bubbling cauldron, that is the color of silver. With a tarnished and pointed finger the aged woman motions for Hanna to bring her focus even closer and Hanna concentrates on the cauldron where she sees an image of her own face, and from her face she can hear her own voice speak the words, "I am a seeker to learn the wisdom of the dark."

The woman chuckles and begins to stir the hot contents from within the cauldron; Hanna's face turns and Hanna is peering at an image of her mother who cries and prays for Hanna. Her mother prays for Hanna to leave the dark and to find the Light of God.

"Your mother does not have the same beliefs as you." The woman exudes wisdom and grace despite her age; her mind is still and Hanna can sense an aura of control like the color of a deep orange omnipresent about her; Hanna continues to see what the woman brings to her and she can see Jace who is reaching out to her to bring her into the darkness – to bring her to the other side – to understand that sorrow has no limitations. Her mother Alayna withdraws and Hanna can feel her sorrow; Hanna realizes that she gave up on her mother whereas her mother did not give up on her – and she had no idea of her mother's prayers.

"To heal another," Rhoda says aloud, "you must first heal yourself."

With that message the vision of the wise old Crone recedes from view and with her the images of Jace and Alayna vanish with the cauldron and Hanna is left amid the smoky contents of the pipes that are smoked by the Shamans who do not speak a word.

Hanna opens her eyes, "Brokenness," she says, "we are all broken at certain times in some sense."

Rhoda smiles, "Yes," she says. And Lorde absorbs the tobacco in the pipe and lets the smoke funnel from her mouth as all the villagers begin to talk among themselves. Hanna lets the knowledge settle in her soul and Lorde removes a leather-bound book from a square case and from within Hanna is given her Grandmother's satchel.

"How did you get this?"

"On your journey," Rhoda says, "you will find the things that you need."

Hanna takes her Grandmother's *Book of Shadows* into her hands.

"Put in that book all that you learn and you can pass it on to Alysiah someday."

The wise Shaman begins to sing a song in her native tongue.

"She sings a song about going to sleep and awakening anew," Rhoda explains.

Hanna hugs her in a warm embrace. Her satchel, etched with a burning sun, is Hanna's reminder of the light that she seeks as the cold is evermore present and she can see the frost from her breath. She takes the *Book of Shadows* and places it within the satchel and they prepare for some much-needed sleep.

Chapter Twenty-Two

"We need to rip that woman from the deep and force her..." Bridget feels angry and Alexandra can take no more. She has called a meeting; all witches need to assemble to help now. Rose is not feeling optimistic.

"Being pregnant, I don't know if I can..." she is torn between guilt and their mission.

"That's why we are all here to do it for you." Alexandra is calm as she tries to reassure her daughter.

"She can curse us but we can counter-curse! We do stand a chance against her Rose! We must get that precious baby back into your arms."

"She's never been in my arms." Rose cries.

They congregate at the estate: The Sister's Coven, The Guardians, the girls from the Group Home, and their family. They are given fine wine and cheese platters. Their family is seated at the open round table and their guests are provided with tables about the grand hall. Michael's family has joined them: Lucy and Joshua, their son Jericho, his girlfriend Anna, his sister Allison and her new mate Patrick join together to enjoy fruit and cocktails. Alexandra tries to bring all of them together to convene with good intentions and to raise the energy from a massive low to a highly favorable and more significant positive atmosphere because energy is important in the workings of a witch. She has again invited Chris because she knows the *Daily* will be read by Danica and Lucinda who have also been involved in the legends of Brighton for the past twenty years; Alexandra wants them to see how her own family have been victimized and she hopes to elevate their energy for healing to focus on more salient matters over vengeance.

Rose's status as an un-aged woman has most of the town fretting; they just do not understand the witch community. Many of the town folk feel that all witches in general are capable of evildoing. But Alexandra calls them together tonight with the special intention to discuss creating a peace treaty: the *All Witches Against Violence Committee* to hopefully show the community that they mean no harm.

"They need to understand that not all witches are evil" Alexandra explains.

Sterling is within the room and she looks broken. Torn. Her face is that of a serene expression and she cannot help but feel some sense of guilt like Rose who feels she has abandoned her first child considering the pregnancy with another child. Alexandra does not want them to continue in guilt as that brings the wrong kind of energy onto them.

"We form this alliance for all witches to spread the word that we are against the use of violence!"

"No harm done." Bridget gets it.

The guests rattle their hands upon the table like a drum roll…

"Yes!" Alexandra raises her fist, "we can call for peace – because a fight for peace would be too ironic!"

They laugh subtly. The humor is contagious like positive energy erupting among the banter.

"We need to live freely as Witches and Warlocks in our community," a voice says among them, a face Alexandra does not recognize and she can see Chris in full momentum with pen to paper.

Alexandra realizes that she needs to address the Witches and the Warlocks outside of the Brighton community – the surrounding towns and neighbors because she does not want the status of Brighton to impede on them. She wishes to cause no harm – and they are correct – they deserve to live freely as a witch as-much-so as the non-witch does.

They convene among themselves to address how they can pass the word of peace. Alexandra feels that as the baby grows in her daughter's womb there is more time she loses with her first grand baby but she keeps the thought in her own mind thankful that her daughter doesn't do so well telepathically; she feels safer in that fact but remembers to concentrate on getting her back.

Arriving late for the dinner are Sarah and Rebecca from the group home and Alexandra has finished her speech. Bridget and Sharon fill them in on their intentions to aid their fellow witches in living a good life who are free from outside scrutiny. The girls love Alexandra and are committed to her in every way.

"The point is to locate the bad witch and make her good again," Sharon says.

"Right." Bridget nods but cannot help but to still feel the fire raging inside of her.

Bridget has always been more of a go-getter with the idea of fighting the fire with fire, but she respects Alexandra and wants to do what is right for all the witch community.

Elenor also joins late and takes a seat aside Sterling and she orders a cocktail from the caterer. Elenor knows that her beloved friend Sterling deserves some restitution from the doings of her own sister and she wishes she could take her pain away.

Some still chat quietly among themselves about how they wish they could just force Goldie from the Catacombs but they too keep quiet as to show respect to a fellow witch.

"Then we have it." Alexandra tings her glass, "We have the initiation ceremony during Samhain when we conduct a ritual so powerful she will be subdued by love."

Sterling chokes down a bite of fish and bites her lip.

"And my daughter will have her child come back to us!"

Rose thinks about how Michael would see his child for the first time, and she tries to smile, but the tension is there in the pit of her stomach where her baby is, and she thinks how her baby will be without a sibling if they never get Elizabeth back.

"We are back to calling her Elizabeth." Michael tries to soothe her.

"Summer if she becomes an angelic child." Rose is trying to be optimistic.

And they turn to Alexandra who can hear them and she wonders why they would ever call her Summer.

Hanna, armed with an Elder's staff, and her grandmother's *Book of Shadows* dreams of a place within the catacombs where Jace holds baby Elizabeth in his arms. Then she awakens, where she is on the cold earth, beside a blazing fire, and the moon is in the position of midnight. The dream provides her with temporary comfort. She still feels a sense of foreboding, but she turns toward the fire and tries to hold the image of Jace with Elizabeth in his embrace, and she thinks about where he is and where he can be going.

Alexandra takes her Coven to the *Mystical Mountains* store along with Sterling while her members explore the various magical tools: Sharon finds a chalice of white marble. It is expensive but she is in awe of its beauty. She is a water sign on the astrological chart and feels the chalice complements her interests. Melissa finds an athame blade with a white handle and believes that carving the magical circle would make her capable of worthy participation with something to offer. It would make her feel like a witch. Bridget chooses a deck of tarot cards for divination and a box of Runes to tell their fortune; with the aid of magical tools she can intuit the future. Celia chooses a pentacle she wants to wear around her neck because silver jewelry fits her personality and a wand made of light oak will help her conjure magic. They purchase their items from Elenor and Alexandra thanks Sterling.

In the following days, Alexandra prepares a sacramental meal before the initiation ceremony. Within her home she sweeps the sacred space and she invites Melissa who chose the athame blade, to trace a circle from within the sacred space;

Melissa carves an imaginary circle at the edge of the stones Alexandra placed before them in a clockwise direction, the motion of deosil, a term Wiccans use to describe moving with the sun.

She next invites Sharon to her sacred place. Her altar is armed with the chalice they use to drink the wine for purification. Next she moves away from her altar, placed at the center of the circle, and sprinkles salt water within and around her sacred space to bless her space with positive energy. She burns incense so the scent of sandalwood creates an atmosphere that's needed for initiation ceremonies. She further cleanses the space by passing along the incense to Bridget who gathers with them and with the energy of the Sun God Alexandra asks that each member is blessed by the Guardians; she lights a white candle and ascribes their names into the melting wax and as the candle burns they are lifted angelically toward the Sun God, overseer of the Celestial City, during the most trying times when the atmosphere grows dark for winter.

The ritual tools are placed upon the altar to represent the four corners: Earth is represented in the North where she places fall foliage from the last harvest; Air for the East where the incense burns; South is represented by fire where the candle burns and in the West there is water within the chalice. At the center is another candle to represent the Goddess who is not forgotten in the times of the impending dark. Alexandra chimes the silver ritual bell and begins her initiation ceremony for the girls who wish to become an ordained witch. She speaks in tune with the mystical energy that surrounds their space during the ritual as she also speaks:

By the powers of the four quarters we charge this great circle with positive energy by the divine light and let no evil enter here!

Guardians of the Four Quarters, I ask of you all to bless this formation in the respect of forming a greater Coven!

Outside there is lightning and the sleet and hail are falling.

They hear the words of the Guardians in unison:

We bless you...

They speak as if through a tunnel in a faraway place.

Thank you dear Guardians, Alexandra says and she begins the initiation rite:

I conjure thee o' great circle of light, we ask that the great Goddess bless us and consecrate this mighty circle...

And the lightning crashes as the Storm Goddess opens a pathogen, a portal, between the worlds as the sky parts.

I call upon your Great Spirit to gather here, to fill this space with your power!

Alexandra's voice grows louder over the sound of the lightning crashing.

The women are lifted off their feet as if they are floating as the energy courses through the room. They fill their lungs with Divine radiance and by inhaling deeply their core soul becomes enriched with the blessings of the Goddess whose light penetrates them; their heads fall back, their mouths open, and the light enters their bodies. As they are placed back onto the ground they still feel light as air as if they are still buoyant.

Alexandra continues:

By the power of the Craft in the name of the Goddess I summon the Sun God to bless these new initiates who gather here to enter my Coven and thus name themselves a Witch! So Mote it Be!

She moves from the center of the circle toward the girls…

I ask of you, Bridget, to drink from this chalice that it will bless your soul and on your journey after departing from this great circle… so that you may become a witch.

Bridget drinks from the chalice and feels the warmth in the pit of her stomach.

By the Craft of magic under the Guidance of the Goddess and in the name of the Sun God himself, I declare your initiation is properly cast!

Bridget bows her head...

"Thank you dear Mother, High Priestess of this Coven, I am blessed."

In the remaining hour, Alexandra properly initiates her girls into her Coven as she repeats the initiation rites as they drink from the chalice and allow their souls to be ordained by a Priestess in the way of the Witch.

The girls can feel the radiant energy course through them and the blood courses through their veins as the warmth from the Sun God enriches the purification water, and the water from the chalice enters each and every one.

Alexandra ends the rites:

I honor you dear initiates for your attendance and I bid you farewell as you depart. I leave you in peace with love in your heart as there is love in mine... Hail and Farewell!

One by one the Four Quarters ignite like smoke to a flame as the Guardians recognize their departure and so the energy leaves the room: first from the Sun God, then the Goddess, onto the Guardians, as the smoke rises, and lastly the warmth fades and they are left with one another to depart from Brighton and aid Alexandra in her time of great need.

Alexandra moves in the rotation of Widdershins around the great circle so that they may leave one-by-one as they prepare for a new day.

Hanna takes long strides on the path told by Lorde the Great Sorcerer; somewhere in the mountains a Great Warrior laid down his staff. They stop beneath a coniferous tree and Hanna's mind is in the past.

"You know Rhoda," she says, as they take a rest, "Lucius and I were wrong; he wanted to split the energy between them, Aly and Lucas, to divert their attention but Goldie was not targeting their energy; she wanted to spill their blood."

"Yes, dear," Rhoda is tired, " and now the Goddess wants a girl child."

"But why?"

"You followed your heart on the path to getting back your daughter in the way that you felt protected and the Goddess entered your daughter to instill in her the energy she would need to survive. It was a kind of sacrifice."

Hanna doesn't get it.

"So now she wants a mortal child to raise as her own?"

"We cannot foretell exactly what the Goddess's intentions are. All we can do is trust her Divine Graces."

"I just think that she wanted Aly in the same way she wants Elizabeth."

"Do not give up hope. The Goddess sends her Divine Graces."

"If that's what you want to call it."

"The birthmark on the wrists of your children is the Divine Mark of the Peace Treaty to make it balanced once and for all."

"Why do they have to use babies?"

"That is the heart of the Dark Ones. We Witches all have our initiation ceremonies and shedding the blood of the most innocent at the highest point North is the gravest of all ceremonies – only the darkest ones are capable of it."

"You have that right."

"I am right."

"We shall see."

"Yes, in time."

Hanna sighs.

"Then you were not entirely wrong," Rhoda explains, "it was hard then too to know what the Goddess wanted with your daughter but you had a vision and that was your soul searching for the answers."

"So after the sacrifice wouldn't the Dark and the Light get what they want?"

"We cannot always get what we want exactly the way we want it and that is true for

389

the Goddess as well. This is the journey to put into motion making it right between the two Spheres."

"What does your soul tell you to do?"

"That is your part. I am a Guardian and an Adept and I excel in telepathy and some divination. I can locate the dark ones but I don't know how to reason with them."

"My question is if the Goddess wants to claim the soul of the child once the sacrifice is complete."

"This may not sound so much better but isn't the present presumption that she wants a mortal child?"

"The Dark as well as the Light are seeking the same child. That much we know."

"Right."

"Just remember you did what your heart desperately wanted to do in order to save both your children."

"Now Rose is in my shoes…"

"Now Rose is in your shoes."

Then the Great Sorcerer speaks in her native tongue…

"She says the ruins of the Temples are in the direction of the East," Rhoda explains.

With the sun setting in the West Sage is already ahead of them – guiding their way – the Temples ahead of them. In ruin.

Chapter Twenty-Three

Hanna wishes she could connect with Lucius telepathically to check on her children, but she realizes he must be busy working the lifts and training as an EMT. The children are safe with Reese and Luther, she feels certain. As Rhoda struggles with the mere walking stick Hanna hands her the Great Staff given to her by the dearly departed Bernard who she hopes is also their guide in the form of Spirit – and then she thinks of Jace – and wonders if Bernard can pass into the Celestial City without him. She then thinks of retrieving her magical tools that belong in her satchel, and she recalls the hex and the fact that she could not practice magic and in that moment she is thankful for Rhoda whose strength aids her. The staff that Rhoda uses is infused with immense energy and Rhoda can sense that too. Light of any kind can be felt by those who are sensitive enough to perceive it and that light can be directed with intent and purpose; the beholder of such a staff is a powerful vessel and Hanna realizes too that she needs another Witch to accompany her – one who is most able to practice magic safely. The School of the Temples, once hidden in the majestic mountains of Vermont, has fallen in the wake of the war between the worlds.

Somewhere in the recesses of the mind, Sydney has a memory, and Rhoda can sense it; Hanna is searching the ancient Temples again, and she has not confided in them to aid her this time. Paisley and Priscilla are concerned but she feels they are held back now aided by Alexandra and Rose who are now armed with Raja Jade and Thor at their side. Where Raja is then Sydney feels that is her calling. They know that Hanna must be in the company of another witch and Rhoda sends Sydney a mental message: *We are okay here.* Is all she can say so the dark will not intercept her messages. Sydney can see Hanna by using her mind's eye, the Witches' third eye.

"I can't connect with her," Paisley says.

"If only I knew what she was looking for," Sydney says, wanting to help.

"Just ask them," Priscilla whispers.

"Gandall's staff." Immediately comes through from Rhoda.

Now Sydney feels she can understand but she doesn't know what has happened to Grandall and she thinks time must solve everything.

"Perhaps you need to look beneath the rubble," Sydney sends back like a Morse code.

She does not receive a response but she continues, "Try moving some of the debris away and follow your intuition."

Rhoda understands that message is intended for Hanna and she informs her that Sydney has made contact with her but Rhoda is fearful of the dark's interception but Hanna thinks the dark could care less – they have no problem showing their faces but it is the followers of the Light who cannot locate the Dark ones.

Hanna connects with a low level of energy, not sure what it is.

"The energy may not feel greatly powerful at first," Rhoda assures her.

"It's like a metal detector finding metal," Sydney says, "you are connecting with an energy vibration."

Hanna can connect with Sydney remotely but at a very low level. She thinks about how she would like to connect as powerfully as she does with bi-location.

Hanna feels energy like the pulling of a magnetic force; she holds her hands extended from her body and out front of her she knows instinctively where the energy outside her mind feels the strongest and she bends down to lift some of the debris just like Sydney said and when she lifts the brush a rat brushes past her and Hanna screams. Rhoda motions for her to feel more strongly, intuitively, and reminds her that the staff must be close to her; she begins to help Hanna remove the debris and from the rubbish there is a surge like an immense amount of energy when the feeling rushes through her body and the dirt falls beneath them she grasps the Mighty Staff with both hands and peels it from its dusty grave.

Hanna holds the mighty Staff high above her head when she sends a little telepathic message, "Thank you," her voice chimes within Sydney's mind to which she responds, "any time."

And they lose a connection when Hanna believes she can hear a baby cry. She immediately feels a need to locate her magical tools – but she is unable to practice magic safely – and she does not know what to do. She reminds herself to maintain the intuition but the baby's cry is alarming to her and the memories of Aly in the possession of Goldie and her Demon are haunting. Rhoda holds a finger to her lips so they are both quiet as they intensively listen.

"They are somewhere beneath us in the catacombs," Rhoda says, and Hanna looks anxious.

"Are we ready?" Hanna whispers.

Rhoda is subtle and calm.

"We must strengthen our minds so we can be strong in our calling."

Hanna sees Sage perched on a rock face before them and she feels more subdued.

"The baby crying is a sign of well-being." Rhoda tries to reassure her.

Hanna says firmly, "She's alive."

Alexandra falls into a deep depression; the witch her daughter befriended has turned against her family. The loss of her granddaughter is ever-so pervasive and she dims the lights within her bedroom to light a candle at her altar.

She beckons:

By the power invested in thee, I call upon the dark Goddess, aid me in my fellowship to the dark – I call upon the dark ones in this consecration…

Her candle's flame grows bright, and by the flame she consecrates her athame blade – with the blessings of a dark warrior, the Goddess peers through the flame with tranquil green eyes.

Welcome friend, Alexandra says to the Green Goddess – the maiden of the dark ones reveals an earthy layer to her persona that is not entirely dark, and Alexandra is comforted.

I ask for your blessing to do for the dark what no other can …

"What is it you wish to do?" The Goddess has a stern and courageous voice.

I Empower the Great Goddess with best wishes - that in a time of need I will find my beloved Granddaughter.

"And what can you do for the dark ones?"

I will take down the darkest witch who wishes to destroy you. To overpower you.

"Wish to destroy my power over the night?"

Yes.

"That is very courageous of you… what exactly will you do?"

I will first take her ruby-studded wand and with it I seek to destroy her.

"That is the doing of the darkness."

Yes. Alexandra is morose.

"You have my blessings." The dark Goddess speaks now in a faint and faraway voice.

Alexandra blows out the candle and the smoke stirs among her in a cloak shrouded in darkness. Her hands shake but she can feel the power of the Goddess – to which she will not allow a witch to have more power than herself.

The *Daily* sits beside her cauldron within the room and the feature shares the Alliance of Witches who stand against violence.

Alexandra doesn't feel regret. She feels the power of the Goddess, and in this way she feels like Bridget – that her heart yearns so remorsefully that she'll do anything to get back her beloved granddaughter; the power of the dark burns within her soul while Hanna feels the force from within.

Grandall's great and mighty staff burns in a hue of yellow when it is being used for Celestial purposes; its powers are immense – if she pushes, it pulls, if she pulls, it does the opposite. If she twirls the mighty staff above her head she levitates; a tilt to the left, and the sparks fly out of it; move it to the right it absorbs the light.

The staff is mightier than the sword, mightier than the athame blade; the athame blade is never to be used for cutting, but for only carving the great circle within a sacred space; the staff too must be used for Celestial purposes. The staff is longer than Hanna is tall; she wonders if she is the right beholder of such a powerful object.

Rhoda perceives her thoughts and moves her staff, Bernard's staff, above Hanna and Hanna ducks; when she moves it low, Hanna jumps. When she moves it halfway, Hanna shields a block.

"Never wonder if you are good enough before you have the chance to test your strength."

Alexandra drinks from the Mugwort Potion to aid her in her quest; on the night of the full moon when the veil is thin between the two worlds, on the night of All Hollow's Eve, she will evoke the Goddess of the Light to serve her what she asks: bring her child's daughter back! She continues to meditate before her altar, thinking of her grand baby and on each end of the altar, she has two black candles and in the center, a red candle burns. Her cauldron bubbles over the fire within her space and she withdrawals a piece of parchment and ascribes the deepest of intentions; that baby Elizabeth be given to her with no harm done. Then, Alexandra burns the paper and sprinkles the smoldering ash into the cauldron as she blows out each candle; outside there is light from a three-quarter moon and she peers out the window

401

as the smoke filters through the screen into the night so that the Goddess of the Celestial Light will receive her request – and she will learn for once and for all just exactly what the Goddess bestows for a child she calls Summer.

May my request manifest! So Mote it Be!

She   hollers   into   the   night.

Hanna smells smoke.

"Do you smell that?"

"Something is burning," Rhoda acknowledges.

"Yes…"

"Winter is upon us… smoke is in the air."

"But I don't see the smoke."

"Something may be burning from within. What is on your mind?"

"Summer."

Rhoda has a faint chuckle, "hard not to want the warmer weather I suppose."

402

"No, I mean the baby girl - the one they want to sacrifice for the dark!"

"You sense that she is connected to the fire?"

"Yes, somehow connected to the fire or the smoke."

"It is important to follow your instincts. The way will become clearer to you."

Alexandra takes her bag of Mojo and ties the satchel around her waist. She walks into her home after bidding the night farewell and she closes the window to shut out the cold once the smoke dissipates. She enters the great room and her Coven convenes with her there. They drink wine to replenish their soul's energy when Rose turns to her mother, her abdomen is visibly more pronounced, and she lays her head upon her mother's lap.

"The dowsing rod says that we are to have a boy."

"Boys are fun too, my sweet angel."

"We knew you were busy Alex," Bridget says, calling her by her nickname, "so we brought the baby shower to you."

Rose sits up gently and looks to her mother; the girls have brought gifts. Sharon and Bridget also made meals. Melissa and Celia made desserts. The women are in awe of one another; it feels old to be in one another's company. Kyla, Isabella and Jasmine put their money together to buy a swing for the nursery. Sharon put together a cake made from diapers, burp cloths and bibs. Celia bought bottles and clothes. The Sister's Coven brought an assortment of blankets, bath towels and pajamas. The cookies were baked in the shape of a cauldron. The cake is yellow cake batter with butter cream icing that features a boy in booties and a necktie.

Michael drops in; the men are in the parlor. He kisses his dear wife and winks, "Just checking on you girls." He says and steps outside the door and follows Edgar down the hall. The men are going ice fishing.

"The new little guy will have good company among those men," Alexandra says, but she hides her alliance with the Goddess of the Dark. Her bitterness and resentment takes precedence over her emotions; Goldie is a dreadful, and most hateful witch.

She ponders the idea of the alliance against violence and in some regard, she can see no other way – she feels she will do whatever it takes to bring Elizabeth back to her beloved Rose.

Rose is thankful she can conceive again, and she looks to her mother knowing she sees a change in her; her tone is different and she has a different kind of energy in the presence of all the girls. Her aura has subsided, and the light doesn't shine through her eyes.

The following day Rose sits by the river as the snow permeates the landscape. She speaks out loud to the crisp, clear, open blue sky.

"Why couldn't my protection spells work?" She asks as if the Goddess should be listening.

She thinks about the potion she drank before they removed her daughter from her womb – thankful she did not know while they cut her. Thankful they did not want to harm the baby then – thankful that she still has a chance to find her. To bring her back. She thinks about Duke – that he likely experienced death by choking. She feels that if her protection spells had worked then perhaps Goldie would be her friend; she would be a witch with love and compassion over hatred.

The air is bitter and cold too. Rose shivers. The neighboring town by Brighton has calmed some, and the protests have subsided. Silver has been able to work without the fear of her store burning to the ground – so she hopes. Rose knows the fury Danica and Lucinda feel after having lost their daughters to a witch. To black sorcery. Rose hopes that she can otherwise convince them that not all magic is evil. She yearns to make it alright for once and while she is happy about her baby coming, she thinks about how Edgar became her father – how he had been brave enough in the face of estrangement – to make things right within the home. She has a father after all, and she thinks about Hanna – and she wonders if Elizabeth can be saved. She shuts her eyes as she thinks about Michael, alone in the dungeon of the catacombs, feeding on rats, and how he endured the labors of hell just to see his family again – and she feels deeply that he deserves to see his beloved daughter. They feel dire inside all-the-while trying to be happy. She cannot help but to consider William Banks and how she can honor her husband and feel for him the connection she got to experience with Edgar – her family so sullen now was at one time so complete. Rose kicks up the snow and Thor idles from behind the snowbank and licks her hand. She knows that when she returns to Brighton that her mother will be preparing for the biggest festival yet, Samhain, in a ritual to bring out the dead. She wonders if her mother will summon evil to go with it.

Chapter Twenty-Four

Lucy finds Rose by the river; she heard from Joshua that Rose could not be found at home.

"A bit cold out here isn't it love?" Lucy says and rubs her back.

"I just needed a walk outdoors," Rose says, and she hugs Lucy with a ripe abdomen between them.

Alexandra sweeps the debris from within her home. She knows that the dead awaken on Samhain and the two worlds converge to make communication efficient between the living and the dead. She has become smitten.

"Will the Divine Goddess allow her to kill your baby and then take her?" She says aloud while sweeping. She has sided with Bridget and the paranoia of the Goddess's intentions has gotten to her.

Lucy agrees aloud too as if her inner intuition connects with Alexandra's mind.

"She's some Goddess..." she says with disdain.

They are losing faith.

Alexandra feels certain that they only have each other and she feels a disconnect from the brilliant light of the Celestial City.

"We have our own light." Lucy says as she hugs her. "We have the light from within – all that is sacred."

Alexandra feels a warmth and a light touch and returns to vigorously sweep the floor.

Samhain is approaching and she has been writing the ritual that will bring her out from the land of the dead, somewhere beneath the surface, where she is in the company of rats. Alexandra is livid while wanting to find Goldie; she is not afraid of the wretched witch and her blood boils. She and her daughter were always a good witch, but she cannot help but to consider where that got them. She understands Lucy's and Bridget's contentions and the more she thinks the madder she becomes:

"That man left me at the age of twenty, pregnant, alone!" She sweeps again.

Sharon, Melissa, Celia and Bridget, her forever Coven, collect items for the altar. They go to Sterling's store to pick up oil, candles and incense. Isabella, Kyla and Jasmine bake pies and make an assortment of desserts. Lucy goes to the store to collect wine and ale. The men are gathered within the parlor where Edgar smokes on a cigar.

"My dear wife and daughter," he says in the doorway…

Michael, Jericho, Joshua, Samuel, David and John listen intently…

"I believe the two of you can do this," Edgar says reassuringly.

"We think so too, Pop," Samuel says.

The men intend to back their women.

Hanna is deep within the catacombs alongside Rhoda; Lucius works the resort and Reese and Luther care for the babies. Aly plays happily by their side in the lodge while Lucius builds with blocks. James Edgar

411

drinks from a bottle; Hanna is missing them and wishes she could be with them. She tries to hurry for her sake and that of Rose. The catacombs are dark, omnipresent and eerie. She can hear the cackle of laughter and chatty voices of women, but the echo of voices come in all directions and the tunnels are vast. In their lair the Demon is starving. The way Michael was starving but their intentions are more grave than death alone; the hunger pains are a driving force for devouring an infant at the mercy of dark sorcery and Hanna knows he won't be able to hold back. Hanna recalls that they will only feed him on the night of the Winter Solstice when the dark is superior and the night will shed its power onto them. When the daylight succumbs to darkness, so shall the Demon succumb to wrath. Then her magic will be most intense and powerful and she plans to overcome the light.

"What does she get out of this?" Lucy asks since she has returned from the store.

"She will be Queen of the Night, overseer of the darkness, and indefinitely immortal as a very powerful witch and High Priestess."

Alexandra has for the time being left out exactly how her feat will be achieved.

"She will be able to move freely between worlds if the light is unable to stop her." Alexandra stops and thinks for a moment, "It's in the Handbook of the Dark Craft and Sorcery. Her intentions oppose all that is just and good – followers of the Light are to use magic for the highest good of all and with no harm done." She goes back to sweeping. She has been vigorously sweeping for over an hour. Her mind whirls. She thinks of the hug she could feel between her daughter and Lucy but her mind succumbs instead to needing the Goddess of the Night.

She feels that educating her Coven members is important, but she also knows that intense fear is the hindrance of the Light which helps the Dark. She refrains from saying too much. Her dark intentions are of her own accord and she wishes not to bring them into the vast empty pit that is the lair of dark sorcery.

Rose begins to peel the potatoes. At the time of the festivity, they will feast as a sole unit who convene to conquer the Dark Ones and to forever bind the Dark from interfering in the way of the Light.

"That's it," Alexandra says, breaking her concentration as she escorts the broom back to the corner.

"We go in and take out the Demon..." Alexandra is flush.

Rose looks up from the pot of potatoes, "What if they hurt her?" Rose isn't certain they should move forward because what if she in fact is sacrificed but her soul is taken by the Goddess to live out eternity there?

Rose addresses her concern.

Alexandra thinks for the moment. "Our intention is to take back what is rightfully ours."

"Maybe we do just that." Lucy is candid and maybe naively optimistic.

The women return from the store and place their burlap totes, filled with Witchcraft booty, upon the kitchen table.

"There's enough of us," Amber says as the Sister's Coven enters the room through a portal from the cold outdoors – they got the memo to prepare for Samhain and have made their arrival festive, "so we separate them and bring them back to Brighton."

"You underestimate her intense power." Rose is grounded in reality.

"We know she is pure evil," Sydney says.

"She's capable of doing anything…" Paisley adds but Sydney gives her a nudge.

Priscilla takes the cue, "She'll do whatever it takes to secure her status as a Dark Witch, but that doesn't mean we can't stop her."

"Well said," Alexandra is pleased. "We will begin with three days of protection spells." She concedes after rationalizing the extent of Goldie's power on behalf of Rose, but Rose is too well aware that protection spells did very little in the past; Rose is intensely afraid.

"We will go there and find that baby girl." Alexandra can sense Rose's admonition regarding Goldie and her powers.

The girls all nod and procure to reach such power for themselves.

"We fight fire with fire." Alexandra is fuming but she settles down a bit to keep the good faith of the Light in the face of all the girls.

The motivation is coursing through their   veins.

Hanna finds a locked door.

"This is where they have him detained." She can sense his presence because she is especially connected to the suffering just like being connected to Michael at one point. She notices however that the

416

voices have stopped. Their own breathing sounds heavy amid the silence. There is a smell of smoke smoldering from somewhere in the area.

"Someone has entered the catacombs," Leisha says. She and Goldie are secure within the dark underground. The smoke rises to a high vantage point within the deep, dark cave but their location is obscured by the thick of the expansive outdoors but Hanna can sense she needed to be in Vermont and it turns out her intuition was right. Lorde was a key component in finding their location but Hanna thinks of her grandmother's *Book of Shadows* in her satchel and she wonders if something within those pages can aid her in what to do or where to go next.

Goldie is standing over a bubbling cauldron that permeates the space with dead newt fragrance to ward off unwanted guests but Rhoda and Hanna hold their nose.

They appear as if they could vomit.

"Oh well, we can let him have a snack." Goldie speaks in a hissing voice as if her tongue was forked and she could devour rats whole.

"This close to the dear little infant's sacrifice?" Leisha has a dark and decrepit soul.

"He's starving though – don't you think we should let him have a taste?"

All joking aside, "Herschel Beecham is still only half man and half beast. We cannot compromise the sacrifice."

"What do you know about the Demon?" Lucy is getting inquisitive.

"She keeps her pet she plans to use to fulfill the darkest prophecy." Alexandra considers her word choice.

"To shed the blood of the most innocent on the night of the full moon, the day of the Winter Solstice, when the darkness can become the most powerful. She plans to sacrifice my baby for the night!"

Rose is desperate. She wonders if they can pull off such a feat.

"We don't exactly know the Goddess's intentions." Alexandra is looking for the positive to comfort her daughter.

"She wants her soul. Will taking my baby's soul fulfill the prophecy? Will my baby's death fulfill the pact to bring order between the dark and the light?"

"No." Alexandra is lost for words. Her daughter's logic is sound, but she must help Rose to remember that she is a witch and witches must use their senses.

"Remember your senses."

"I sense exactly that" Rose says and she exits the room.

Alexandra turns to the room full of women "We will perform a ritual with the best of intentions." She hopes to keep them on board.

"It's like a case of déjà vu again" Paisley says to Priscilla.

"We have to remember that we did succeed once" Sydney says.

419

"We must succeed again." Amber is adamant.

"Tell me about it." Alexandra's voice is a whisper.

"Hanna's child was to be sacrificed on the night of the Winter Solstice…" Sydney explains.

"Upon the top of Mount Katahdin…" Paisley adds.

"On the highest point North." Priscilla sighs.

"Is that her intention now then?" Alexandra contemplates aloud.

"We destroyed the mountain…" Sydney is trying to be soft.

"We destroyed the mountain but we let Goldie go." Paisley looks morose.

"We're so sorry…" Priscilla's voice chimes, "if we didn't let her go…"

"This wouldn't be happening," Paisley finishes her sentence.

"Don't be sorry," Alexandra says, but she cannot hide her angst.

They become aware of a sigh around the corner and find Rose who is sullen.

"Yes," she cries, "Goldie is repeating history."

"Well, let's come together this time…" Alexandra says and she removes a red candle stick from the burlap bag and she escorts them to the altar in the great room.

"This one is for the Demon they keep locked away."

Outside the Ravens are stirring.

Alexandra begins cleaning and consecrating her magical tools that are to be instilled with their intentions.

Hanna jolts as a hand touches her back – "June!" She says too loudly.

The walls of the cavern produce an echo. Rhoda hushes them and Malaki comes into view and crouches beside them.

"How did you find me here?"

"We are only lucky after finding this…" June holds up Hanna's original satchel.

"Jace must have lost this." Hanna is using her senses as she feels the satchel in her hands and she can sense his energy as if he had it in his possession.

"It was lying on a pile of dirt. I opened it and found the athame blade and the wand I only remember you using."

"Thank you."

"I tripped right over it."

"But why are you here?"

"Because I had a note – worthy of being written by the greatest teacher – and it was written that if the note was found then so too was his great staff and we are to meet in the catacombs."

"We followed the energy of the staff."

Hanna holds it in view.

Rhoda waves her hand yielding the light before her face "The sorcerer told us we would come in contact with your magical things on this journey."

The Ravens are retreating. Alexandra peers out the window and nods that the time is approaching.

The voices in the catacombs are diminished.

"Is it possible," Hanna says, as they listen intently, "that they want to hide until their sacrifice is complete?"

"Most certainly," Rhoda says, "they wish to perform the most heinous crime and they do not care to be bothered by petty interruptions."

"Then they think we are no match for them."

"Contrarily, Hanna," Rhoda says, "they know we are a match for them."

"She won't stop until she kills one more person…" Hanna says.

"Or a dog…" Hanna recognizes Sydney's voice who is communicating with her telepathically.

Hanna closes her eyes for better reception. She can see intuitively using her third eye that back at Brighton they are preparing a ritual and Hanna can feel the intensity of Alexandra's demise in her grief to take back baby girl Elizabeth.

The baby cries but she cannot be heard.

Why does Hanna suddenly feel so far away? At this moment she thinks about Jace when a light appears at the end of a tunnel.

"That might be for us," Rhoda says as the light dims and then turns to black.

"Should we follow it?" June says.

"Not yet." Rhoda whispers, hoping to find the little yellow bird.

That would give her great comfort, then she searches her soul, and her heart hoping that her intuition will tell her of the light when Hanna speaks.

"The Goddess wants a baby… maybe she…"

June coughs.

"Is here too." Hanna finishes.

Malaki points to Hanna's satchel, "Is there anything in that that can help us?"

"I'm not sure," she says, "it's my grandmother's *Book of Shadows*."

Then she considers that she and Rhoda have two great staffs.

"The light we just saw could have been a celestial body."

"Or the magic of a great staff?" Malaki is following her thought processes.

He recalls the light Grandall exuded from his being when he was in possession of the staff.

"The Goddess says Grandall has been reborn." Malaki remembers his wisdom well.

"Conception produces a glow like that," Rhoda nods.

"Something just happened," June says, but it is unclear to them exactly what has occurred.

"Then let's go find out." Malaki is firm.

As the day gives way to night Alexandra opens the sacred circle with her athame blade; she carves a mighty circle as the women place candles upon the floor to mark its place and they etch a pentacle at its center. Alexandra places a red candle in the center of the pentacle and she lights the wick.

"We will not be calling upon the Guardians in this rite." She lowers her head.

The women follow her lead; she extends her hands with the athame blade piercing the night so she begins:

Hail to the Goddess of the night!

Hear us! We call upon you in this rite, from the underworld we bring you here to aid us by thy will be done.

There is a full moon outside the window.

The Goddess of the Underworld came to us.

The lightning crashes. The Goddess of Storms parts the sky where a great vessel moves across the sky like an ancient ship of the dead. As the ship lowers, a blue light is cast outward and from the ship, the Goddess of the Night is cloaked in a dark cape and she emerges from its stern. She does not speak, but she extends her hands outward, and the blue light extends from her fingertips. They

426

become enamored by the blue light like a thread that is woven from them.

Why have you called upon us in this darkest night? Her voice is piercing.

The thunder cracks and the massive vessel hovers over them.

The Great Goddess peers with eyes of turquoise green and her iridescent flesh is pale against blue skin like the light that she emanates.

We call upon you for a certain witch wishes to rise above your great power.

No witch shall be greater than the Goddess of the Underworld. She frowns. *She will abide by the laws of darkness.*

Sydney thinks of Jace at the moment and tries to telepathically join Hanna in her pursuit of Goldie and her bed-ridden Demon.

What is it that you wish?

The dark Goddess means business. She does not lightly entertain being summoned.

For the witch to give up the baby that is not her own.

427

She wishes to sacrifice the blood of the most innocent?

Yes, she does, great Goddess. Alexandra admits.

But only a Demon can do so.

She has already created the entity to perform the deed.

Alexandra does not fold beneath her immense power. Rose shivers in her great power as the electric blue light engulfs the premise and surrounds them with the aura of the dead. The Goddess's flesh is made of this light and Rose considers how they have summoned the dark one over the Goddess of the Celestial City – not knowing her intentions for wanting a human child for herself. Or the energy of one after a sacrifice? No one knows. The Darkness is cold and the electric blue light is the lifeline of the Goddess in the earthly realm. The Goddess has locks of flaming red hair that curls beneath her cloak. There is a breeze in her presence and Rose shivers. The rest of the women shiver too as Alexandra has called together her newest Coven to coincide with the expertise of the Sister's Coven as they work to channel energy back to Hanna. But Sydney cannot maintain a connection particularly because the energy of a dark one is not so open. Alexandra grows with the hope that the dark ones will put a stop to the efforts of a measly little witch.

The blue light turns to smoke that casts over them like a thick fog and the Goddess leaves them without speaking another word. She lifts her hands and the vessel outside rises and she retreats toward it.

Continue She says from her vessel that hovers amid the parted skies as the Storm Goddess aids them.

Hail! Alexandra says upon her command thinking only of Baby Elizabeth who she will not call Summer because her granddaughter is not the child of a Goddess.

On this dark night, in this time of dark sorcery – I call upon the witch to grace us with her presence — Goldie Silver we call upon thee! Rise from your place of hiding and come hither by thy will be done! So mote it be!

From a place above them, the women come together to form a mighty circle as they hold hands and the red candle burns at the center of a pentacle – they stand in perfect unity as the darkest clouds part in the night sky. Goldie's face flashes with eyes of red and she sneers as Jace appears from the deep cavernous black hole that has opened in the night sky. Like a vortex out of the ether emerge the bodies of flesh, Kamra and Victoria, who he summoned from the dead and they are shrouded in smoke.

You are blessed, the Goddess says and the dark black sky opens to reveal the rain of hail and strong wind as the lightning fires from among them and the roof begins to shake from the weight of them but the Goddess amid her vessel is still visible from outside where a portal connects them and they are all shrouded in dark energy.

When you succeed, bring them to me! The Goddess beckons as Goldie's wide eyes flash in crimson and from her open mouth she wails as a torrent of rain floods from her mouth and the Goddess of Storms fights back to close the portal and the torrent of water and hail closes causing them to lose Goldie as predicted by the Goddess.

She is a strong witch but one who is entirely out of her place. The Goddess is angry because a mere witch has succeeded in escaping her energy and the vortex opened by the Goddess of Storms – no witch has ever succeeded in controlling the elements – the duties of only the Goddesses.

"Wait!" Jace shouts. Goldie held him prisoner along with the dead he awakened but Goldie made one slip up and closed the portal with the powers of the elements before she could bring Jace and the cousins back to the black hole she kept them in.

Your work is yet to be done!

The Goddess is angry and she retreats backwards like leaving time in her wake, and she enters the dark void where time ceases to exist – like Grandall being reborn after giving Sterling another chance at life.

The Goddess's face becomes a hint of smoke and the ether closes to leave the elements to the Storm Goddess who sends the wind and the hail into a fury and Rose breaks the perfect circle to approach the window, now that the portal being closed separates them. She peers past the glass to find Jace alongside the girls Kamra and Victoria who have materialized from their ethereal bodies; all Rose can think is that their mothers, and their families, would never accept the presence of their newly made bodies no matter how much they miss them because such things are the workings of a witch.

Then they hear the cackle of laughter from Goldie as the thunder hammers like the sound of rain falling on a tin roof; each piece of hail sends them a fury of sounds so alarming they know the anger of the

Goddesses but Alexandra is content in knowing they have gained the attention of the Goddess of the Dark.

"We are sorry." Victoria cries.

Weak! Goldie's voice hisses, *weak pathetic little brats!* She can see from the orb of glass.

Goldie is shunned by the Dark Goddess herself but Jace and Alexandra both know there is yet magic and sorcery to be done.

A flash of light sends them an electrical shock and Kamra's and Victoria's bodies glimmer revealing that their energetic bodies are materialized but are that of energy and not biology.

Alexandra falls as the energy drains from her body and she feels the fatigue that overwhelms a witch after summonsing a powerful entity like a Goddess.

Alexandra loses her hope as she has lost faith in the Goddess of the Celestial City.

Chapter Twenty-Five

Hanna takes the cold stone wand and begins to charge it with the power of intention until Rhoda swipes it from her hands.

"The curse..." she reminds her in a whisper.

"I forgot..." Hanna's voice is soft as she considers the fact that she cannot practice Witchcraft as if learning for the first time. The idea stings still.

They can lift a curse but the energy is never the same. She can feel the weight of the Dark piercing her every intention. A curse can be counter-cursed but that is the workings of Darkness. Witches and Warlocks know that only love and compassion can heal the Dark. Hanna must resolve her family's struggles to keep her dear children from the same fate placed upon her.

Hanna gives the Mighty Staff of Grandall to Malaki who uses the staff to tap the wand three times; the wand begins to glow and Hanna watches as Rhoda chants and the coolness of the wand turns warm in her hand and even Hanna can feel the heat. The warmth radiates down her arm and they become subdued by its beauty and majesty.

"I don't see how the Goddess can be bad," June says while watching the glow.

"We cannot take a chance … it's like a leap of faith… and if the Goddess is in her right mind then she would understand our intentions are of the highest good."

"We need to take Summer and get out of here." June affirms.

"That's all fine … but what are we going to do to keep Goldie from kidnapping another infant?"

They sigh. No one has that answer.

Alexandra does not have the backup from the Goddess of the Celestial City – it seems they are all gunning for the same infant but for different purposes. Sydney tries to assure her that they are in the right place

435

as Hanna is working within and they are working outside with the intentions of helping them locate baby Elizabeth especially since Sydney can telepathically communicate with Hanna and if that doesn't pan out then she can intuit from Rhoda.

Hanna pushes forward to find the baby the Goddess calls Summer. She is persevering, however, to take baby Elizabeth back and give her to her biological family. She is left with reasoning that two entities, a witch and a Celestial Goddess, have expressed their own intentions with her.

"The light was someone exiting the Underworld; leaving the place of the dark for the place of light." Hanna ponders, then her intuitive mind veers to the thought of Jace – how is anyone able to make the conversation from a dark state to a light state without his aid in transitioning?

She thinks that Jace must still be with them wherever that may be.

"If only we could follow the baby's cry," June says.

Rhoda has her own thought, "The Sorcerer said the Dark Ones dwell where there was a seed planted."

"We can only go so far as to tap into their minds," Hanna adds as they try to muster a plan.

June and Malaki continue to follow their lead; their minds are sharp when it comes to intuition and telepathy.

Then they come to a dead end. The door goes absolutely nowhere.

"They have done this on purpose." Rhoda says.

"The Catacombs are full of these." June has the epiphany as the past with Alysiah is at her heart.

Hanna guides them in retreating the way they came. When they find the light of day they are on top of the mountain despite the cold. They have the most majestic views, and June cannot help but to think of Mount Katahdin in Maine, named *The Great Mountain* and how they had to destroy it to protect Aly. They destroyed a mountain but they let Goldie go. They failed. The evil Witch has returned …. The Mountain could not get back despite turning back in time. They could only preserve Sterling through Grandall who gave his own life for another. Hanna also thinks how a place of such immeasurable beauty could be a place of such horrific happenings such as the sacrifice of something so innocent and pure.

Alexandra suffers as the women try to console her. She, like her daughter, is losing faith, even in the Craft. Their spells don't seem to work and their desires seem to fall on deaf ears. The Goddess of the Underworld has left them to deal with Goldie – a witch against a witch – and Alexandra cannot help but to fret that her magic is not strong enough against a witch so ugly as Goldie. She wishes Grandall could be among them. She considers that his staff may not be so mighty as it is not with the majesty of a Great   Elder.

Hanna can still feel his energy through the staff. The wand is now warm with a glow as Rhoda has blessed the tool and charged it with positive intentions. The tool radiates in a kind of Celestial Excellence.

The energy of the Mountain changes and another warm glow appears to their side.

"Hello Hanna," Sydney says as she steps through a portal.

The air is cold but the warmth of the wand and the staff make teleporting possible. The energy is high among them whereas back in Brighton the energy is dismal and low; that is the place where Jace is to be – a new kind of energy that is like the Underworld because the souls there, like Kamra and Victoria, are not ready for the light – or were they?

"There was a light in the Catacombs," Hanna informs Sydney, "maybe some kind of transition."

"Keep the faith. You are right. Jace transitioned with Victoria and Kamra…"

"And then what?" Hanna is eager.

439

"They were absorbed back into the Night. Hostage not to Goldie herself, but the Goddess of the Underworld!"

"And Jace? He was so cold…"

"Still freezing I'm afraid. We got nowhere. Nothing from the Goddess of the Dark and she took Jace and the girls I'm afraid."

"Jace is so powerful…" Hanna's voice is a whisper.

"Goldie is evermore."

The Underworld has essentially become Brighton or vice versa. The rest of the Sister's Coven move through and Sydney flashes them a warm smile that reveals her hope for finding baby Elizabeth. She doesn't say that she believes the Goddess wants the energy of a sacrificed child – she doesn't say a word, but her smile radiates hope.

The snow blankets the trees; they admire the landscape out of the catacombs because the simplicity of the cold, caused by the position of the sun, is not like the cold of the Underworld; the landscape does not possess the bitterness of that kind of energy.

"We have to get inside her head."

June thinks how they are all on the same page.

The girls remove their backpacks and they light a fire from kindling wood they stored, and they warm their tea over the embers. They have small amounts of food and some blankets. Sydney presents her story recollection to Hanna and June listens. They reminisce on their first experience and how Aly was saved. Nothing of their first experience tells them how to find Elizabeth. This experience is entirely new and Sydney also relates Alexandra's evocation of the Goddess of the Underworld, how the awakening startled Jace from his imprisonment in a cavern where he was lured by the baby's cry.

"That was almost us too then..." Hanna says thinking of their excursion through the mines and the caverns. All built some time ago by man. Now a refuge for the most devious and sinister witch they have ever known.

Hanna thinks that Helga is not aiding them this time because she is waiting to possess the energy of the child once she has been sacrificed. She thinks that even the most Celestial body with the intentions of the Highest Good can go astray – not just from a lust for power – but for an intense desire.

Helga wants a daughter and she calls baby Elizabeth Summer. Hanna tries to understand what her intentions and motivations are exactly but the Goddess is in rogue or so elusive that she cannot be reached. Hanna shakes the feeling as Sydney interrupts her mental pondering.

"How can we get into her mind?"

Hanna considers that Sydney is aware that Goldie is more adept in prying into their minds, even Rhoda's, than they are capable of from their end.

"Why are some telepaths better senders than receivers?" Rhoda says aloud.

Her questioning makes them consider their experiences and their strengths as witches and only Rhoda can call herself an adept. The rest are learning.

Grandall was an adept. Hanna thinks. She then wonders what she can do with the power of the staffs and the newly charged wand. Her grandmother's wand. She thinks an adept like Rhoda can use the energy for good intentions despite the curse.

"It's not typical of a good witch to exert mind control over another witch," June says.

"No, we're not that kind of adept." Rhoda agrees.

"How can we use our minds against her?" Priscilla asks.

"Can we control her? The way she does it to us?" Paisley adds.

"Maybe not completely," Hanna ponders, "but it's worth a try."

"And we do have Rhoda," Amber says, and looks toward her, the most adept witch among them.

"I have never used the mind for such things," Hanna says, and she is nervous.

It is now Halloween back at Brighton. Or Samhain for the Witches. But Danica and Lucinda have formed a communion in a candle-lit vigil outside of *Mystical Mountains.* They use the holiday of a non-witch against a witch and Sterling is alone. She enters the back room and she finds comfort in the altar she has created among the boxes of supplies. The back room is not what it used to be when it was the place of evocation, performing spells and raising the energy of the dead. It was a place of performing rituals – now it is the place where she prays over the altar. She is seemingly a lost witch due to the circumstances; her sister used Black Magic spells to cause a heinous crime against the non-witch community – a spell so evil it caused death by choking. Sterling considers all things and feels the presence of something dark has shrouded her love and passion for The Craft.

The protesters' raging outside can be heard.

"No more Witchcraft," one of them says, but Sterling cannot place the voice.

"We stand against your sorcery." Another says.

Sterling considers momentarily that if they knew more, or knew better, that they would stand against Dark Sorcery such as that that is practiced by Goldie but then she kneels at her altar and she prays to the Goddess of Celestial Light. She prays for Elizabeth. She prays for her sister. She prays until it becomes a chant – until the witch in her feels alive again despite the moment and she rekindles her courage...

Bless be the child Elizabeth she says
By thy will be done no one will harm anyone!
So Mote it Be!

The fire of the protest outside is raging, and there is a communion of bodies outside the store doors who protest the contents of a magical store. A store not just for selling magical things, but a store that is in itself a magical thing and Sterling begins to feel the warmth of positive, radiant energy exuding from within her and extending without in her environment. To Sterling that is the blessing of the Goddess Helga.

To Hanna, the radiant energy of positive light is the radiance of the Celestial City itself despite the Goddess. Despite her wishes for a child and whatever her intentions might be.

There are innocent children going door-to-door to collect candy.

The night is brisk but the children feel safe.

Sterling wishes that all children could be safe on this night. She does not know what Goldie is planning and if it is to take place on Samhain when the Veil to the Underworld is its thinnest, when evocation can take place – when an evil Witch can summon the energy of a more powerful Dark Goddess – or worse, a Demonic entity. But Sterling considers that there is none for

Goldie to evoke – she is in herself entirely the most evil anyone has ever known.

She is the Witch who kidnaps an infant child, who wishes to be the most powerful entity, and one who can starve a Demon to bring out her own self-absorbed desires.

Then she feels the light in her own abdomen. She feels the energy of Grandall. Intuitively she knows it is him who speaks with her from within. The Light of Grandall is now Sterling herself. She knows not what to do exactly, but she knows her prayer of good intentions can be heard.

She thinks of Alexandra who is falling into despair and with that kind of energy comes the darkness. There is Jace presiding over her. There are Kamra and Victoria, alive as the dead ones from a materialized body; the energy of the dead permeates Brighton. But the Dark Goddess has taken them. Sterling intuits with the energy of Grandall filling her soul that Alexandra is presiding with the Goddess of the Underworld who, once manifested, seeks to control the souls of the dead for evil deeds in order for the dark to preside over the Celestial City. Over the Light.

Sterling knows that the Goddess of the Underworld is taking Alexandra's soul and even Jace is being controlled by the energy. She thinks that no one, especially the non-witch, should find their dead child alive again. She doesn't know how to make it right again. She does not feel worthy of having the enchanting soul of the Elder within her.

"Sister," Sterling says, kneeling behind her altar; the scent of sandalwood fills the room.

She focuses her positive, radiant energy on her sister; she imagines her face when they were five; she surrounds her sister's image in her mind's eye with love.

"Malediction," Sydney says, "when a witch directs psychic attention with an evil intent..."

"A hex," Hanna says, minding her cursed dilemma.

"We can do the opposite." Sydney says as if Sterling's energy is contagious.

"What do you propose we should do?" Hanna is trying to be safe.

"We find her heart."

"If she still has one." Amber isn't buying into it.

Silver takes her lit candle from her altar and enters the outdoors.

"All we can do is pray for you." Lucinda still has tears.

Danica stands beside her sister. She quietly bows her head and raises her hands to the air as if to reach out to God.

Sterling knows that they, like her, can pray for safety. She wishes for them to see that not all witches are evil. That most witches pray, or chant, or meditate for the Highest Good of All with No Harm Done to None.

That is the Mantra of the Good Witch.

She yearns to heal them. She does not know how so outside in their vigil she prays too because perhaps the God, in the Witch realm, Atlas is listening and so, then, perhaps the God will convene where the Goddess has gone astray.

Beneath the light of a full moon, while the innocent children of the town outside of Brighton trick-or-treat for candy, the witch prays with them so that all might find the Light of God.

Chapter Twenty-Six

"Pray she finds the Light of God," Danica says and they commune to raise their hands. Sterling can feel their energy and it is a positive kind of light. A light that she knows was vacant for her sister when she was being harassed by the girls who they prayed for but now they pray over the sister of the evil witch. Sterling joins them because she too can pray for her sister. She yearns to find her heart.

She does not realize that she is commencing in the same attempts as her Coven Sisters and she thinks about Rose and Alexandra who are at home in Brighton and she begins to pray for them to stay in the Light.

"We have prayed for the souls of our girls…" Lucinda says.

Jace can feel them too. He holds steady to the girls' materialized bodies.

"We have prayed for our girls..." Danica says aloud to the members convening outside.

"We pray their souls have found the light of God," Lucinda continues.

Sterling realizes they all wish for the same thing.

Rose shudders over her mother as Alexandra falls to the depression and her yearning for her granddaughter overtakes her being and Jace contemplates what he needs to do to bring together the Treaty that he knows must happen to balance the Light and the Dark for good.

"They have," Sterling insists, "because you have prayed for them."

Sterling is grateful her store is not burning – that they come in peace. She silently says an enchantment to wish them blessings from the Goddess. She firmly believes that Helga is good.

Rhoda removes a precious plant from her bag of mojo: a Mandrake Root that is known to possess magical powers.

"I was saving this," she says as she stirs the kindling for the fire, "now, going within to seek answers begins with meditation." In a deep trance Rhoda helps Hanna to find the passage into the light as she connects herself to her psyche and two minds become like one. In a small portal, like a bright circle of light, Hanna finds her guide: Tia.

"Welcome back," she says in her soft, angelic voice.

Hanna moves fluidly between walls made of light as her ethereal body detaches from her physical body; she shimmers against the iridescent backdrop. There is in the distance a great cascade as the water can be heard gushing over rock formations. Everything is splendid and beautiful. Rhoda concentrates as she too leaves her body to join Hanna in the circle of light where they find themselves in awe of their surroundings.

If only Goldie could see the light, she thinks but in the body of light thoughts are things and can be heard by all. Rhoda nods. There are angelic people, spirits of the departed, moving beyond the wall of light that encapsulates them. Hanna finds a pair of golden doors and Tia motions for them to move toward them; they float in a gentle drift and notice the doors look solid as if made of the Earth's gold. Hanna uses the hook loop to knock gently on the door but a sound like an organ is made and the doors open before them. Tia guides their spirit bodies through the doors and they enter a kind of enchanting cavern like a castle nestled in the rock face of a gigantic mountain. Hanna recognizes the Angelic City before them and she finds a throne within the Temple. A new Temple. One she has never seen before; she can feel the weight of immense power. The Souls of the Elders gather before them and they guide their way to the Goddess herself; Helga moves swiftly like a gentle breeze; she is the most brilliant light anyone has ever seen; she is made of colors that cannot be found on Earth.

Hanna wonders why they have been graced with her presence and she wants to inquire about baby Elizabeth.

Helga speaks, "You know that it is my wish to behold a precious child," and she motions with the spreading of her wings where there is also the God, Atlas, who oversees the Celestial City seemingly far away.

"You can't love her…" Hanna finds herself saying because she is not entirely subdued by her beauty; she maintains a firm composure of one who almost lost her beloved daughter to a Witch and her Demon.

"Hello again, Hanna," Helga says and the walls seem to pulsate with life. She remains calm with the composure of a very smooth cat. "I have the most Divine plan…" she continues and the light reverberates in a rhythmic motion as if they are living and breathing.

455

"Such hatred could cause these walls to crumble…" Helga is firm.

A hole opens in the wall made of light and Hanna is moved through it like a tunnel that acts as a vacuum and she is led outside the Celestial City and through the Darkness of the Ether where anger cannot hold up the walls and Hanna can feel the shifting of the Celestial City that moves beyond the realm of space and time where they find themselves.

She turns to Rhoda who uses telepathy to communicate, "You feel strongly about the baby…"

"To remain with her mother."

"Then we must trust the Goddess…"

"Anger can damage the walls…"

"Damage the walls of the city like your anger, Hanna."

"So she kicked us out."

"She assures you her plan is Divine."

"To take a murdered child and raise her in the City of Light …. To keep her from her mortal birth mother?"

"We don't know…"

"No, we don't… but she also did not bother to explain herself either."

Amber finds Jace; in the vastness of darkness he floats in an endless drift. Amber is once again in awe of him; the way he exchanged his life for his daughter makes her think differently about him.

"I'm surprised you're not Hanna," he says with mild curiosity.

"No, I'm not Hanna." Her voice carries like an echo in the Ether.

Amber's physical body breathes mildly as her ethereal body joins Jace and she pulsates subtly like the light that wavers to sound.

"Why are you here alone?" She asks.

"To get out of the way."

"What do you mean?"

"I can help Hanna better this way."

"I don't understand."

"I can help her help herself better."

"By stealing her magical tools?"

"I was only following directions."

"What directions?"

"I can't say."

"Why not?"

"Only when the time is right can I help Hanna."

"Why do you continue to help her?"

"Why are you here to help me?"

"I didn't say that."

"True."   He   says   flatly.

Rhoda pulls Hanna onward to the realm of the Shamans; her people have long believed in the human spirit that lives a dual existence with the physical body: one made of the light (or the dark) and the other that is made of matter upon the Earth. Rhoda shows her a garden and within that garden there are passageways.

"Depending on one's enlightenment each path offers a different destination."

"I'm not sure of my path then," Hanna says.

"Even if not known by the physical self, the spiritual self can be more advanced…"

"I can't believe I'm doing all this without the aid of magic…"

"The Curse can be cured and all can be right again because the mind is another vehicle to salvation… just intuit where you are to go."

Hanna uses the energy she feels in her light body so that the spirit can direct her on where to go while the physical body stays at home base. It takes a moment when Hanna grows brighter with a purple hue and she finds Tia again and Hanna finds a glimmer of hope….

"Goldie must have a spirit body here as well."

"Oh?" Rhoda muses, "a light body?"

"This is the realm where the mind is. It might be a mind of long ago… but it is the mind none-the-less."

Hanna hovers in her spirit body within the garden; the layers of existence are raw, pure and full of energy and matter – the two states of existence.

"The Shamans have created this magical place through their spirit journeys." Rhoda explains, "the layers of existence are vast."

Then Hanna realizes that she is to reach another layer of consciousness and she turns toward a deeper kind of trance and together they enter the level of awareness that could shed of times past as Rhoda joins Hanna into the depths of her psyche.

Hanna and Rhoda are calm and Tia is a smidge of light within the garden but Hanna begins to burn brighter as the level of her awareness deepens and Hanna finds first that she can perceive Alexandra's thoughts; she is thinking about black magic, about forcing baby Elizabeth out of her wrath – if only she could become more powerful within the dark – to become an ever greater dark witch – she would give herself to get her granddaughter back to her mother. Hanna shutters. Alexandra would become like Jace in that case. Even dark thoughts feel like dark things like insidious crimes. As Alexandra sleeps she thinks and dreams of dark crimes; she is at the edge of despair and she wishes to take her revenge on Goldie. Then Hanna thinks again how her own anger could damage the walls of the Celestial City and she feels concern now for Alexandra who is falling into depression.

Hanna feels the presence of someone else within the garden, and she has a vision of Goldie before adolescence. She has the epiphany that she can reach into Goldie and locate her dreams and desires prior to Victoria and Kamra – before they turned her heart to cold stone. As Hanna transcends time and space, she has a panoramic view of the catacombs that exists physically as if right below them in the place they dwell as if the gardens are there looming above them.

Rhoda perceives her thoughts immediately…

"The Shamans built this Garden after you saved your daughter from the Demon and his evil witch…"

"But I learned that they were not just evil…

"There was a time when they were innocent…

"No matter how young."

"Yes…"

Goldie doesn't flinch. She resides in the caves of the underground awaiting the Winter Solstice when she can sacrifice baby Elizabeth as she starves the Demon who will do the deed at the highest summit North – this time in Vermont.

"Not even destroying a mountain could stop her." Hanna says.

"No, not even destroying a mountain was enough…" Rhoda agrees.

"So what can be done without destroying her?"

"That is for you to decide."

"Why me?"

"Why you?"

"I feel compelled."

"Yes…"

"She feels rigid and cold."

Their garden begins to become colder still as Hanna locates her mind. In Goldie's thoughts are only the desire to murder baby Elizabeth. To shed her blood and offer her sacrifice to the Goddess of the Underworld.

"But she wants too much power."

"What else do you feel?"

"Alexandra has made a pact with the Goddess of the Dark…"

"To do what exactly?"

"She will slay Goldie and offer her body to the Goddess of the Underworld and promise to serve her always."

"Anything else?"

"The Goddess will take her…"

"Goddess?"

"Helga and the Goddess of the Dark dual over the thoughts of having her."

Suddenly Hanna's aura turns to a darkened gold as if the light and the dark are folding and the layer of the surface turns to something of mud.

"We are firmly merging in a state between the light and the dark," Rhoda says.

"Like Samhain."

"The Veil between the worlds becomes thin."

"What can be done here?"

"We are officially at war now."

"This is the existence of the duality between the Worlds…"

"Where the war is not on land but of the mind."

Hanna can feel Goldie as if she is all around her. Her mind is vast and dark and empty other than the contemplation to sacrifice the blood of the most innocent. Hanna can feel too that Goldie is not as strong and powerful without the Wisdom of the Old Crone. The energy surrounding Goldie is like a brick wall…

"But even bricks can crumble…" Hanna says.

"How?" Rhoda tests her further.

"Like we did to the Mountain."

"It takes clear focus and clear intention."

"So Mote it Be." Hanna confirms. "So Mote it Be."

But Goldie is too fast witted and she finds them there and as she disrupts their consciousness the walls of the angelic garden begin to crumble and Tia takes the only portal back to the Celestial City before the Garden can crumble completely and Hanna is no longer in her mind.

As Goldie finds a portal to her soul, she finds that Hanna is not an open vessel and is more like an adept witch when she concentrates vigorously and she finds not one mind, but two, and she realizes that Hanna is attached to an adept and she is not working alone.

"The one whose mother doesn't want her." She tries to break Hanna.

Goldie is menacing and her voice is like nails to a chalkboard.

Hanna is however unfazed.

She thinks of the Curse. Of the Peace Treaty.

"The one with the grandmother … a weak little witch that one was."

She reminds Hanna of death by choking and she thinks of her physical body sleeping.

"Cursed just the same as she."

Goldie confirms Hanna's fears.

Hanna tries not to think. Tries not to let her into her psyche. But Goldie has a tight connection to Hanna and she hears her cackling voice again, and the sounds of rats' nails scurrying across cavernous walls, and Hanna knows they are just below – but the powers of the mind do not have physical boundaries, only imagined ones, if they do not let the garden crumble – if, at war in the mind, they can extract her or find within her a memory of something bound to the light. Hanna concentrates and finds the rhythm of her mortally beating heart and it is through that opening where she intends to channel

her energy and find the glimmer of a soul that
once was not so dark.

Chapter Twenty-Seven

Goldie forces Hanna to view an image of her grandmother lying dead on the ground – a warning to what is to come for Hanna if she folds under the weight of Goldie's own mind and memories. She is unable to breathe and soon her heart will stop, but Hanna does not lose her concentration. She does not focus on the image of her grandmother nor the threat that she is cursed to the same fate as her grandmother, Rose, Victoria or Kamra – that for once Goldie is bound to lose. Then Hanna finds a memory; Goldie is lying on the ground too. Her nose is bloody and she has just been beaten by Kamra as Victoria stands over her body scathing away insulting Goldie as nothing but ugly and vile.

"So she became vile…" Rhoda affirms the coincidence.

"She became as others perceived her," Hanna says as they continue to channel mental energy.

"The only one to pay attention…"

"Was Leisha."

Hanna thinks she hears Goldie's words as she continues to be subdued within awareness of what it was like to be the girl sobbing on the ground with a bloody nose, chastised and scorned as pitiful, low, and ugly. Hanna can still feel the pulsating of her thoughts being imposed on Rhoda and she can attach her awareness to the rhythmic breathing of her physical body.

"Be careful." Rhoda warns, "Do not connect with your physical body."

Hanna shutters at the thought she almost led Goldie to her.

"Thinking of your body will open a portal. Stay focused. Stay grounded."

Momentarily it is as if they have the upper hand over Goldie.

Hanna has a thought as she brings her awareness back to the central body and the energy created by the mind: can she imprint a thought onto Goldie the way Goldie can do upon her mind?

She remembers Jace and although he is not present, she feels him within herself; she thinks about the pact to reconcile their differences – how in the end it worked for them because he would give his own life for his daughter – how Grandall gave his own life for Sterling. Hanna knows she has to somehow find a common ground to balance the light and the dark. She sends an image of the two halves of a crescent that make a whole unit with a celestial staff running down the center. The image burns in her mind's eye and begins to glow; Goldie's mind pulsates like a beating heart. Hanna can feel the throbbing between her temples back at home base, but within the cave where they sit in silence in a deep trance-like state, the ethereal body is able to go on journeys and to teleport and move through walls unlike the physical body. June can feel Hanna; they can also see her entrance into the depth of the spiritual realm but their own minds stay grounded within the cave; beyond that her mind is in a precarious state as she searches for a body – for Goldie, who would appear like a dark and hollow figure as an a ethereal body – but her own mind is like a single light particle. She does not want Goldie to perceive her without Hanna knowing first where she is located. She is a faint glimmer small enough to intrude on the conscience of another. Hanna focuses still while her body is at rest just as Rhoda has instructed and while Rhoda and June and Malaki think of maintaining the energy by imagining positive energy engulfing Hanna's second body within the cave – while her mind tries to impede in the body of Goldie. Consciousness takes on many layers, many forms of body and mind mastery. They focus on sending Hanna light and love but not too immensely so as not to overwhelm the aura of Hanna's mind. There is a faint mist engulfing her physical body that keeps her ethereal body strong within the cave and her mind equally strong as she searches for a way that Goldie might let her in involuntarily but without harm. Hanna can feel the coldness of a blank stare as the coldness is daunting but her mind does not shiver from the cold the way her body would. In this way she does not have to practice magic as she too needs to find a way to lift the curse. Hanna also searches for love – is Leisha's love enough? She directs her energy too on Leisha while the others focus on Hanna to shed their light and love upon her – energy needs to be contagious – as Hanna has learned the depth of being an adept in the way of Witchcraft through the mind and not just by magic.

She has learned how to leave her body. She has learned how to project her mental state into the awareness of others who are willing such as with Sydney, now she must learn how to effectively find the light of love within the mind of not just an adept, but the darkest of all witches. Hanna considers that at the end of every tunnel there is a glimmer of light and with that ounce of hope she presses on to locate Goldie's mind while she concentrates on the goodness of her sister – how Sterling fares at home within her store with the sanctity that the protestors are reaching a resolve – she uses that positive energy to find resolve within Goldie. She must find a way that Goldie can feel love despite being tormented by childish and foolish school girls – Goldie must find a way to see love over everything she endured. Leisha might be that vehicle of love and hope.

Rhoda begins to hum with the voice of a songbird with her attention turned to Hanna as she uses her third eye to open a channel within Leisha as an access point. Rhoda locates Leisha's mind herself and finds her childhood while Hanna still searches to enter deeper into Goldie. Leisha shows no indication that she is aware of Rhoda invading her mind and her memories. She finds Leisha as an only child. She finds too that her dear cousin Goldie is her only friend. From Leisha's point-of-view Rhoda learns that Sterling, like Rose, were popular within the community and paid very little attention to them. Goldie and Leisha became inseparable. They felt they only had one another.

Hanna has another clear thought as she works her way into Goldie's mind; Leisha, once, after stealing Alexis away from her duties as Guardian, declared herself as a dark one out of her devotion to her dear cousin. Hence, they wonder if she is truly the balance between the darkness and the light – and they consider if she can be the portal into Goldie's mind as they access that speck of light through an act of love. Does Leisha abide by the laws set forth in the decree to balance the light amid the darkness as a gateway to Goldie's heart – can they help her into the light simply by making her aware of an act of kindness as opposed to having an alliance with the dark? Hanna shivers momentarily at home base as her physical body flutters and she takes a deep breath to keep from shuttering and her ethereal body maintains the sitting posture; she projects her mind onto the mind of Goldie and together they work from within the underground to once again bring Goldie from the trenches and into the light of day.

Amber remains with Jace. Together they float in an endless drift.

"This is sorrow," Jace explains.

"It's a dark kind of peace," Amber says.

She realizes that Goldie does not even belong to the dark; the dark can be a vast place for growth that allows restless souls to heal but Goldie instead seeks to gain power. She wishes for the dark to have immense power over the light. Amber then thinks this is the place where Goldie needs to be. Leisha too. So that they both can heal from their childhood traumas.

Sydney is receptive as she communicates telepathically with Hanna and she receives thoughts outside of the ether in the state of the Shaman's Promised Land –

the space above the catacombs. The space of light and love they created to practice magic in the form of sorcery – the place where June and Malaki reside just outside the cave, the place where they can project mental awareness onto Hanna. Sydney perceives Hanna and Rhoda's ethereal body within the cave; June and Malaki in the Shamanic Temple outside the cave, and then she locates Hanna's mind and within her mind is a small connection with Goldie but not a complete and total entrance into her psyche. They do not want Goldie to feel their intrusion.

Hanna speaks telepathically to Rhoda from within the cave, "This place is too light and too buoyant for Goldie to reside."

But Rhoda cautions her not to communicate because the energy connection between them and Leisha and Goldie could be broken. Despite their ethereal bodies being together, Hanna feels very alone and Sydney can perceive that thought so she helps Hanna to stay grounded. Hanna feels her presence and her physical body takes another deep breath.

"She is not ready for an elevated place of peace," Sydney sends to Hanna as if Hanna's own mind has the thought. Hanna nods. They discontinue communication now that they are all on the same page. Hanna is relieved that June and Malaki are at peace within the Garden Grove created by the Shamans to protect them from the frost of winter where they go to retreat. She wishes she could feel Jace but Sydney intercepts her thought and projects the place of the ether into Hanna's mind's eye. Hanna receives an image of the ether and Amber has joined Jace to aid him within the space of darkness where sorrow goes to mourn – to the place where they hope Goldie will find herself. They wait patiently. Hanna understands Jace's place as the Overseer of the Dark. She understands Amber's love for Jace but not how they can find themselves together. She thinks of Kamra and Victoria who he resurrected from the dead who have cold, physical bodies like he once had. She does not feel that their presence from the dead will shed light on the situation with their mothers' mourning. She wonders how she can help them to heal too, like Goldie and Leisha. She wonders exactly what can happen to bring them all together.

"We need to take smaller steps." Sydney projects the thought onto Hanna whose heart breathes rhythmically in strides and Sydney sits in a meditative state upon the comforts of her couch where she is surrounded by her Coven Sisters; Priscilla and Paisley hold each of her hands as they project positive energy upon her so that she can have the energy to maintain a connection with Hanna. Entering Goldie's mind is a daunting task and they each hold onto one another in the mental capacity as being with Goldie physically is not enough. It was not enough to destroy a mountain, nor to find peace within her Demon – it is within her heart and soul where they need to help her to open her heart like a vessel and to aid her soul in finding peace. But Goldie is a stern and vile soul and they are up to a challenge like none other before; this time is ever more difficult because they have to find within her the desire to heal.

Hanna begins with that. She sends Goldie a slight thought of finding love. But Goldie's mind shutters and throws Hanna a message as if Goldie has the argument within her own head – her only love is to gain immense power and that thought makes Goldie smile. She sits within the catacomb not thinking about being on the highest summit North in Maine but being in the highest state while she contemplates sacrificing the blood of the most innocent – this time to spite the God of the Celestial City as she will return his efforts in blessing the child of Spring with that of offering the blood of the sacrificed child to the dark that will be devoured by the Demon she keeps locked away and starving. She no longer promises power to the Demon but takes full authority over his being and intends to dominate the darkness with immense power, power that will trump the power of the Goddess of the Underworld, where Jace and now Amber awaits. Alexandra too awaits at her altar contemplating becoming the follower of the Goddess to challenge Goldie and to somehow claim her granddaughter before it is too late.

The thoughts of the mind are instantaneous and Hanna can feel Sydney within her mind and she feels at ease knowing that she is not utterly alone. Together they imagine light and love; Rhoda looks for a channel within Leisha; June and Malaki hold Hanna in light and love; Jace and Amber await her arrival and still Goldie's mind projects the deepest regards of hell onto them and all they can feel is hatred at the highest and darkest level. They shutter. They can feel the intensity of desire to offer sacrifice blood to the dark, and they cannot hear the cries of the infant screaming and they wonder if she is alive at all.

"But she must be," Rhoda says after perceiving their thoughts to give them both hope. Goldie is stone cold like a great piece of ice over the North Pole.

"She is so far North she'll offer the child's sacrificed blood from the cavern," Sydney speaks telepathically to Hanna and Rhoda too perceives the thought.

They are cautious and careful, but they do realize that Goldie is focused and determined that she cannot perceive them being within her mind.

But they are wrong and Goldie eyes flutter in the midst of the intrusion, and she finds them impeding her mind with thoughts of love and she dismisses their inquiries with a spell she chants from the projection of her own mind *by the power of three I banish thee!*

The portals between Hanna and Goldie and Sydney and Goldie are severed and Hanna's physical body begins choking. She is suffocating on black smoke that Goldie sends her from the fire at home base in Vermont. The lodge is billowing in a black

481

cloud and Lucius is alarmed; he finds his wife's gasping body upon the bed; he removes her without waking her and takes her to the porch made of glass; there, he lays her body on the floor without waking her and whispers into her ear: "Stay there," he says calmly, "the children are well with Reese and my father." He strokes his wife's hair to soothe her and outside the glass enclosure on the back porch the Shaman community gathers outdoors, and they hold a vigil led by candle-light to aid Hanna in her efforts to restore Goldie with love and they chant for peace over her soul.

Lucius enters the indoors to put out the fire that is smoldering with black smoke; Goldie was willing to sacrifice the Ravens that blocked the chimney escape causing the flames to smolder rather than escape. The Shamans outside become surrounded by the Ravens – those that did not act in the efforts of suicide – a theme for the adherence to the Dark. Hanna thinks that even Jace was an act of suicide and that of Grandall who may have given their lives for the light, but they too were essentially an act of the dark.

She thinks there is a glimmer of hope in that thought because the light and the dark can be similar. She rests with that thought and her physical body stops choking. She is at rest on the rug in the room made of glass and although the Ravens are startling them the Shamans continue their chants and songs of peace.

"We are at war with the dark." They nod in unison that they understand and amid the Ravens the Shamans hold their lighted candles that are symbolic of the light that fills their nights. Clover finds Hanna through an opening in the door and as she rests upon Hanna's chest Lucius closes the door and looks for Thor.

"Stay strong." Rhoda encourages Hanna.

They are still connected mentally within the cave that shelters them and the rest of the Shaman community have joined June and Malaki in the Grove that still grows the wild flowers that surround them; they have found a way to surround Hanna in the physical and the state of her spirit body – now they want to find a way to be of her mind to make her mind strong as Rhoda has suggested.

Hanna looks for Jace; she thinks gently of luring Goldie to the peace and mild tranquility of the ether. June and Malaki take a deep breath too and exert their mental projections onto Hanna; they try to assist her in the effort to take Goldie from the safety of the catacombs, and into the ether, where they feel she can be in the safety of the darkness led by Jace. In the place where she can heal, and baby Elizabeth can be safe from harm, and they can get her back into her mother's arms.

Chapter Twenty-Eight

Outside the cave in the place of the Garden Grove that is held together by a mental capacity the Shamans work to open a portal. There are saplings that grow amid the winter in the place they consider as enchanting as the Celestial City – the place that is a kind of Heaven for the Shamans – they are willing to risk this place to aid Hanna in finding Elizabeth the way they had two years before with baby Alysiah. They too hope to help Goldie in finding happiness.

"It's like taking a walk down memory lane," Rhoda says. "There was something that made her happy once."

"Something other than ruling in the Darkness," Hanna suggests.

They stay calm, and the vigil outside Hanna's doors stays strong and Clover rests upon her chest and the followers of the Light remain at peace and plot how to bring Goldie into their world because in the past – they failed her.

The ether is quiet. Jace feels proud that Hanna thinks she can bring Goldie there as the thought is delivered from Sydney onto Amber and she shares her mental energy with him. The image Hanna projects to Sydney is that of a boy who once was nice to Goldie before Kamra and Victoria beat the bloody snot out of her. He was gentle with Goldie but then he moved away. His name was Matthew, a neighborhood boy, when they were just eight and they rode their bikes to the creek because they had parents who did not watch over them. Hanna then reaches out to Sterling to confirm the memory. She realizes that the memory is coming to her from Rhoda – a memory that Leisha has within her and Hanna finds that Leisha did in fact meet them there, and they ate fruit from the apple orchards and played by the Creek – the three of them there as if then they had no worries in the world.

Sterling is receptive to Hanna's thoughts. From the quiet of her bedroom while she reads from a book she sends Hanna the mental message: she plans to use a scrying mirror to locate the boy that Goldie once felt affection for. She wastes no time and exits her bedroom where she enters her Great Room and beside the piano she sits at her scrying mirror to channel an image of the boy, now a man, that her sister once used to know.

"I didn't know that she was so hurt," Sterling says with compassion in her heart. "We just were not close because we were so different."

"Do you know this boy?" Hanna maintains an image.

"I find it hard to remember, but I enjoy the vision and I think Goldie would too."

"Matthew went away," Hanna explains, "all we can do is to somehow get Goldie to take this memory with her to the ether where she can heal."

"Only upon her death?" Sterling cannot help but to hope for the change of heart in her sister.

"We don't think so necessarily..." Hanna says.

"There has been enough death already." Rhoda tunes into their energy vibration.

They yearn for Goldie to find the image of a long lost, and possibly long forgotten friend. Hanna hopes that it would be enough to free her mind from the years of hatred that collected in her soul. That is when they all begin to hear the baby crying and their hearts jolt knowing she is so close to them.

Alexandra kneels at her altar, and she thinks of the Goddess of the Underworld who could bless such a menace to society and she also thinks of Helga who wants a child. She considers that she now has the blessing of the Underworld and contemplates how the dark can be manipulated to free Elizabeth while destroying all of the dark for eternity. She stencils in the wax of a dark candle, *eternity* as she plots how to cause the dark underworld to crumble. Hatred stirs in her own heart the way it does for Goldie and their energy center, the solar plexus, begins to appear the same. Her heart aches for the baby that rightfully belongs to her daughter. She sees no other attempt working to fill the task of getting the child back to her birth mother because without her sacrifice an evil witch will possess immense power. She kneels before her altar that is decorated with dried flowers to represent the seeds of life feeling that there is something important within them. She places her magical tools upon the altar and waits for news from Hanna.

This time, Hanna thinks, they are all connected telepathically and together they can accomplish the task to bring order to the dark. They have commenced in a psychic network because Goldie cannot be handled this time in any other way than to mentally tune into her mind, soul and heart's desires.

Alexandra notices that the Ravens have gathered outside her door and she feels intuitively that they surround them because they are that close to Goldie – they appear when Goldie herself is surrounded too – she wonders why they would be such a dead giveaway but fathoms that the dark is desperate for victory even to the extent of making themselves obvious and known.

Sterling is nervous. She asks over her scrying mirror that the Goddess bless them in their efforts and their rite of passage to locate baby Elizabeth and to find her way home. Clover cries over Hanna in a sound like a song of peace as together they begin to pray, chant, evoke and summons with the fullest of intentions: Jace, Amber and now Alexandra oversee the dark – they feel they have Goldie cornered and the sounds of the baby crying and the fleeing of the Ravens means they are close to fulfilling their intentions.

Alexandra notices that the Lily of the Valley upon her altar begins to glow with an intensity – possibly a blessing from the Goddess of the Underworld or Helga but at this stage she does not know precisely because her own aura is a saturated state of Gray as the dark and the light become a kind of blur upon her.

Lucius is greeted by a tap at the window as he hovers the body of Hanna and he finds Sage and within her beak there is a letter. As he opens the window Sage enters while being pecked and surrounded by the Ravens that are vigorously trying to disarm them; Lucius battles each one until they fall upon the cold earth and he can let Sage in to feel the warmth of the fire that burns among them.

The letter is from three days ago and written by Hanna; they have been atop a mountain in Vermont and are among the Shaman community where Rhoda has taken Hanna on a vision quest; where together their ethereal bodies work to locate Goldie;

but they have decided to locate her in a mental capacity to shield their own bodies from rapture at the hands of the evil one who wishes for their deaths and her reign as the Highest of all Order. Hanna explains that Rhoda is a strong sorcerer and it sets Lucius' mind at ease knowing that Hanna is being guided by a great adept. He hovers over her body with the letter and tells her softly that their children are safe, not to worry, and to carry out her mission because the Shamans have gathered despite the intensity of the Ravens that surround and haggle them. They are covered by shields and do not dare to use force if there can, this time, be another way.

She describes the Shaman's Holy Land where June and Malaki await with the Shaman community; Lucius feels her beating heart and feels immense relief knowing that his wife has prepared this letter at the time when it is most needed. They have been within the mind trying to locate Goldie for days and intend to return to their bodies only if and when they have Goldie herself and restore order between the dark and the light which appears that both have become greedy.

"I hope she knows what she is doing," Reese says over Hanna and Lucius' children as she tucks them into bed as the night becomes darker and the moon casts an omnipresent glow out their window; the night is calm and reassuring and the Ravens do not gather there. Luther enters the room and takes Reese by the hand where they exit the room with their sleeping grandchildren and they gather at the fire to send thoughts of positive energy to Hanna and Rhoda.

Outside there is snow, but within the Shamanic community the Holy Land was created after the destruction, and they maintain this place to be of great importance to those who try to mend the dark one's lost soul.

Goldie feels the weight of the gathered mass and she prepares her own altar with a black candle. She carves into its side the insignia of a pentacle turned upside down – a kind of talisman for her Demon who has long been ready to feed; "The only way now is through the dark," she says and Leisha stands amid her intentions and as she lights the candle the atmosphere surrounding Sterling becomes thick as a fog – Goldie challenges her own sister — with a message that she is commenced in the darkness that surrounds her. The air around her becomes dense and cold but she continues to use the scrying mirror to locate an image of Matthew…

Hail, Goldie says to evoke the Goddess of the night but Alexandra feels strength in knowing that she has been blessed by the Goddess herself and she maintains a focus on the thought of bringing Elizabeth home – by all and any means! She holds the image of Goldie in her mind's eye because it is Goldie who is now opening her own mind to let in the dark and it is a portal now for Hanna, Sterling, Alexandra and Rhoda who have come together collectively to challenge her.

May the Dark prosper again, she continues to speak aloud over an altar with the burning candle that is anointed with Demon Blood – an offering to the Goddess of the Underworld but she has not risen and Alexandra feels assured she can evoke the Goddess to do as she desires – anything to get her grand baby back.

Outside there is a deluge of water that stirs from the cosmos – the intention to drown out the Shamans and their attempts to free baby Elizabeth – but why, they wonder, would the storm Goddess create the rain?

They continue to focus on their intentions because within the Holy Garden Grove the rain is welcome but outside where Hanna's body lays upon the floor in Vermont the rain is not a friend and they begin to freeze.

"This is the war between the dark and the light," Rhoda says firmly, "the Storm Goddess is impartial and thus the rain is currently friend and foe."

"What do we do?" Hanna says telepathically.

"Keep calm. Maintain composure. Meditate with the fullness of positive energy to bring Elizabeth back to her mother."

The Ravens clamber about within the trees and caw among them to drown out the sounds of their song.

Lucius opens his doors and hastily the Shamanic community take cover indoors at the lodge as the mountains of Vermont become engulfed by the Ravens but they are shielded and take cover indoors where they can gather, and lay their hands upon Hanna, and give to her their blessing from within in a vigil for positive change.

As the High Priestess of the Dark I profess my allegiance to the Dark and Hail to all that is mighty and powerful!

Goldie wishes to summons the energy of the Dark Ones and in this moment she seeks the blessing of the Goddess of the Underworld in connection with the great storms. Alexandra counteracts her intentions and pledges allegiance to the Goddess herself but Goldie is not shy and thus she continues and amid her altar in the cavernous underground Leisha kneels aside her beloved cousin; they focus their intentions on aligning themselves with the Darkness as the child cries for her mother and the Demon whales to be fed.

Her cries echo from within the cave and can be heard by all. Rose and Michael jolt from their bed as they know intuitively that is their daughter and they take flight to their altar where they too kneel and pray over a candle that burns white to honor the Goddess and her love for their daughter.

Hanna concentrates on sending Goldie an image of her love for a friend named Matthew – what if she could find him again? The Shamans chant, pray and sing over her body and Hanna's mind in turn feels strong.

Unleash the beast of the dark! Goldie's words too echo through the cavern and they know now that midnight is upon them and Goldie has the highest energy of Night outdoors where the full moon is aglow and the Storm Goddess makes it hail but inside the Garden Grove they are protected, and indoors at the lodge they have the warmth of the fire and they burn their own candles with the light of love around them.

I shall be the Queen of the Night … Goldie gets greedy … *and my dear cousin shall be mother to us all.* Goldie's words hiss with intention before an altar that is for conjuring the Dark but the Goddess of the Underworld does not stir and Alexandra beckons before her altar. *I offer myself to you in exchange for the baby girl who is crying for her mother.*

Alexandra is intense. She shutters and her body begins to flutter as the energy of the Dark Ones fill her room. Her altar becomes shrouded in dark energy and she knows that the Goddess of the Dark Underworld has unleashed her souls upon her and Alexandra feels the energy of the Dark Souls enter her body as her head is thrust backwards and with her mouth thrust open she inhales, literally, the energy of the Dark Ones as a blessing from the Goddess herself.

Well said dear sister. Leisha nods as Goldie continues to chant her rite to the darkness regardless of not having a blessing from the Goddess of the Underworld. Her evocation has landed in the throne of the Storm Goddess instead who provides the hale of the night and the rain showers to the Garden Grove because this is a war among the mortals and only they can decide how to make it right. Even Leisha thirsts for power while Alexandra has offered her own sacrifice to the Dark Goddess in exchange for the child who is to be sacrificed by the Dark Witch who yearns for total power – and for that reason Alexandra has her blessing. She is literally fed with the souls of the Dark.

Alexandra begins a ritual within her room while Rose and Michael are within their room kneeling at their altar. They are not mentally connected but Rose can feel her mother's dark energy and so Rose prays for her mother, "Dear Goddess of the Light," she says, "Helga will you bless us on this journey to get my baby back..." she feels her stomach as the child grows within her, "I want you to know your sibling," she whispers and Michael holds his wife. He feels deeply that if he can find his way out of the catacombs, then they too can free Elizabeth from the confines of the Dark Others.

Go to sleep my dear daughter, Alexandra whispers at her altar feeling that her daughter is praying for her; she can feel her intuitively and so she speaks out loud in an effort to comfort her daughter because she is willing to sacrifice her soul to the Dark Goddess in exchange for the mortal child that is to be sacrificed by the darkest of evil witches to gain the greatest of power – immortality and total control and power of all who must bow down to their Master of Great Sorcery or die at her hand for disobeying her every command.

Goldie is pretentious, but she is not weak. Then the lightning crashes and threatens to devastate the Garden Grove. June and Malaki along with the Shamans take cover within the catacombs and the Ravens, satisfied, follow them into the depth of the caves as the storm whirls from outside and they have no choice but to take cover all-the-while chanting and praying to recover baby Elizabeth without Goldie's intention to consume total power manifesting.

"My little angel, I am here for you," Rose says over her altar. She can feel her mother too whose soul is darkened. Rose shutters, not wanting to lose her mother, but yearning at the same time to get her baby out of the possession of a delusional witch whose own greed could devastate the mountain of Vermont that sustains them.

The Full Moon becomes shrouded by dark clouds and the light cannot fall upon them and they do not succumb to the dark but take refuge from the elements. They continue to pray and chant to elevate the energy from the dark to the light and they work together to bring Goldie from the catacombs and into the place where her soul can heal.

Thor scrapes the ground before their bedroom door and Rose lets him in – he is a welcome sign to feel the safety of his familiar face because Jace cannot be there to fight the dark as he dutifully awaits the passage of either Goldie's soul or her mind to make an appearance where he can best serve the Goddess of the Underworld and give the darkness an eternal peace for the souls who recover from trauma – the way that Goldie herself needs to do.

Thor places his head to her chest and she cries into his fur while praying that the Goddess of the Light will bless them in finding her daughter so that her own mother does not have to give herself completely to the dark.

Chapter Twenty-Nine

Her abdomen stirs quietly with the life inside of it, and she thinks about the life that is inside of her and the life that is seemingly beyond her reach. Michael rubs Thor's head and wraps his arms around his neck. The animal familiarity is a sign of hope as Thor found them on the Night of Terror.

Lucius shields Hanna's physical body as Sage sits upon her chest trying to shed comfort to her as Lucius leans into her and whispers, *You are protected in body, mind and soul, my love.*

Clover wraps at the window as Sterling sits in front of her scrying mirror trying with all her might to locate a boy that once showed love to her sister.

The Ravens are startled in Vermont and they also hover outside the store as Sterling tries not to be startled by their presence and she knows that Clover is a sign of her good fortune – her only hope that she can find an ounce of love within her sister's soul.

Goldie's eyes flash in a shade of crimson and stands before the altar and she takes up her athame blade and begins to chant as the Demon emerges from the confines of his cell and she beckons: *Dark beast of night, you must feed on the blood of the most innocent, a child of a precious little twit, to sanctify my allegiance as Prime Overseer of the Dark!*

Not even the Goddess can stop you sister...

Leisha advises her as the only sister of their Coven that shows their greed and thirst for power.

Alexandra calls out...

Goddess of the night, hear me! And bless thee in this consecration!

The skies part and the Phantoms emerge; they stir within the catacombs as they can feel the weight of the darkness upon them but they do not retreat, they remain grounded and in unison they begin to focus love and compassion upon the dark ones; aside from Alexandra who has taken an allegiance with the Dark to fight Goldie in her own wrath. The Shamans and the good witches together chant and pray as they summon the energy necessary to defeat them.

The catacombs turn to an immense cold as not just the frigid air of winter is upon them but the Phantoms surround the entirety of the Night in Vermont but their power is insurmountable and Rose and Michael shiver too as they intuitively feel them within their soul. Rose begins to cry as she knows the war between the Dark and the Light have commenced nearing full power. This is not a physical war, but a war among minds and it takes great energy to contain them.

Hanna takes the Great Staff into her ethereal fist and bellows … *Sterling keep scrying!* Rhoda focuses intently and uses the Mighty Staff of the Elder within her own grasp and sends Sterling the message *she too knew love once.*

The staffs possesses great energy from the lives of the adepts that used them and Hanna's physical body begins to choke as the curse tries to invade her body again and Goldie's eyes gleam in the Dark confines of the Underground where she is housed and cannot be located because the tunnels of the catacombs are immense; the others stay grounded in the Garden Grove and Hanna and Rhoda maintain their energy within the Cave that conceals them from the Phantoms that beseech the Mountains of Vermont and Alexandra continues: *Goddess of the dark Underground I evoke thee!*

Goldie stands composed and firm at her altar and she holds the athame blade thrusts upward to what would be the night sky in its darkest hour with even the light of the moon shrouded in the thickness of Dark Energy...

The cries of the infant are in the open as Leisha takes baby Elizabeth into her hands and Goldie conjures the most

Harrowing of Evil in the *Book of Shadows* that should never have been opened.

May the blood of this innocent child be used to attest my adherence and utter allegiance to the Dark Sorcery of the Night and to the immortal Goddess may I preside over thee to become the Great and Powerful High Priestess of Evil …

May the blood spill out and onto the earth as I become Mother of the Dark!

She raises the blade and the lightning crashes from outside. The Dark Night is thick and Alexandra turns blue before her altar. Her breath is a frost despite the fire that burns in her home in Brighton.

Rose can feel her mother dying and she shutters. *Mom, stop!* The Darkness frightens her and Michael takes her into his arms as he cradles her bulging abdomen and he can feel the dense frost from the window pane and he keeps her from running to Alexandra because even he hopes the Dark Ones can deliver his child – that there is just one soul who is not so possessed to keep his child. They feel the Goddess Helga has failed them and they shutter as Alexandra may have found the only way to help them but as Goldie speaks out of Evil and Malice Rose speaks out of love and yearns for her mother. The Light cannot be found among them and they wonder if Helga would possess the soul of the disenchanted child and keep her away from them in the Celestial City and leave the mortals to fight the Dark into Eternity.

The Winter Solstice is now upon them again and a portal to the Underworld opens and from it a rat emerges where Alexandra lays before her altar and as she suffocates in the thick of Hell a letter of her last words falls to her chest: *I give to you dear Goddess of the Underworld, the blood of this rat instead, to offer to you my allegiance to the dark on this Night! Take from its blood my signature in writing and I offer to you myself instead!*

Goldie sniggers and the catacombs floods with rats that scurry in a haste and the

Ravens are startled from outside as the Dark Underworld opens for all to see and the Phantoms stand to dutifully carry out the Deed of the Most Righteous Dark as they howl in the mist and the thunder rolls and as the lightning crashes Goldie's athame blade comes down and the Demon lunges for them to devour the shedded blood of the most innocent one…

Now feed on this pitiful child and make us rein over all things Dark! By thy will be done!

And a portal opens like a great vortex into the deepest pits of Hell and Wrath but the child has stopped screaming and Goldie peers before her at the hand of her Cousin who is bleeding and the athame blade has pierced clean through to the other side of her own hand.

You have missed the child and have gotten me instead …

Goldie's eyes grow wild as the Demon lurches and Leisha drops the child and as she is falling the Demon is in full gallop as he takes her head into his gaping mouth and together they fall into the Great Portal toward Hell.

Goldie stands alone amid the portal to the Underworld, unable to deliver the blood of the most innocent to the Demon she left starving and instead watches as the Goddess of the Underworld emerges and she takes the child into her own immortal hands and rubs her head gently, *no one has ever tried to defy me*, she says with piercing green eyes and jet black hair and an aura of the darkest Noir.

Hanna begins to chant: *Blessed be! Dear One! May you too find love…*

And Sterling holds the scrying mirror with both hands as she beholds the image of a smiling Matthew long ago who holds out his hand to a childish Goldie who has stumbled and fell. As she feels his hand she can once again feel the warmth of his hand and she thinks of her dear cousin Leisha who she has murdered with her own hand and she begins to cry as Rose is left sobbing in her husband's arms and the familiars take to the outdoors where the Ravens are retreating and the Storm Goddess closes the portals in the skies and through the portal the Goddess of the Underworld takes baby Elizabeth and the mortals are left standing in their mix of love and fear.

The daylight breaks over the horizon and the Longest Night turns to the Shortest Day and the shamans return to their jobs at the resort as if nothing of a War had started. Hanna and Rhoda are swooshed back into their physical bodies and they awake with a great gasp and Lucius scoops her up into his arms and she lays her head upon his shoulder, *she's not dead.* She says and they take comfort in that, but they know not what is awaiting them next.

The Garden Grove is a place of great refuge but with the retreating of the Night its walls crumble as the Shamans had known that it would be a place of much need during the Holy War and Goldie is left alone within the Catacomb with the feeling of a generous warm hand upon her and she is left to decide if she wants to enter the light of day as they gear up for the pending Summer Solstice in a festivity to honor the emergence of the God Atlas as they wonder if the Goddess herself will receive her wishes.

The Lily of the Valley grows in Brighton where Alexandra is laid to rest as she offered herself to the Goddess of the Underworld so that as she is laid the child may emerge. Rose cries over the headstone of her mother and she takes to her husband knowing that their child is due any day soon and she sulks thinking of her mother at their table as she holds in her hand the letter her mother had written realizing that her mother gave herself in exchange for the blood of the most innocent and the Goddess of the Underworld gave her blessing.

With her grave fully covered and the flowers blooming Rose can only think what has happened to her precious child and wonders if Helga has found Summer

513

because her mother has given herself for Elizabeth. They are all left confused because they know not what the Goddess of the Underworld has done with baby Elizabeth then Hanna remembers Jace and she thinks perhaps this is the time he was speaking of.

With that thought Hanna goes to the outdoors where the Lily of the Valley is plentiful and she whispers toward the radiant sun … *it has been six months. You must come out now.*

Sterling stands in front of her scrying mirror and wipes away the stain that tarnished the mirror with her sister's face as if the image is set in stone and she peers at her image and she imagines with the fullness of her intention the love Matthew showed for her. On the Longest Day of the Year she yearns for her sister's soul and that is when the bell clangs at the front door and she is greeted by her old friend Susan who stops in to buy from her store crystals and incense as she plans to concoct a spell to make her dear nephew feel love again.

"Who is your dear nephew?" Sterling asks.

"One witch cannot ask another witch how she knows." Her dear friend laughs heartily.

"I could feel it the moment you walked in."

"My dear nephew is Matthew."

Sterling drops the mirror.

"Oh?"

"Are you alright dear?"

"Yes, I'm sorry. It's been a hard past six months."

"The winter storms were strong this year."

"They were indeed."

"How are you faring? I've seen the tabloids. All those protestors."

"Yes."

The bells clang again and Sterling's face nearly hits the floor.

The girls before her are none other than Kamra and Victoria.

"What are you girls doing here?" Her voice shakes.

"We want to find Sterling."

"Well you have found her."

"We were told that you could help us."

"Who?"

"Our mothers."

"I'm sorry?"

The air is different and Sterling feels in the pit of her stomach that something else is different and she collects her thoughts to think what in the world must be different.

"We were not nice to your sister the other day…" one of them says. And Sterling takes a seat in her chair wondering if the air is not just in tune with the Summer Solstice but something else….

And with another clang her heart jolts.

"Matthew," her dear friend says and she hugs him.

"Matthew?" Sterling wants to leap from her chair.

"We almost lost him." She says.

"What do you mean?"

"He was in a car accident. Years ago. Been in a coma…"

Sterling cannot believe these words.

"But you just said … my sister, yesterday…"

"Yes." Matthew chimes in. "I had a rough week since coming out of a coma and everything but I met your sister…"

"You met Goldie?"

"I did. It was kind of like a weird state of déjà vu." He scratches his head. "I was coming out of my coma by the hand of your sister… a very surreal kind of dream. But I'm trying to find her again."

With those words Sterling begins to sweep the shards of glass made by the scrying mirror.

"But you girls said you just saw her yesterday."

"We did. By the river," Kamra says.

"She bloodied her face." Victoria was solemn.

"We want to apologize." Kamra explains.

"But why? Why now?" Sterling tries to hide her confusion.

"We thought she was a weird witch…" Kamra huffs.

"Coming out of the catacombs…" Victoria insists.

"She was coming out of the catacombs…" Sterling is a near whisper.

"As I was coming out of the coma she appeared," Matthew says. "I had a great deal of admiration for her years ago."

Then it strikes Sterling earnestly that the girls don't look a day older than their teens, but how when time has not stopped? Then she thinks, time has a weird way of surprising people and for them it did stop. For them in their deaths, for him in his coma, for her sister in her solitude in the catacombs and when the door chimes again it is Goldie who has the most earnest smile on her face when all she can see is Matthew who takes to her and they go outside the door without speaking to anyone else.

Kamra and Victoria shrug and make their way into the beauty of the daylight.

"What did you need for that spell?" Sterling suggests.

"What spell?" She laughs, and they both laugh and Sterling takes to the window to see her sister who has fallen in love with Matthew all over again as if for the first time. And Clover is above them in the rafter making a nest as the new buds of summer are upon them and Sterling shutters once more … *but what about the baby she calls Summer* she says aloud.

"Who?" Her friend says.

"The baby." Sterling breathes mildly as she watches Matthew take Goldie by the hand once more and they walk together toward the river toward all the things Goldie had done wrong but that she can make right again.

Hanna whispers again to Jace *where are you* as Rose and Michael are walking toward her and Lucius brings their children into the outdoors.

"Was my mother's death in vain?" Rose says.

"I don't think so." Hanna tries to assure her.

"My mother gave her life for my child."

"Yes," Hanna is receptive, "the father of my first born gave his life too."

"They must all be together. They have to be," Lucius says as Luther and Reese join them in the outdoors.

Reese takes her grandchildren into her arms and although she never did have children of her own, the grandchildren she enjoys with her dear husband Luther fills her heart with great joy.

"The Peace Treaty," Hanna says.

"What?" Rose is still hopeful.

"The Dark and the Light are not at war any longer... but they are making a treaty. Tia told me."

"Who?" Rose still feels numb but tries to be in great spirits over the child she is about to have.

"The magical pixie of the Celestial City."

"Thoughts are things," Lucius says, and he points the way.

There is a portal that has opened, and there is light emanating from within it when they see the spirit body emerge and it is Alexandra who walks through an aura of light that is greater than the sun and she carries with her an infant child.

Rose and Michael are stunned and proceed slowly.

"Mom?" Rose is both in awe and confusion.

"This is your immortal daughter Rose," Alexandra says.

"I don't understand," Rose says.

"I'm sorry my beloved Rose," she is cautious, "she died when she hit the floor. Her little brain could not take any more."

Rose cries in earnest. "You have my baby?"

"Yes. I do."

"But why did Helga…"

"Name the immortal baby Summer?"

"Yes…"

"Because it would be the Summer Solstice my dear Rose when the immortal child would be given back to its mother…"

And with that Rose's abdomen becomes warm and the spirit bodies of both Alexandra and Elizabeth become like water vapor in a bright light that Rose can feel in her abdomen and as her stomach grows fuller and brighter, she knows in her soul that she is about to give birth to twins. And all is right again.

And from the tree line among the shadows emerge her closest confidants, Phoenix the great horse and best friend Duke, because Jace always knew the past could be alive again. In the end, not just the dark is egomaniacal, as they learn because even the Goddess herself can have human-like intentions and in that they balance the Light and the Dark; like Grandall, and Jace before them, Alexandra could give her life, and only then are they equal because they bestow what others wanted to take. And only then is the greatest sacrifice unconditional love.

So Mote it Be.

About the Author

Candace Meredith earned her Bachelor of Science degree in English Creative Writing from Frostburg State University in the spring of 2008. Her works of poetry, photography and fiction have appeared in literary journals Bittersweet, The Backbone Mountain Review, The Broadkill Review, In God's Hands/ Writers of Grace, A Flash of Dark, Greensilk Journal, Saltfront, Mojave River Press and Review, Scryptic Magazine, Unlikely Stories Mark V, The Sirens Call, The Great Void, BAM Writes, Foreign Literary, Lion and Lilac Magazine, The Green Shoe Sanctuary Literary Journal, Setu Magazine, Impspired Magazine and various others. Candace lives in Virginia with her two sons and her daughter and fiancé. She earned her Master of Science degree in Marketing and Communications from West Virginia University. Candace is the author of various books titled Contemplation: Imagery, Sound and Form in Lyricism (a collection of poetry), Losing You (a novella collection), Winter Solstice (book 1 of a 4 book series): The Crone (book 2), The Lady of Brighton (book 3), Summer Solstice (book 4) and her published children's books A-Hoy Frankie! Your Riverboat Captain, Matilda Gets Adopted, Who Farted?, Andre the Broken Tea Cup Goes to the Market, Nola Plays Baseball, I Ain't No Bully, Little Blue Shoe, After Life and Before Evolution There Was Creation. Also out on the market is a Young Adult Drama Girls Drive Jeeps. Candace's novels and stories are being adapted for film.

Check out her websites for all published titles at:

www.candacemeredithbooks.com

www.turningpagesbookpulishers.com